COLD FRONT

To my loving wife, my anchor in a storm.
The light that guides me home.
Without you, I would be adrift,
lost to the sea.
Thank you for supporting me in a way no one else ever could.

To all the heroes in blue, and sometimes in multicam.
The ones who risk it all every day so that others may live.
Semper Paratus.

"The true warrior fights not because he hates what is in front of him, but because he loves what is behind him."

G.K. CHESTERTON

COLD FRONT

A LOGAN CROSS THRILLER

D.M. WEBBER

DEEP WATCH
PRESS

Library of Congress Control Number: 2025921293
Hardcover ISBN: 979-8-9990159-3-8
Paperback ISBN: 979-8-9990159-4-5
Digital Book ISBN: 979-8-9990159-5-2

PRINTED IN THE USA

CONTENTS

AUTHOR'S FOREWORD

Sometimes the right choice is not the easiest one. At its core, this novel is about the integrity, grit, and determination needed to face difficult choices in life.

While this is a work of fiction, the choices we make in our everyday lives will have parallels to the themes presented in the pages of this novel. How far would you go to protect others? Would you put your own life at risk? Would you put the life you've built at risk?

For the protagonist in these pages, Logan Cross, these are no longer hypothetical questions. The fight arrives at his doorstep. As he works to uncover a greater conspiracy, the risks amplify. The choices he makes have consequences, and the deeper he digs, the greater the danger.

The men and women of the United States Coast Guard make decisions like this every day. On small boats, cutters, aircraft, and during high-risk maritime boardings, these dedicated professionals make choices to execute dangerous missions, knowing that the cost may include their own lives. There is no trophy, no promise of accolades, only a drive to save others, which overrides self-preservation instincts. The old service adage proclaimed, "You have to go out; you don't have to come back."

While policy has changed to provide greater safety to the men and women in uniform, the mentality remains behind each insignia and nametape.

My greatest hope is that as you read through the pages of this novel, you can relate to some part of Logan Cross and his journey through the darkness. Maybe you've faced those difficult questions in your own life. Perhaps you've experienced personal tragedy or seen someone you love to face a tragedy. If you haven't, maybe it helps you assess your own willingness to respond to difficult situations.

Most of all, I hope you enjoy the ride. Buckle up, there are rough waters ahead!

D.M. Webber

March 2025

THE WIND WHIPPED across the waters south of Manchester Harbor and Great Misery Island at nearly twenty knots. Forecasts predicted an easing off as the sun rose that morning, but it was still blasting across the open water, turning the sea into a washing machine of choppy waves with rippling whitecaps. Tony Rivetti gripped the wheel of his boat, knuckles turning ghostly white with the strain in his hands. He wasn't all that skilled at operating a small boat, certainly not in conditions like this. However, his employer was clear that this trip was simple, and it had to be done solo to avoid suspicion. He wouldn't tell his employer no; that never ended well. He had been ordered to rendezvous with a gray and white center console to take delivery of a shipment of drugs for refinement and further distribution. He had cash in a small duffel on the deck behind the operator chair. After he exchanged the money for the drugs, he would be back in Manchester before noon.

As the ten o'clock rendezvous came and went, he complained to the open sea that the other boat was late. He wondered why they were keeping him waiting and if it was some kind of power play. There was no way to know the real reason, so he told himself to be patient and try to hold his position.

For forty-five minutes, Tony alternated between tapping his foot on the deck, drumming on the wheel, and occasionally pacing when it was calm enough. It was a vain attempt to somehow speed up time until the other boat suddenly became visible on the southwestern horizon. As the boat drew closer to Rivetti's position, he watched it rock and roll on the waves. It was as unstable as his own craft in this wind and chop. It was another seven minutes before the boat was close enough for Rivetti to see two people on board: a driver with long, perfectly-parted hair and a sun-kissed tan that made him look a little like a character from some '8os action movie; the second man was behind the first and had huge arms, a bald head, and a mean scowl on his face. He resembled a professional wrestler or a bouncer. He looked as uncomfortable on the boat as Tony felt. The two men looked like they were ready to give him a beat-down instead of a simple marketable goods exchange. Rivetti shook the thought from his mind and tried to focus on not vomiting on the deck as his boat rolled violently in the chop.

The other boat closed the gap to a foot, and the second man tied a line to Tony's boat as they continued to drive forward, putting both boats into the choppy waves. It was clear the other operator had far more experience handling a small boat in rough weather.

When the rolling hulls settled into a synchronized lazy back-and-forth pitching, the other operator called out with a slight accent that Rivetti couldn't identify.

"What you have for us?" There was no inflection in his voice, just ice.

Rivetti glanced at the man, but he stared back blankly. There was no emotion, not a thing. Rivetti felt a nervous charge of energy run through his entire body. He reached for the duffel, trying not to look threatening or nervous, even with his palms slick with sweat. He held the duffel close at his side, then asked, "Got the stuff we need?"

The operator pointed to the back deck, raising his eyebrow as if to say, "What, you don't trust us?"

Rivetti felt that feeling again; he couldn't shake it. It wasn't the ocean making him nervous. He spoke a little more tersely than he would have liked. "Put it there," pointing to his back deck, "then I'll hand the cash over and we can be done with this."

Action Hero nodded at Wrestler, and Wrestler took the sign to do what he was asked. It wouldn't matter, not to Rivetti anyway. He started moving bag after bag, slowly filling the other man's deck with them, until the last bag fell loosely on the pile. Rivetti watched carefully, then put his arm up with the duffel outstretched toward Action Hero. *What a bunch of creepy guys,* he thought.

Action Hero grabbed the bag, carefully putting it behind his console chair, turning his back for a moment. He spoke barely loud enough for Rivetti to hear over the wind and waves, "You're about to... how you say... serve greater purpose, Tony."

There was that feeling again, cold, creeping through him like ants under his skin. "Why?" His voice projected confusion and fury. "What the fuck is that supposed to mean?"

"It means, enjoy the afterlife," Action Hero said, and before Tony could react, there was a suppressed Glock pointed at his chest, and a muffled shot rang out.

Tony Rivetti heard the shot, felt it, but his brain refused to acknowledge what had happened until the second shot rang out, punching through his chest next to the first. He stared blankly at Action Hero for a moment, blinking in pained disbelief as it suddenly became clear. It was far too late for action. He now knew why he couldn't shake that nervous feeling. Rivetti opened his mouth to speak, but blood sputtered where the words should have been as his lungs collapsed, and he grabbed his chest, struggling for a last breath he'd never get. As he lost consciousness and his world turned black, his last view of life was of Action Hero's icy eyes staring at him while still holding his pistol at his side.

●●●●●

The gunman holstered his pistol without ceremony, casting a final glance at what, moments ago, had been a man. He wouldn't think of Tony Rivetti in that way. Rivetti had been a small part of a greater plan, one he didn't fully understand. Apollo was supposed to plant drugs, kill the man to make it look like an exchange gone bad, and case the Pickering Wharf Marina in Salem for a specific boat, as well as the general layout, which he had done before he had left this morning. Of course, he'd worn a disguise to throw off any facial recognition at the marina, so it would be nearly impossible to tie him to what had taken place out here, south of Cape Ann.

Subconsciously, he drove back to the southwest to pull the boat at the ramp. It would likely take an hour or more to get back, but it could be less since they weren't heading directly into the wind. Ox spoke up, realizing Apollo had come out of whatever trance he was in. "They won't figure this out, will they?"

"No chance. Cops do not give a damn about—how to say—pusher. Their... uh... investigation will lead no place. We did them favor."

Ox grinned as they bumped through the choppy water toward Pickering.

As predicted, the return trip was shorter. They pulled up to the boat ramp a little under an hour later. While Ox walked up the ramp to get the truck, Apollo pulled his phone from his pocket. It rang three times, then a man answered. The reply was simply, "It's done." The man on the other end of the line thanked him for his services and told him to keep his phone nearby. There will be more work soon.

PART ONE
UNCERTAINTY

"True genius resides in the capacity for evaluation of uncertain, hazardous, and conflicting information."

WINSTON CHURCHILL

1

UNITED STATES COAST GUARD STATION
GLOUCESTER, MASSACHUSETTS, MAY 2022

DUTY SECTION SWAP took place an hour earlier. The usual griping took place by the starboard section; their counterparts in the port section were looking for excuses to keep them stuck scrubbing and polishing instead of being home with their families. It was the same at nearly every small boat station in the Coast Guard.

Boatswain's Mate First Class Logan Cross had to admit he wouldn't trade it for any other post. As port section leader and law enforcement and weapons petty officer for the station, he shouldered responsibility for almost everyone, including gear requisitions, training schedules, and ensuring that everyone in his section, and many outside it, had what they needed to survive. Although a gunfight in coastal Massachusetts was unlikely, he knew how quickly routine safety boardings could go off course.

He left MSRT, the elite Maritime Security Response Team-East in Chesapeake, Virginia, a few months earlier to report early to Station Gloucester. He didn't leave because he wasn't good at it. He was. He was one of the best. But after years of high-stakes, adrenaline-fueled operations, late nights, long deployments, and near-death encounters, he and his wife Melanie wanted more: a home, a kid or two, a family, and a more peaceful life. It would be hard to do that if he didn't come home one day. So, he made the toughest trade of his career: danger for duty.

Cross recertified as a coxswain, a boat driver, in a few weeks. The small twenty-nine-foot response boat was used for law enforcement and shallow water search-and-rescue operations; piloting it was second nature. Then he knocked out his boarding officer recertification to take over the LEPO/WEPO role he now held. Next up would be the forty-seven-foot motor lifeboat later that summer, and the heavy weather cert in the winter. He planned to be fully certified early the next year. He was spacing it out intentionally, taking care of his crew first. The command noticed, and so did the crew. Cross could feel their trust in him grow.

Logan Cross was obsessed with military history and tactics even as a young boy. Even in his earliest school years, he had this feeling that he would end up joining the military at some point. He remembered his dad telling stories of his father, who was a tank commander in the Second World War. He was stunned when he was told the story of how his grandfather got part of a finger blown off by a German rifleman; the German got lucky as Cross's grandfather was getting a wind call prior to a major engagement outside some random French village. Though his grandfather died long before Cross was even an idea in his dad's mind, the legacy was seared in young Cross's DNA, and it would never leave. As he matured, his interests ranged from military history to military thrillers, and then to intelligence and even interrogation techniques.

When Cross mentioned the idea of joining the military in the shadow of his late grandfather's legacy, his parents advised him to attend college first, perhaps hoping that enlisting would lose its luster after a few years of earning an undergraduate degree. The concept only strengthened in Cross's brain, and as he put his energy and focus into classes on the origins of terrorism and historical revolutions. He excelled at those topics. His final paper for his revolutions class offered a deep analysis of the impact of the Iranian revolution on modern-day terrorism in the post-9/11 world, which earned him the best grade in his entire collegiate career.

Boring temp jobs in nameless office buildings with zero excitement cemented his desire for adventure and a life of greater meaning. Logan Cross didn't want a career pushing paper. He considered joining the Navy SEALs, but there was a steady pull in the other direction. He pulled away from the fight and toward saving lives. Partially emulating one of his favorite literary characters, Chief Boatswain's Mate John Terrence Kelly, he joined the Coast Guard instead of the Navy, determined to become a boat driver. The decision put his parents at ease. At least he'd serve in a non-combat role and wouldn't be a target for insurgents.

Fate, however, possessed a strange sense of humor. As it would turn out, the young boat driver had skills in law enforcement that were appealing to some folks on a little-known team out of Chesapeake, and a call from a former instructor of his didn't hurt. Cross landed a slot on the coveted MSRT on a service-wide all-rates solicitation and ended up being shot at anyway. The unusual path shaped him into someone who took nothing for granted—someone who could see the big picture, even when concealed in fog.

The call came in after 1100, as the cooks prepped for the noon meal in the Can-Do Café. The smell of spices, fresh chicken, and veggies permeated the small space. The Can-Do Café was named after the crew of a pilot boat who had risked their lives and paid the ultimate price to save an active-duty boat crew from the station who found themselves in trouble on a rescue of their own. The history and legacy of this station were palpable, which appealed to Cross on a deep, personal level.

Cross heard the radio come to life in the communications center at the back of the station overlooking the boat docks, but that wasn't a confirmed call. It was only people wondering about a boat adrift. The watchstander received a call from an unlisted number on the station landline, indicating a possible medical emergency out past Great Misery Island off Manchester Harbor. The reporting source gave little information before hanging up. The unreachable number didn't have a caller ID that registered on the old-school digital landline receiver.

When Cross was called into comms, he checked his Garmin watch, an Instinct model he had chosen for durability under the rigors of combat operations as well as functionality. It was 1106; it was a perfect time for a case to kick off. The seaman who was standing the first watch described the call as "weird," which made Cross a little curious about what he might be missing.

"What do you mean," Cross asked. "Weird how?"

"I mean...," Seaman Robertson said. "They called in saying there was a medical emergency, provided no further information, and hung up before I could ask questions."

"No information at all, not even the type of medical emergency?"

"Not a thing, only a location."

"Okay, Robertson. Thanks. Keep an ear out for anything else related to the case. We'll be underway in a few minutes."

As he toggled the search-and-rescue alarm switch and announced underway orders for his boat crew on the response boat, Cross hoped the reporting source was around long enough to answer some questions. Great Misery was about fifteen minutes on the RBS, maybe a little more with the current wind state, so it wouldn't be long before they were on scene. He had more questions than answers, but Cross knew that was frequently the case with search-and-rescue cases until more information was developed en route.

Cross filled out a quick mission record with the minimum information he had, listing his crew, mission, boat number, and cell phone in case they lost communications with the station. He grabbed his ready gear bag, leaving the station at a steady run to beat his crew to the boat. As he made his way down the brow to the pier, he noticed the twin Honda outboards on his boat puffed steam, and the discharge water streams shot out. He knew his good friend, Machinery Technician Second Class Nathan Sutter had beaten him. He was onboard firing up all the boat's systems. Cross stepped onto the boat, and Nate joked, "You're getting slow, old man!"

At thirty-five years old, Nate was two years Cross's junior. He was an inch taller than Cross at a full six feet. Nate was tall and athletic with dark brown hair cut short in a crew-cut with a little gray creeping into the temples. Nate started to show the age of a man with three kids and a wife to support, but was, nonetheless, a high performer.

"Shut up, Nate," Cross said with a smile. "All those gray hairs don't come from being *younger* than me." They'd met a decade earlier while in another unit and somehow made it to Gloucester together.

"Okay, fair point, but most of them are from my wife and kids. I'm still faster than you."

"Maybe by a whisker, but I'm not quite settled in yet. Does anything feel off on this one?"

Nate took a slow sip of his energy drink before responding. "No, buddy. Like what?"

"I don't know, a feeling. Maybe it's nothing."

"What was it your old man used to say? If something feels off —" Nate started.

Cross finished the statement without hesitation. "It probably is off. I know. Let's keep heads on a swivel, okay?"

Cross put his inflatable low-profile life jacket over his body armor and shirt, then slipped on his gun belt, snapping the belt keepers in place. Nate did the same. The rest of the crew made their way onboard. Boatswain's Mate Third Class Cody O'Donnell readied himself, and Seaman Lauren Davies was right behind him.

Cody was fresh into his twenties, five-foot-ten with light brown hair cut high and tight, with a mustache, and a lean physique. Lauren was just over eighteen, having joined the service right out of high school. At five-foot-five with a slight frame, she had dark brown hair pulled tight into a regulation bun. Lauren was still finding her place at the unit.

After Cross announced the information about the reporting source hanging up, Cody spoke up. "Boats, they gave that little information and hung up? That sounds strange. I mean, I know I'm a new boat driver, but that sounds weird to me."

"Thanks, Cody, I appreciate your insight. You've got a keen eye for those details. Keep trusting it. For the moment, with so little information, we treat it as SAR until something proves otherwise. Head on a swivel, folks. Don't assume anything. Let's get going."

The seasoned crew went through their accustomed risk assessment and were off the pier less than ten minutes after the initial call had come through. The watchstander informed the station's officer-in-charge, Chief Warrant Officer Bill Grayson, of the mission on the crew's behalf. As Cross called back to clear lines, he received confirmation that they were no longer attached to the pier and ramped up the throttles. He said to himself, as he always did, "Go baby, go!"

Their course took them past Ten Pound Island and its iconic lighthouse. They passed the Dog Bar break wall and then traveled along the Cape Ann coastline toward Manchester. Cross was at home on a boat, the water splashing under the hull, the wind blasting through the open windows, and the twin gas outboards humming behind him as he drove his boat at max safe speed toward the last reported position on the south side of Great Misery. He dodged lobster pots every few seconds, and the boat danced among the assorted white and yellow buoys like an experienced skier in a slalom. He maintained situational awareness to avoid hitting one of the many submerged rocks and shoals. It wouldn't help the person in distress if he ran his boat aground due to a lapse in judgment. The other challenge was the wind. It was kicking up choppy seas that should have eased off earlier this morning but hadn't. Weather reports were always off. Today, the wind-driven chop was sending occasional bursts of salty sea spray onto the windshield, and Cross was forced to use the windshield wipers to maintain forward visibility.

As the RBS approached the target area, Cross looked back at his crew. Only a few minutes out, they were alert, aware, locked on, and appeared ready to take on anything the day threw at them. He was proud to have such a great crew to be with on this mission.

It wasn't long before Davies called out, "Surface contact, bearing three-three-zero degrees, about a mile out!"

"Damn good eye, Lauren," Nate said, "I have it in sight, white on white center console, appears to be dead in the water. Cross, you got eyes on?"

"I have it," Cross confirmed as his eyes narrowed to focus on the boat. It was drifting with the seas on its starboard side, aggressively rolling side to side, as if no one was controlling it. About a quarter mile out, he slowed his approach to allow time for his crew to assess the situation. No one spoke, but everyone likely got that same weird feeling.

Where was the operator?

Cross took a breath, considered the possibilities, and realized there was only one thing to do. "Rig lines for slip. Making my approach, starboard side."

He'd slide the RBS into position on the other boat's port side rail, putting his starboard side to theirs to assess the situation, and tie off so they could leave in a hurry. He would then send one of his people to assess the severity of any injuries on board. It weighed on him that the other boat never replied to Station Gloucester. They were close to shore towers, so he wondered why they weren't answering.

His thoughts were suddenly broken by his crew.

"Ten feet and closing," called Nate. "Speed good, approach angle good!"

"Roger. Standby lines!"

Cross carefully eased alongside the other boat at a chosen contact position.

Nate called the approach, "Five... four... three... two... contact!"

The RBS bumped the center console softly with a mild chirp as the collar of the Coast Guard boat contacted rubber and fiberglass, and the inflated fenders took the remainder of the contact force.

"Pass all lines and take out slack, I'll steer us into the swell in a second!"

"All lines made and tight!"

"Roger. Coming around!"

Cross skillfully positioned both boats with bows into the shifting seas so they could at least have a halfway decent ride while they figured this one out. As soon as they were stable, Cross ordered, "Nate, step over, tell us what you see!"

Nate grabbed his helmet from the armrest, snapped it on, and then stepped onto the aft deck of the RBS. "Stepping over!"

Cross nodded.

Nate instantly slipped and lost his footing inside the other boat. The crew watched as Nate moved in slow motion, nearly face-planted, and grabbed the console rail at the last second. He then jumped back about three feet.

His face was ghostly white. "Motherfuck!" he screamed, his eyes darting around the deck.

Cross felt a sudden chill despite the seventy-four-degree temperature.

"Nate!" Cross somehow knew the answer to his own question, "What do you have over there?"

Nate paused for a little too long, then said in a voice too beaten for his usual energy, "Buddy, you need to see for yourself."

The risk of leaving the boat with only two crew members was not as severe as the trauma Nate was experiencing on the other boat. "Cody, on the sticks, I'm going over." The fellow RBS Coxswain calmly took the kill switch lanyard, meant to shut down the engines if the operator was pulled from the chair for any reason. He clipped in without a word.

Cross snapped on his helmet before carefully stepping over to the other boat.

Once on board, he caught sight of a man lying on his back in a sticky pool of blood. Two bullet holes marked his chest. His mouth was open in a silent scream, matching the stare of his open eyes. It almost looked like he'd been shot mid-sentence, caught completely by surprise. His pale face seemed drained of blood. Cross pulled a pair of disposable gloves from his belt, then carefully knelt, trying not to get any of the man's blood on him, and checked for a pulse. *Nothing. Dead.*

The rocking boat, the wind, and the sea spray suddenly gave Cross the feeling he was trapped in a hurricane. The suspicious phone call pulled his thoughts like a wild current. The lack of follow-up response was like an added gale-force wind. Now there was a dead body. The white tops of breaking waves were about to crush him to cap off his thoughts. His mind was overwhelmed with so many details that it was difficult to rein it all in.

Cross stood and stared at Nate. His jaw tightened, and his eyes went cold. When he finally spoke, his voice came out flat. "What was that you said about something not feeling right?"

"Jesus, Cross. Medical emergency, my ass. They fuckin' put two holes in his chest!"

As they silently considered the situation, Cross looked over the deck of the boat and noticed some bags stacked along the side. His instincts told him what they contained, and once again, his experience anchored him and told him to think differently about this case. He quietly reached for his phone as he looked back at the victim. Cross felt his blood run cold. The victim looked vaguely familiar. The realization smacked him in the face like a bag of bricks. Tony Rivetti was a known drug and weapons trafficker operating from Massachusetts down to Virginia. Rivetti's face danced in front of Cross's eyes like a specter, remembering all the time he and the MSRT had spent trying to hunt him down. They had nearly caught him once.

Rivetti was known for being the rendezvous guy, the one who would meet for an exchange of goods for money, but he didn't usually run solo. Someone else would drive the boat, and Tony would conduct the business.

Why was he out here alone? Why Gloucester?

It wasn't adding up. Cross felt the pull of his conscience. He had to do something outside the bounds of normal operations, but it might help him get some real answers. While Nate and the rest of the crew briefly turned away, he opened his phone's camera, snapped a couple of pictures of Tony, the wound, the scene, and the bags of what he suspected were drugs. He slipped his phone back into his pocket and asked for the operations camera. A moment later, he took the same pictures plus a few more without disturbing the scene.

Cross felt his stomach twist into a tight, painful knot. The weight of this case tested his professionalism and composure.

"Nate, let's get back on the RBS, contact station, and let them know we have a crime scene. Request state troopers meet us out here."

"Yeah, Boats. No problem." Nate sounded as if the magnitude of the discovery had broken something in him.

They both stepped back to the RBS, taking a moment to dip their boots in the water to remove the blood before stepping back into the cabin.

"Station Gloucester, Station Gloucester. Rescue two-nine-one-eight-three, rescue two-nine-one-eight-three on channel one-six, request you switch and answer working channel, over." Nate was still all business, even if he wasn't in the best headspace.

A moment later, the secure VHF came to life. "One-eight-three, Station Gloucester on working channel. Go ahead, over."

"Station, one-eight-three, we have an adrift boat with a deceased operator with two gunshot wounds. Notify command and begin notifications to state troopers and CGIS, over."

Nate glanced over his shoulder at Cross.

Cross felt his eyes staring at nothing. He felt like he was searching for an answer in an abyss. He might not be able to find what he was looking for.

Nate shrugged his shoulders.

Just hope for the best. We're doing it by the book.

One minute went by with no reply, and Cross knew there should have been one by now. He had taken Nate's place and was about to call again when the silence was broken.

"One-eight-three, station," came a gruff voice of a seasoned maritime professional.

Cross immediately recognized the voice of Chief Warrant Officer Bill Grayson.

"Station, one-eight-three, go." Cross was apprehensive about what was coming. He felt his heart race; his palms were slick with sweat, and his instincts reached for distant possibilities.

Grayson's taking over was outside normal operations, and Cross felt unnerved.

"One-eight-three, station. Civil authorities will not be meeting you out there. You are to tow the adrift boat to station, tie it to our inside slip. We'll figure out what's going on with civil notification later."

This wasn't protocol for a homicide or suspicious death in any form. Every part of Cross's being screamed that something was off. Grayson's order wasn't unorthodox; it was dangerous. However, challenging the officer-in-charge over the radio would only create friction, maybe even isolate him before he had facts to back up his gut. His thumb hovered over the mic key for a second longer than it should have. He could feel the sweat collecting on his brow. He sensed the eyes of his crew watching to see what kind of leader he was in this tense moment.

"Station, one-eight-three copies all," he finally said, calmly but abruptly. "Returning to station with adrift boat. Nothing further, out."

He slowly slipped the mic into its overhead cradle. A lump formed in his throat. *What the hell is the old man doing? This isn't caution, it's control.* Cross had spent enough time in combat zones to know the difference.

2

UNITED STATES COAST GUARD STATION
GLOUCESTER, MASSACHUSETTS, MAY 2022

CROSS AND HIS crew followed Grayson's orders and returned to the station. They tied the center console boat to the inside slip away from prying eyes. Nate had to admit Grayson's directions didn't sound like a request; it sounded more like an order.

Grayson met them on the pier, helped handle lines, and then patted each crewmember on the back before telling them he would guard the boat and body until an officer from Sector arrived to start the investigation with local law enforcement's assistance.

That wasn't protocol for something like this, and Cross said, "But sir—"

Grayson snapped back, "But nothing, Boats. Get your crew some chow, and don't come back down here. I've got the watch. That's an order."

"Aye-aye, sir." Cross walked after his crew, unable to shake the thoughts that this was way outside of policy. Everything about this felt wrong.

●●●●●

Cross had seen death before—dealt with it before. Gruesome injuries were no mystery. While his stomach was unsettled, he got through the lunch of grilled chicken, mixed bell peppers, and rice pilaf. His crew barely touched their food.

Nate endlessly mixed his rice with his fork. Cody took one bite of the chicken and stared at his plate as if searching for a deeper meaning to life. Lauren looked almost frozen in time and space. Her hands were flat on her thighs. She sat unblinking, staring at the wall.

Cross finished his meal quickly and then went and sat down with each team member in turn to check in. He had learned over the years that no one was ever as strong as they portrayed. He had lost two close friends from a previous unit to suicide, neither of whom gave Cross the impression that they contemplated that most final solution to life's problems.

Nate was shaken, broken, after seeing such a graphic death. "Cross, why? What was the point of that? Leave a guy for dead in a boat off Salem? I can't get it out of my head."

"I wish I knew, Nate, I really do. It's hard to get it out of my head, too. What do you think you need?"

"Time," Nate said with a sigh. "Just time, buddy."

Cross paused for half a second too long, and Nate noticed. "There's something else, isn't there? Please tell me you didn't recognize the dead guy."

Cross couldn't mask the look of admission on his face. He wouldn't lie to his friend and engineer. "Yeah, Nate. I did. He was someone we tracked on the team. We almost got him once. This whole thing seems shifty."

"Christ, Cross! Now what?"

"I don't know yet. I can't figure that part out yet. All I know is I have to run it up the chain of command."

"Got it. Let me know if you need any help with that. These guys sometimes need some convincing."

"Thank you," Cross said with a nod, "I appreciate it."

Cody was much the same. Younger and less experienced, his reservations came out immediately. "BM1," Cody said with his head cocked to the side in confusion, "can you clarify something for me?"

"Sure, Cody. What's bugging you?"

"Nate said 'medical emergency my ass.' Was that the call here?"

"That's what it was supposed to be, yes."

"But it was a dead body instead. Why the discrepancy? Why didn't we know earlier?" The look on Cody's boyish face made Cross wonder if his subordinate was ready to go kick in Grayson's door himself.

"Cody, I don't have any answers on this yet. I'm going to get there. In the meantime, is there anything I can do to help you cope with the case and fallout?"

Cody spoke in boat driver terms for a moment with a brief smirk, considering the trauma of the situation. "I'll be fine in the long run. It'll take time and distance to get this in the past. But I need to know that this wasn't some kind of weird setup. The whole thing just smells off."

Cross briefly saw Tony Rivetti's face flash through his memory again. "Cody, I agree with you. I'm not sure why it was off yet, but I'm going to figure it out. Promise."

"Thank you, Boats. I suggest you go check in on Lauren, too," Cody said with a subtle nod to their youngest crewmember, who looked like she was a hollow shell of herself, "I don't think she's okay."

Cross moved toward Lauren. As the youngest and newest to the Coast Guard, she graduated from basic training in Cape May, New Jersey, only a couple of months ago. She looked like she'd seen a ghost; she was pale, stoic, and didn't say much. Cross figured she would need some help to process what she was feeling. As he sat down with her, he cautiously put a calming hand on top of hers. "Lauren, I'm so sorry you had to witness something so graphic. Talk to me. What's going on?"

Lauren's eyes misted over, and she looked at Cross with a face that showed equal parts sadness, shock, and uncertainty. "BM1, I don't know. I—I've never seen something like that." She sighed and pulled her hand away. A tear rolled down her cheek. "When I went through basic training, they said most stations are relaxed, other than occasionally being busy with cases. No one ever said we'd be witnesses to murders."

"If it helps," Cross said with a sympathetic smirk, "they didn't say anything like that when I went through either."

"Kind of," Lauren said as she wiped the tears from her cheeks. "I'm just trying to make peace with the fact that it had to happen on our watch."

"I completely understand. This is a difficult situation to handle."

"Doesn't the Coast Guard have resources to help us with this? It's not all on you, BM1."

"They do, Lauren. I'll get those lined up. Please ask if you need anything else."

"Thank you for checking in, BM1."

"In case you wondered, there's a reason I'm so invested in you, Cody, and Nate. Years ago, I witnessed one of my fellow non-rates at my first unit sexually assaulted. Four fellow service-members, people she knew and trusted, snuck into her room at night. I felt helpless. The next day, when she told me about it, she made me promise not to say anything. She later reported it, and all the offenders experienced the wrath of a commanding officer who wouldn't tolerate that kind of behavior. After seeing the trauma that it caused, I made a promise to myself that I would never let my crew deal with the ugly things alone. I would always have their backs."

Lauren wore a look of disgust and horror. "That's horrible. I had no idea. But now I see why you want to take care of us. I know I appreciate it, and I'm sure the rest of the crew does as well."

Cross felt strongly that he should take his crew off the board and let another boat crew handle operations until his crew got the help they needed. The conversation with Lauren confirmed it. He wasn't going to lose more friends and shipmates to things he could help resolve by being a good leader and friend.

●●●●●

Cross marched into the executive petty officer's office, next to the communications center, and knocked. Chief Jonathan Drazen answered, "Enter."

"Chief, my crew is torn up over what happened. I recommend an immediate stand down and critical incident support."

"Absolutely. You'll have what you need before the end of the day, and your crew can sit it out. We'll recall people if necessary. Are you doing all right?"

"I've seen more than I care to, but it's not the worst thing I've seen. I think I'll be okay, but I'll check in with the chaplain when he gets here to be sure."

"Smart man. Don't assume you're bulletproof. It takes a toll on everyone."

"Thank you, Chief. I appreciate all your support."

"You're welcome. Let me know if I can do more."

Cross left feeling like he had the ear of his chief and a strong ally.

As Cross returned to his team, he noticed an unmarked SUV drive up to the back lot of the station. He slipped into the communications room to observe.

The SUV pulled into a spot across from the building, and an

officer in short-sleeve dress blues stepped out, adjusting his formal cover. Cross could barely make out the rank: lieutenant. The man made his way to the pier like he knew where he was going. He descended the brow down to the boats and disappeared.

Cross thought it was strange that the officer didn't check in with the station or chief first. He slipped out the exterior door and casually walked to the deck shop, a little outbuilding by the edge of the pier. He snuck to the back window and cracked it open, hoping he could overhear the conversation.

"Nice to see you, Bosun."

"Nice to see you too, sir, though I wish it were under better circumstances," Grayson replied.

"Tell me about it."

"Not sure what these guys were thinking, it wasn't careful at all."

"I'll reach out to them and make sure they know."

"I'll talk to them. They'll listen to me."

"Fine, where do we stand here?"

"Waiting on locals so we can call this a drug deal gone bad, nothing more to talk about, sir."

"Understood, I've taken steps with Sector. You shouldn't get any heat from them. I'll leave you to your job."

Cross crept into the office and turned his phone to silent. No sense giving himself away. He heard the lieutenant stomp up the brow in his dress shoes. The SUV revved to life and drove away. When Cross thought the coast was clear, he slipped back into the station and walked into his duty room. His thoughts went in two directions. *What was Grayson into, and who was the lieutenant?* He could think of one way to check his suspicions. Tony Rivetti was a known quantity, not just some random pusher. Cross felt compelled to find out why he ended up dead in such an unlikely place.

Cross waited a sufficient time to allow Grayson to return to his office and to a normal rhythm. His instincts calmed the storm inside him and gave him a subtle nod that he was doing the right thing. Waiting would allow breathing room—an intentional pause. He walked to Grayson's office ten minutes later, his heart racing slightly. This conversation could reveal something or nothing, depending on how Cross chose his words.

He stopped at the doorframe and knocked twice loudly.

Grayson spoke quickly. "Enter!"

Cross squared the corner into Chief Warrant Officer Grayson's spacious office with its natural wood desk made from local timber decades earlier and an array of nautical memorabilia befitting a man of Grayson's position and title.

"Sir, do you have a few minutes to discuss the case we just encountered?"

Grayson was unreadable in his facial expressions, and his answer revealed nothing. "Sure, Boats. What's on your mind?"

"Is there some reason we had to break protocol on the investigation?"

"You mean the lack of local resources?" Grayson grinned.

"Right. Is there a reason we had to take it on our own? Shouldn't we be pushing more buttons on this?"

"How would we do that exactly?"

"Calling up and down the chain of command until someone answers. Banging on doors like boatswain's mates until someone helps us out."

"I understand your position, I really do. Let me give you some insight. I've learned in my time here that local resources are somewhat unreliable. Sometimes we're required to act independently. You know that as a trained boat driver. Sometimes you need to make a judgment call on your own. Totality of experience, right?"

"Well, sir, I get that. I'm just saying, shouldn't we be pressing to not compromise a murder case so there's a proper investigation?" Cross folded his arms over his chest. He couldn't help feeling confused about why Grayson wasn't seeing reason. There was still nothing to read in the man's reaction.

Grayson was listening with no emotion on his face. He grinned as he said, "Listen, I get it, but I'm not going to burn bridges here. These resources we have here, Gloucester Police, Essex Sheriff, and Massachusetts State Police, they're unreliable, as I said. If I bark at them, I risk open hostility between cooperative agencies."

"But sir, if it's their responsibility to—"

Grayson abruptly cut him off. "Cross, listen, I'm not compromising our limited cooperation for 'could have, should have.' I need you to stand down, and we're going to reach out as soon as we can and let our professional law enforcement partners do their jobs. Are we clear on that?"

"As a bell, sir."

"Good... dismissed."

Cross walked out of the room, feeling more confused than ever before. Grayson's actions were odd, even suspicious, but the words left no path to anywhere other than a dead end. Grayson said he would contact local resources, and there was nothing more to chase.

●●●●●

That night at the station, Cross checked on his boat crew again. Chief Drazen delivered on his promise of critical incident counseling, and the coroner took the body. The crew was still shaken and bagged for further missions this duty cycle, per the chief's concurrence with Cross and his judgment. Still, they seemed like they could move on, given some time off the boats. As for his own needs, Cross simply needed to clear his head.

The next morning, he stepped into the dim station gym while most of the crew was still asleep. The air smelled faintly of rubber mats, old sweat, and a worn resistance band that hadn't been replaced in years. He didn't bother turning on the overheads; he worked out in the pale glow of emergency lights and his fury.

He started with a mile run on the treadmill, Metallica's Until It Sleeps blaring in his headphones.

The words echoed the pain he felt, staying right by his side.

The rhythm was out of sync with his run. His legs moved, but his mind focused on the adrift boat, the blood, and the supine dead man staring him in the face from the deck of the Boston Whaler.

The man had a name, even if he didn't want to say it out loud on the radio. Tony Rivetti's face danced in front of his eyes like a fuzzy projection on a dirty white board. Rivetti had a dossier in the team intel shop, complete with pictures of a man who had been on the wrong side of the law for his entire life.

The curse of his crew seeing that bloody murder matched the words, and it remained seared in his brain.

He dropped to the mat and pushed through burpees, pushups, and kettlebell swings. He worked fast and hard with no rest. His shoulders burned, but it still wasn't enough. The image of Nate's white face, slipping in blood, burned into his skull like a bad tattoo.

He thought about how Tony Rivetti could no longer harm anyone. Of course, he couldn't; he'd taken two bullets to the chest.

He moved to the heavy bag and hit it harder than usual. Jab, elbow, knee. Again. Then he took karambit strikes—three tight arcs aimed at an imaginary throat. Again. He tried to clear his head, but it wasn't working. He had visions of the team as they geared up for a takedown to bring in Rivetti to face justice. The rattle of rifles as rounds racked into chambers, the chirp of radios as they were checked for proper encryption, the buzz of their night vision as they checked focus. The mission failed that night because intel had been off, and Rivetti was long gone before the MSRT showed up.

He lost control mid-combo. His fist clipped the edge of the bag and slid off awkwardly, jamming his wrist. "Shit," he hissed, shaking it out.

The bag swayed in front of him, taunting him like the specters of his past life on the team.

Cross leaned forward, rested his forearms against the vinyl, and let his head drop. The silence in his ears rang louder than the music. The chaos he was trying to sweat out remained.

He breathed hard, shutting his eyes.

Slowly, he pushed off the bag, finished his set out of sheer stubbornness, and finally stretched more to hide the tremble in his hands than to loosen up.

He was still rattled, but he had a crew depending on him. At least that was something he could still hold on to.

He went back to his duty room and showered, trying to process what he had witnessed during the last twenty-four hours. As the hot water ran over his muscles, he let the events of the day filter through his head like a spin cycle.

As he pulled on his uniform, put on his dependable GoRuck MACV boots, and grabbed his karambit, Cross paused with the karambit in his hand. He unfolded it, feeling how perfectly balanced the knife felt. His thoughts wandered to four years earlier, when the blade had become a part of his persona, woven into his identity.

●●●●●

Jakarta, Indonesia, 2018

The air in the dimly lit training hall was thick with the scent of sweat and incense. Cross's bare feet were stuck to the worn wooden floor; his shirt was soaked through, and his lungs dragged in the heavy and humid Southeast Asian air. He gripped the dull training karambit, trembling slightly. The curved blade still felt foreign in his hand.

Pak Hendra moved like smoke. He was fluid, agile, diminutive, and terrifying at the same time. The older man circled Cross in silence; his eyes were sharp and unreadable.

Cross lunged, sweeping the blade toward his master with nearly perfect form. In a blink, Hendra sidestepped, redirected Cross's momentum, and twisted his wrist. The karambit clattered to the mat. Before Cross could recover, he was face-first on the ground, and the edge of his master's trainer blade pressed against his neck. It was the fifth time that night that Hendra had effortlessly overpowered his student.

"Again," Hendra said, stepping back.

Cross pushed himself up slowly, clenching his jaw. He was bathed in sweat. His shoulder throbbed from the landing.

Cross retrieved the blade and reset.

He paused more than long enough for Pak Hendra to notice.

"You hesitate. Why?"

Cross wiped his forearm across his brow. "Because I keep screwing it up."

"Good. Now you are learning."

"What do you mean?"

The master approached, slowly and deliberately. "The blade is not your strength. It is your mirror. If you strike with ego, it will show your overconfidence. If you move with fear, it will display your fear for your enemy." He tapped the karambit in Cross's grip with a calloused finger. "This is not an American knife. It does not forgive arrogance or ego."

Cross lowered the blade slightly, breathing shallow. He didn't know what to say.

"You came here thinking you were already dangerous. Now you are being remade."

For once, Cross didn't argue.

That night, after drills, Hendra handed him a live karambit with a tiger-striped finish. Cross turned it over in his hand, feeling the sting of failure with every bruise.

"You are not yet a master of this blade," Hendra said with a sage nod. "But tonight, you finally stopped trying to be."

From that moment on, the Gerber folder stayed in his pack, forgotten. The karambit never left his side.

3

CROSS AND MELANIE MET ONLINE. The modern cliché had not escaped most of their family and friends, and it would be a regular joke within their small inner circle that they had both been online shopping for a spouse.

There was an instant connection that only improved when they finally met in person. Cross was instantly captivated by her. She was five-foot-seven with light brown hair that flowed like a pristine river over her fit shoulders. Her brown eyes occasionally flickered to hazel in different light. Cross felt her eyes could swallow a man whole. Her curves befit a young woman who takes care of her body. She was stunning, and Cross knew right away he wanted a life with Melanie.

He had a year left at his unit, and Cross heard rumblings of orders to the MSRT. Not wanting to leave Melanie in the dark, Cross told her after a few dates what might be on the horizon. She took it better than he had expected. Her initial discomfort with Cross being in harm's way transformed from a prolonged conversation into a sense of peace. Her father had been a man of action like Cross, so it was familiar and comfortable like an old blanket. When Cross asked Melanie's father about his line of work, he remembered the old line. "I work for the State Department." Melanie and her siblings had always suspected it meant something else, but never confirmed it. Cross knew right away, especially after he and Melanie discussed her upbringing full of martial arts, fitness, shooting trips, and survival skills training.

After less than a year of dating, Cross proposed at their favorite local restaurant. He stepped away to use the men's room, handing the ring to the waitress with a plan to surprise Melanie. He walked back to the table a couple of minutes later. The waitress came up behind him, not thirty seconds later. She said he dropped something. He stood up to take the ring box from her and turned around to find Melanie with a confused look as he dropped smoothly to one knee, asking her to marry him. She was a deer caught in the headlights for a moment, which seemed to stretch into eternity. Cross thought she was almost about to say no, and then she nearly screamed, "Yes!"

The whole restaurant erupted into applause and whistling for several minutes as the couple kissed and hugged.

They were married a few months later in a quiet ceremony with a handful of family and friends. After a honeymoon in Hawaii, they prepared for their future together. The new marriage was a happy one, but the specter of a tour with MSRT loomed over them like a storm cloud. When the orders came through, Cross was confirmed as a selectee for the MSRT and ordered to join a four-year tour. By the numbers, he would be an old man among youngsters, hard-charging career law enforcement men and women from MSST, TACLET, and other high-speed, low-drag units where MSRT typically hand-picked their recruits from. Cross was an oddball. Melanie worried about his safety, but he assured her that his age also meant greater wisdom and maturity, which would help him maintain a safer career.

●●●●●

Beverly, Massachusetts, May 2022

When Cross got back home, he gave Melanie a hug and a kiss that pulled some of his stress away like cobwebs brushed off an old book. He set his belongings in their appropriate spots and returned to the living room. Having known her husband since before his days on MSRT, Melanie could sense something was eating at him. Her degree in forensic psychology helped her see the little flags more easily. He quietly sat at the table until she pressed, "Okay, what's going through that battle-tested brain of yours?"

Cross stared at the grain of the wood table for a moment, tracing slow circles with a finger. "We got a call a couple of days ago. It was supposed to be a medical emergency." He paused, thinking of all the times he had been forced to conceal information about his job to keep Melanie safe, and the heavy guilt of not being able to share enough with her. After a moment's thought, he put his palm flat on the table. "Turned out to be a dead guy."

Melanie exhaled slowly. "Jesus. You and the crew.... Are you all right?"

"They're shaken. Nate slipped in the blood. Cody's pissed. Lauren is broken."

Melanie studied him. "And you?"

He didn't answer right away. He rubbed a hand across his face. His eyes were tired in a way that sleep couldn't fix.

"I keep seeing his face, the guy in the boat. Tony Rivetti. He was a trafficker; we know that now, but he was still human. Someone executed him like it was nothing."

Melanie gave him a silent space.

"I told myself that I was done chasing ghosts," he said in almost a whisper. "Done being the guy who dives into the storm just because it's there. I wanted peace. I wanted you, us."

She reached out and took his hand.

"I'm apprehensive," he admitted. His voice cracked slightly. "Not only of what's happening. But of what I might become. I feel like I'm slipping back into that guy I had to be on MSRT, angry, distant, always on edge. It's so easy to go back to that life. You remember what I was like back then."

Melanie's thumb traced a slow arc across the back of his hand. Her soft eyes finally fixed on his. "I remember, and I remember why you did it. I also remember the man who came home and tried like hell to build a life with me. You forget, it was familiar to me. My dad was gone all the time, like you. State Department, whatever that really meant. Then he came home, trained me in martial arts, weapons, and personal security. The thing is, he always came home and tried like hell for a normal life. I recognized that in you the moment we met."

He looked deep into the brown eyes he'd frequently been lost in as his mind slowly digested her words.

She wasn't judging. She was anchoring.

"You don't have to be perfect, Logan. Just be honest and smart. If this thing goes deeper than a dead body in a boat, then yeah, I want you to chase it, but not alone—not at the cost of who you are."

He nodded as he felt a weight leave his shoulders, almost as if he was removing his body armor. "I think I needed to hear that."

Melanie smiled with warm affection. "Good. Now go make yourself useful and take the trash out. I'm not letting this house fall apart because you're lost in your own thoughts."

"You're right," Cross said, the smile finally returning to his face for the first time in days. "I've got a phone call to make. I know someone who might know what to do with this one."

●●●●●

Officer Jake Harper was a good friend during their time together in Portland and continued to be long after the two moved in different directions. Cross came to rely on Harper when things went sideways, or even when he needed an honest assessment, someone to tell him he was going to die on the wrong hill. Harper held Cross in the same high regard. This was one of those times for Cross. He needed someone to help shape his next move, so he didn't die on the wrong hill due to any errors in judgment.

Cross could remember a case in Portland where they truly connected. They were taking a break from underway operations, getting a few extra drinks and a pit stop on a day so sunny and warm that it should have been a vacation, not a duty day. The radio blared angrily to life with a report of a medical emergency on a fishing boat. They responded with lightning speed and no station authorization, knowing every second counted. A Good Samaritan responded before the Coast Guard boat could reach the scene, and Cross was told to stand down. When the station got wind of the response on no prior command authorization, Cross took withering attacks from the officer-in-charge. It didn't matter to Cross or Harper. They knew they had done the right thing, even if they were told otherwise. That mentality of doing the right thing no matter the cost carried forward in both men long after they went their separate ways.

Cross secure-texted Harper, asking if he had some time to help him resolve something. He hinted that Harper might want his detective hat buckled on tight for this one.

Harper responded enthusiastically that he always had time for a good mystery. Jake Harper never turned away from a challenge.

> Cross: Here's the crux. We were called out to a vague medical emergency with no further info or contact. Found a victim with two bullet holes in his chest, left dead in the boat with bags of narcotics.

> Harper: Who was the vic?

> Cross: Tony Rivetti, known trafficker.

There was a significant pause after this, and Cross wondered if Harper was called away on other urgent business.

> Harper: Okay, that's not an accident, that's a murder through and through. Any other evidence of something suspicious?

> Cross: The drugs on deck suggest a swap gone wrong. But my OIC locked me out, then met with a lieutenant I didn't recognize the moment it happened. No contact with the rest of station or XPO.

> Harper: That doesn't sound like a coincidence; already sounds damning. Problem is it may be out of your hands now. And it's isolated. Unless something else happens.

> Cross: I know. I hope this is the end of it, but I don't think it is.

Harper had two recommendations. First, he thought it would be a good idea to take a pause from the case. It would allow time for the dust to settle. Then, in a week or so, he advised Cross to make an outside inquiry to the state troopers to see if they had an open case file. If they didn't, it could mean the case had been quietly put to rest at a lower level, suggesting possible foul play. The second recommendation was simpler but would take more patience. Harper suggested casually observing the OIC's demeanor, his dealings, visitors, phone calls, if possible, and any unusual absences more than would befit a commander of a busy search-and-rescue station.

They were exceptional recommendations, and Cross felt compelled to play this smart. He needed to develop a pattern on Grayson. If something truly dangerous was in play, the only good way to resolve it was to build a proper case with good evidence. The conversation ended with Harper asking if Cross had any pictures of the victim and scene, which Cross transmitted securely. Harper said he would start digging around and see if there was anything pointing to a larger threat than what he already knew. He also pointed out the most obvious part of this whole situation, one that Melanie had already mentioned. He stated bluntly that Cross could either do the right thing or walk away; he had never known Cross to walk away.

4

UNITED STATES COAST GUARD STATION
GLOUCESTER, MASSACHUSETTS, MAY 2022

WHEN CROSS ARRIVED BACK on duty for the weekend, he felt like his head was largely clear of all the events of the last duty period. He still thought about the scene, the body, the blood, but they were subdued thoughts, almost as if they were partially concealed in a late August fog bank. He was still fit for duty. He had done some punishing workouts the last couple of days, mostly to stay in exceptional condition, but also to clear his head of any unnecessary thoughts. He had a mission, a career ahead of him, and a mystery to solve.

To keep attention at a minimum, he planned not to bring up the inconsistencies in the case. If someone else brought it up, he would suggest it wasn't worth lingering on, making everyone at the unit, and especially his command, believe he was ready to move on. He wasn't, but for now, no one needed to know. He would do his job the best way he knew how, by continuing to look after his crew. He would portray the outward visage of a boatswain's mate first class with a good heart and head in the game.

It was a typical Friday, warm enough to be comfortable but not oppressively hot. Cross got his crew underway for a short training mission and a couple of quick law enforcement boardings to get them back in the saddle and doing the same amazing job they always had. After their training and boardings, he committed to sitting down with them at the picnic bench outside for lunch and follow up on the conversations from earlier in the week.

He approached Nate, who was disembarking. "Hey, Nate, are you doing all right?"

"Yeah, buddy," Nate responded, a look of uncertainty still on his seasoned face. "I'm trying not to think about it too much, honestly."

"I understand. It was a rough one. Let's get the boat crew together for lunch outside. It's sunny, warm, and we can get everyone engaged a little bit. You good for it?"

"Sure. It can't hurt. I need to quickly enter the boardings, and I'll meet you there."

"I'm going to sign the boat in, see you back here in ten?"

"Sounds good." Nate then walked toward the boat haul-out building to do his work.

They made it back to the Can-Do Café about the same time and found Cody and Lauren eating in silence by themselves. The quiet energy felt like a curse covering the two. Cross approached them and said, "Grab your food, and come with us to the picnic bench so we can chat."

They all sat down, and Cross said, "Thanks for joining me. I wanted us to enjoy the sunny weather, and I wanted to check in on all of you. You three are my priority here. Everything else is a distant second. Have you gotten the help you need?"

There were silent stares for a moment as if everyone was trying to size up Cross and his motivation, and then Nate spoke up. "Thanks, Boats. I appreciate you looking out for us and trying to get us back in the saddle. We've all gotten help from critical incident support. I honestly think we need some time to process it, but I can't speak for anyone else fully. Lauren?"

"I think I'll be okay, but that's the worst thing I've ever seen." She looked like she was in another world, cold and distant.

Cody quickly chimed in. "Boats, you know what I need? I need to know what the hell that was all about. Nothing about that felt right at all. No one coming to peaceful Gloucester signed up for violent murders. That's not the type of area this is."

Cross shook his head as he felt the weight of Cody's assessment hit him like an elbow to the sternum. "No, we didn't. But we're in it now, and how you handle adversity defines your character." Cross looked each of his crew in the eye to gauge their reaction.

These kids, his crew, trusted him to lead them through storms and shootouts. This was fog—a minefield—and he had no charted course. He wasn't sure what scared him more, telling them the truth or lying to protect them.

Cross could feel Cody's anger boiling to the surface and knew he would need to tread carefully. He didn't want to dismiss his feelings, but he also couldn't risk leaping without looking. Cross chose his words carefully as if trying to sidestep a tripwire. "Listen, I'm sorry you all had to deal with this. It's not something any of us hope for." He took a deep breath to center his mind.

"I agree, it felt off." He exhaled, letting the words hang in the salty air. "Truth is, I don't have answers right now. I've got suspicions, but nothing that would hold up. Not yet."

He looked at each of them in turn, jaw tight, a friendly but serious expression on his face. "You all handled yourselves better than I ever could've asked for. I don't say that lightly. Cody, your gut instinct out there? You nailed it. Don't ever second-guess that."

Cody blinked rapidly. "Thanks, Boats."

"Just let me work through the details on this case. I'll fill you in as I get more. Does that work?"

"You've got it," Nate said.

Lauren nodded beside him.

Cross knew he could still trust his crew. It felt like the number of people he could trust with this was exceedingly small.

●●●●●

The weekend duty was relatively quiet, with only a couple of minor SAR cases and a handful of boardings. The worst thing the crew dealt with was a diver, who surfaced too quickly and got a minor case of the bends, causing some heart irregularities. Thankfully, they resolved on their own within about ten minutes of the RBS arriving on the scene.

The other case was a typical sailboat owner from the area operating on their gas inboard engine who ran out of gas. When asked why he hadn't put up his sails, the operator said with a sheepish grin and an embarrassed chuckle that he had no idea how to do that. That was a common problem compounded by sailboat owners who seemed to have more money than brains. The crew ended up towing him a short distance to the nearest harbor with the motor lifeboat under Cody's command. If not for their timely assistance, the sailboat would have ended up on the rocks between Baker's Island and Great Misery.

On the duty swap Monday morning, Cross noted the station rhythm, which had almost returned to normal. The clatter of chairs being moved in the galley, the cooks cleaning up after breakfast to the sounds of dishes and bowls clanging in the deep sinks, and the shuffle of boots as the crew moved through the halls was the same as always. The murder hadn't come up at all, which was a little surprising. He planned on calling through Signal to the state police office later that day to see if there was an open file on the murder, like Harper had suggested. Cross let his next moves swim through his mind like a school of cod off Cape Ann's pristine waters. He knew his next move would be driven by his conversation with the state police.

Cross left after he had passed all appropriate information to his counterpart in the other section. He attempted to make the mental shift from uniform to civilian life, but it felt like his old Acura was stuck in between gears. It was as if the shift was blocked, closed off to him in that moment.

When he got home, he gave Melanie the usual hug and kiss. He felt some of his stress lift like a morning fog with her soft touch. She asked how things were going.

"The crew is improving, but they're concerned about what happened and why. I don't have answers for them." Cross felt the burden of the situation as if it was a lead weight on his chest. His crew was looking for direction. But his brain had been put through a spin cycle, scrambled on the missing pieces.

"This will take time," Melanie said reassuringly, "it's like Harper said, the right case needs to be built from the ground up. That doesn't happen overnight. How many murder stories have I read? You know how many were prosecuted in days or weeks? None. Not one."

"I know," Cross said. "Work the problem. Prioritize and execute. I have a call to make."

He stepped into his garage, adorned with the memories of units past and present. There were old, decommissioned boat flags, an old monkey's fist cut off a heavy weather heaving line, and a spent casing from a MK-127 illumination flare. His gaze paused above his workbench, where he lingered on a parting gift from the crew at the MSRT. They had ordered him a SOG SEAL Strike, a vicious-looking blade with a partial serration and a gut hook spine. It was a unit tradition that held deep meaning for everyone involved. On the side of the matte black coating of the blade was engraved:

"Iron Cross" 2018 - 2022
Night Stalker Team

Cross reached above the bench and removed the blade. He felt the balance of the finely crafted weapon. His mind flooded with adrenaline, and his heart thumped in his chest as he thought of high-risk boardings, raids to capture or kill high-value targets, and every near-death event. He returned the blade to its rack and paused as he reflected on the experiences that had led him to this moment in time. His mind told him that this was all a strange nightmare, but his heart told him there was a reason he was thrown into this mess.

He sat on the stool at his bench and dialed the state police barracks in Danvers. He waited while it rang a couple of times, and then a man answered. "Massachusetts State Police. How can I help you?"

Cross knew he needed to identify himself; otherwise, he would get nowhere with this conversation. He would be risking some minor blowback if this got back to the station, but he didn't have a choice. "This is Petty Officer Cross with the US Coast Guard. I'm checking into something, wondering if you can help with a little information."

"Sure thing, Petty Officer Cross. What can we help with?" The voice was friendly, engaging, and full of an energetic passion for service.

"Well, I'm trying to see if you have a case open for a homicide that happened off Cape Ann a little under a week ago." Cross hoped he wasn't giving too much away about the reasoning behind his questions.

"Hang on," the trooper said. "Let me dig it up and see what we have."

After a long pause, Cross heard what sounded like the trooper taking a sip from a mug of coffee.

The trooper cleared his throat and then said, "So, I'm not seeing anything. You're sure it was off Cape Ann?"

"Yes," Cross said. "If you don't have it, you don't have it."

"Wait, back up," the trooper demanded with sudden forcefulness. "Are you saying there was a murder last week that we didn't know about?"

"Seems that way," Cross admitted. "But is it possible local or county took on the case? It could have been an unknown victim or not high profile." He was digging a hole, but he also needed to figure out if the investigation had stalled somewhere.

"I suppose it's possible," the trooper said hesitantly. "But they're still supposed to notify us in case there's something they can't work on their end. It's unusual for a local department to hold notifications; they always seem to need help with something."

"Thank you for the help." Cross had part of the information he needed, and he had to end the conversation before he revealed anything significant about his intentions.

"What boat station did you say you were from?"

"I didn't." Cross hung up before the trooper could ask further questions. He knew he might have revealed he was working outside his command, and that might get back to Grayson, but it was possible the inquiry would at least be delayed if it happened at all. That might buy him some time to figure out how to handle any fallout without drawing any further attention to his course of action.

Cross's inquiry went from Troop A barracks of the Massachusetts State Police to the Essex County sheriff's department; the state trooper in the operations center had deemed it suspicious that a murder wasn't reported any higher than local police. Essex County sheriff informed the trooper that they showed no record of a murder, and they not-so-politely requested the state police find out why. The next call would be to the Gloucester police department. They had a good reputation, so the trooper couldn't figure out why they would keep this to themselves.

Upon an inquiry to Gloucester PD, the trooper discovered there was a brief investigation into a murder off Great Misery Island. However, since the victim was an unknown drug pusher, and no next of kin existed, they were forced to close the investigation. When asked who ordered them to close out the investigation, Gloucester PD stated the order originated with Chief Warrant Officer Bill Grayson, Officer-in-Charge of United States Coast Guard Station Gloucester.

5

UNITED STATES COAST GUARD STATION
GLOUCESTER, MASSACHUSETTS, MAY 2022

CROSS WAS BACK on duty a couple of days later, wondering if his inquiry would result in a tongue-lashing from Grayson or the chief. Cross stepped outside his chain of command, seeking answers about the murder, and came up short, finding out that the investigation stalled long before reaching the Massachusetts State Police. It was unclear where the investigation stalled, or if it had to do directly with Grayson. Cross needed to monitor the situation. He hoped the outside agency inquiry hadn't alerted Grayson that there was someone on his trail. The thought elicited a memory of his earlier years, learning to read his environment. He was doing the same again, just on a different scale and in different surroundings.

•••••

Shenandoah Valley, Appalachian Trail, Virginia August 2008

Leaves rustled through the trees, dancing in the late summer breeze. The sun peeked through gaps in the forest cover. Cross put one foot in front of another, his legs burning, his heart and lungs pumping to suck in precious oxygen to keep him going.

Now was not the time to stop. The distance hike was to a level camping area, which they had to reach before dark. It was day two of three, and Cross felt stronger than ever. This was one of the longer backpacking trips he had done since his days in Boy Scouts years earlier. He was with some friends on the twenty-four-mile, three-day trek on a section of the Appalachian Trail in Virginia's Shenandoah Valley.

Cross was keenly aware of everything around him. He squeezed the shoulder strap of his trusty, ratty old Lowe frame pack that had been given to him as a sentimental gift from his aging Scoutmaster, who could no longer go on the long trips with the troop. He kept it years later as a tribute to the legacy of old Tony, and some of the most treasured years and experiences of Cross's young life. Of the many lessons Tony had passed on from his decades of life and trail experience, there were two he remembered most. The first was to simply do the right thing, no matter the personal cost. The second was to always be aware of the environment; read the space and people around you, on the trail, and in life.

On this day, Cross was aware of the natural rhythm of the woods and the trail, every chirp of an insect, call of a bird, and every noise of a squirrel running across the dry ground. He would be able to recognize even a single noise outside that established pattern, as focused as he was after all his years honing that skill. It would pay dividends years later, although he didn't know it at the time. Cross was priming himself for life as a maritime first responder long before that decision was made.

The hike was suddenly interrupted by a sound that must have come from something larger than the average wildlife in the area. He stopped dead in his tracks, signaling everyone else to pause with a closed fist in the air. No sooner had everyone stopped moving than a juvenile black bear wandered right into their path. They all watched as the bear paused to stare at the strange visitors in its territory, and then it moved on into the bushes. It was a pivotal moment during that trip that would remain with all the friends for years. Cross continued to hone the skill of reading his environment and the people in it.

●●●●●

A knock on the window of his old 4Runner interrupted Cross from his thoughts. He was in the station parking lot after having driven to Gloucester completely on autopilot. He was lost in his thoughts about what set him on his current path, that he didn't see anyone approaching the vehicle. He opened the car door, shaking the past from his mind.

Nate stood there with an inquisitive look on his face. "You ever going to join us for section swap, or sit there lost in space all day?"

"Sorry. Nate, lots on my mind. Good to see you a little more back to normal!"

"Yeah, I figure these things will happen. No amount of feeling sorry for myself will make it go away. Best I can do is try to put it behind me for the sake of my family."

Cross wasn't sure yet if Nate had completely moved on, but there would be time to ask more later. "That's good to hear. Have you seen or talked to Cody or Lauren?"

"They're both here, but I haven't seen them yet."

"Okay. As soon as we get a free moment, let's get together and make sure they're doing all right."

Cross loaded his gear from his SUV to his duty room, got into his uniform and boots, and clipped his karambit to his pocket. He still had a job to do, and he wondered if Grayson would call him in to talk. He would simply need to wait it out, as much as his instinct was to jump into action. This situation required a smart play, and Cross knew from his discussion with Harper how to do that.

As the other duty section went home and work began at Station Gloucester, Cross reflected on his conversation with the state trooper. There was no way it was a coincidence that the investigation of Rivetti's murder had stopped before reaching the state police. Grayson must have stalled it. But why? Was there something else behind it, or was he trying to control local fallout? He didn't seem like the kind of leader to care all that much about the community... or really anyone but himself. It seemed unlikely he was spinning the investigation to keep the local populace from panicking about murders on the waters off Cape Ann. The more he thought about it, the more he was convinced he was clocking Grayson correctly.

The station was quiet for the couple of days of their duty, which surprised Cross, as summer was about to start. They conducted their law enforcement boardings. Cross spent each meal with his crew, learning new things about them, trying to help them effectively move on with their lives after the horror of that murder scene. To his greater surprise, Grayson never called him in to talk, though he had been largely absent the entire duty period, which seemed odd. Cross noted it. He refused to believe it was a coincidence, but things had largely returned to normal, so he decided it would do no good to kick a hornet's nest.

6

BEVERLY, MASSACHUSETTS, JUNE 2022

THE DUTY PERIOD WENT NORMALLY, the crew seemed more like their normal selves, and for almost the next month, the unit was relatively quiet. Gloucester itself was a different story. Summer had fully started, and the tourist crowd was growing by the day. The big restaurants in town, like Minglewood and the Gloucester House, were getting plenty of business from their outdoor eating areas. And the little shanty shops in Rockport were booming nearly every day of the week.

Cross maintained a careful but casual eye on the comings and goings at the station, including phone calls for the OIC and anything else that stood out. In the last month, nothing happened at all. Cross was certain something was going on, and Grayson could be involved, but now he was starting to question his read on the situation. Grayson seemed like he was his normal self, no better or worse than he'd ever been. Equally concerning was that the expected conversation between himself and Grayson had never happened. Cross couldn't be sure whether the inquiry had even reached Grayson. It was the wrong time to kick over new rocks.

If there was some good news, it seemed like his crew was

finally finding a way past the horrors of the murder and was functioning at their usual high level.

●●●●●

On his next weekend off, Cross and Melanie went on a planned overnight backpacking trip. With the weather finally warm enough to camp overnight, they headed to a section of the Appalachian Trail in the western part of the state. They parked the car at the end point and then caught a cab to the trailhead. After everything that had happened, Cross needed some distance from the problem and to clear his head to examine what might come next.

They started out on the trail. Cross wore his in 5.11 pants, a button-down hiking shirt, his Danner boots, and his Eberlestock pack. He had benched the old Lowe years ago. It had become too worn to use, but he kept it to honor his childhood mentor and hero.

●●●●●

Cross would always remember Tony fondly. He was in his 70s when the two met. Cross had just joined the Boy Scout troop in early high school and was looking for camaraderie with boys his age.

Tony looked at Cross almost as if he were a grandson. Where he merely interacted with the other boys, Tony engaged with Cross on a personal level, helping him find his inner strength and drive. Every hike and backpacking excursion with Tony brought the two closer together. Tony was a mentor and friend rivaling Cross's own parents.

Tony had a knack for making backpacking trips enjoyable. One of his greatest efforts was in packing food for dinner the first night on the trail. He taught all the boys how to make a "foil burger." The boys would each make a burger patty, add slices of any vegetables they wanted, then wrap the entire thing in two layers of tinfoil and freeze it overnight. The frozen foil package would be packed before departing for the trailhead. By the time they set up camp, the burgers would be carefully thawed in their own juices. The vegetables seasoned the meat naturally. They would all cook their foil burgers in the embers of an evening fire and have some of the best food a hiker ever experienced.

The greatest knowledge Tony ever imparted to Cross was the ability to read the woods. Most, he said, would "just walk." The smartest and most aware would not only walk to their destination but also use all their senses to interpret what the environment was saying. The woods were a living, breathing, speaking organism. Every noise and smell had its own meaning. It was shortly after teaching Cross the skills of reading the environment that Tony was forced to step back from long hikes and backpacking trips, as he crested into his eighties and his body simply couldn't take the abuse. When he did, in a nearly ceremonial gesture during a scout meeting in his living room, Tony presented Cross with his trusty Lowe frame pack with tears in his eyes. He reminded Cross to always read the environment and trust his instincts.

Years later, with Tony well into his eighties, the two met again on the streets of their hometown. Tony hobbled with a cane, looking frailer than ever. Cross never judged, though it saddened him to see his old mentor looking so worn down. Still, the usual spritely energy crossed Tony's wrinkled face as they met. Both came to the Veterans Day march; Tony served in the Army long ago, and Cross had just joined the Coast Guard. He was dressed to impress in his service dress blue uniform with a combination cover on top of his closely shaved head. Much to Cross's surprise, Tony hobbled up to him, gave him a big hug, and then, with a wicked grin on his face, demanded that Cross sing "Semper Paratus" right there on the sidewalk. Cross, out of a fear of letting down his old mentor, obliged and belted out the words to the Coast Guard anthem for all to hear. Embarrassed, but thrilled to make the old man happy, it was a fond memory for Cross for years to come. It was the last time Cross would see Tony alive. His old friend died a year later while Cross was in Yorktown, Virginia, learning how to be a boat driver. Cross promised himself he would honor Tony's legacy as long as he was still breathing.

●●●●●

Melanie wore her usual Columbia cargo pants, a North Face top, and Salomon boots. She carried an Osprey pack. She had been trying to talk her husband into Salomons for years, but he refused to give up on his "lucky boots."

Several times, the boots had saved his life. Once during a multiple-day excursion, a sudden and violent storm had rolled into the area where Cross was about to set up camp. It started raining so hard and fast that the area flooded in a matter of minutes. Cross struggled to sling his pack over his soaked shoulders in the downpour and scrambled for higher ground. The flooding in the bowl was rising to nearly hip level as Cross started shuffling and sliding up an embankment. He slipped a couple of times as the rain was effectively washing away any hard ground. Undeterred, he kept putting one foot in front of the other, digging his treads into what little solid earth was under him. As he was about to give up and hold his position, he heard a booming crack. Cross sharply looked up to see the upper part of a taller tree, which had been completely blasted from the trunk by a strike of lightning and was now hurdling directly toward him. In one quick move, he grabbed the tree trunk he was next to, dug the treads of his Danners into the muddy ground, and launched himself up the hill another few feet before the massive upper half of the tree landed with a terrifying thud in the exact spot he had occupied seconds earlier.

●●●●●

Cross was back to his usual self, aware of every normal noise on the trail, stopping anytime he heard something outside the normal pattern of life. The great thing about the Appalachian Trail was that it was so well-maintained, he had time and space to spot wildlife long before it wandered into his path. It was easy to take great pictures of wildlife on the trail when there was so much time to react. He and Melanie took pictures of deer, a couple of bears, and a few birds before finally reaching a good spot to set up camp for the night. Another significant feature of the trail was the lack of cell service. They could both completely disconnect from the rigors of life. As an added measure, Cross put his phone in a Faraday bag so no signals could get in or out. He would see and hear nothing from the outside world until he was off the trail and back to civilization again.

Once they took off their packs, they set up the tent and stretched the rainfly over the top. Cross hammered in the tent stakes, while Melanie unrolled the sleeping pads and bags.

With shelter handled, Cross dug a fire pit about a foot deep, lining it with a dozen hand-sized rocks to form a safe burn barrier. Melanie tied some 550 paracord between two sturdy trees, rigging up a bear bag high enough to keep their food and scented items safe from any curious wildlife. Once the fire pit was ready, Cross gathered an assortment of kindling, including dry twigs, thin branches, and larger logs stacked nearby to fuel the fire for hours.

When the fire crackled to life, he pulled out his camp stove and fueled it up while Melanie sat back in her camping chair, sipping water from her Nalgene bottle. Cross poured water from one of his hydration bladders into his portable pot, setting it on the stove to heat their freeze-dried meals.

As they waited for the water to boil, they let the quiet of the woods settle around them. The occasional chirp of a bird, the rustling of wind through the trees, and the crackling of the fire filled the space between them.

"You know," Melanie mused. "I still can't believe you refuse to switch to Salomon boots."

Cross smirked, poking at the fire with a stick. "My Danners have been through too much with me. They're lucky."

"They're old," she countered with a grin. "One day, they're gonna fall apart mid-hike, and then I'll be the one carrying you back to the car."

"You wouldn't make it ten steps," he teased, stretching his legs out.

Melanie rolled her eyes. "Excuse me, I do CrossFit, thank you very much."

Cross chuckled. "Fine, you can drag me a few feet before we both collapse."

The water finally reached a rolling boil, and Cross carefully poured it into their meal pouches. They waited a few minutes before digging in, eating in comfortable silence for a while.

After a few bites, Melanie set her fork down. "You ever think about where you'd live if you weren't tied to the Coast Guard?"

Cross took a moment to think. "I've always liked the idea of having a place in the mountains. Somewhere quiet with good hunting land and plenty of space. What about you?"

"I think I'd like somewhere near the water," she admitted. "But not the ocean—maybe a lake. A place where I could paddleboard in the summer and ice skate in the winter."

Cross nodded. "Sounds nice. Maybe we split the difference, mountains with a lake."

Melanie smirked. "Compromise. Look at you, being all grown up."

They talked late into the night, reminiscing about childhood adventures, trading stories about past camping trips, and debating the best movies from their teenage years. The fire slowly burned down, and they lifted the bear bag, securing it high in the trees before dousing the embers with dirt.

Crawling into the tent, they nestled into their sleeping bags. The distant hoot of an owl echoed through the trees. Melanie rested her head against her husband's shoulder. "No phones, no distractions. I think I needed this more than I realized."

Cross kissed the top of her head. "Me too."

As the fire pit cooled outside and the forest settled into its nighttime rhythm, Cross and Melanie made love, wrapped in the peace of the wilderness and the quiet certainty that, for at least one night, they didn't have to worry about anything but each other.

●●●●●

When they woke the next morning, the golden light of sunrise filtered through the trees, casting long shadows over the campsite. The crisp morning air carried the scent of pine and damp earth.

Cross stretched, groaning as he sat up. "Remind me why sleeping on the ground is fun again?"

Melanie chuckled as she pulled on her fleece. "Because it makes us appreciate real beds."

After a quick kiss, Cross set up the stove again, boiling water for their oatmeal and coffee. While they ate, they discussed their plans for the day: a slow, steady hike back to the car, a lunch stop at home, and then a lazy afternoon doing absolutely nothing.

Once breakfast was finished, they packed up their gear, ensuring they left no trace. Cross scattered the remains of the fire pit and covered it with fresh dirt. Melanie double-checked the area for any stray bits of trash before shouldering her pack.

The rest of the hike was smooth, punctuated by the occasional stop for photos and moments of quiet appreciation for the beauty of the trail. As they neared the trailhead, Cross glanced at Melanie and squeezed her hand.

"Let's make this a regular thing," he said.

She smiled. "I was hoping you'd say that."

They finally reached the parking lot, put their packs in the trunk of the 4Runner, and Cross took the opportunity to pull his phone out of the Faraday bag and check it for the first time since early yesterday. When his phone connected to their data network, nothing came through. They got in the SUV, and Melanie lovingly put her hand on Cross's leg as they started the drive back home.

About half an hour into their return home, Cross's phone buzzed, then again, and then one more time. He was curious more than anything why his phone blew up on a weekend, especially an off-duty weekend. Playing it safe, he pulled the SUV to the shoulder, put on his emergency flashers, and with the rhythmic thump of the flashers echoing in the cabin, he unlocked his iPhone to find three messages on Signal. One was from Harper, who simply said, "Call me when you can. Might have something that could help."

The next two messages were from Nate. The first one said, "It happened again."

Cryptic, what did he mean by that?

The next message sent his refined senses into full alert. "Call me back the moment you get this."

Cross showed the messages to Melanie, and all she said was, "Oh no."

He switched to Signal calls and rang Nate, putting it on speaker.

After one ring, Nate picked up. "Boats, we got a problem."

"Nate, you're on speaker with me and Melanie. She knows. Now slow down, what do you mean?"

"I got word from starboard section OOD," he was referring to the officer-of-the-day, another boatswain's mate running the station and reporting to the command for guidance in their section operations. "They picked up another dead body last night."

"Christ!" Cross said, his head lowering slightly, breathing controlled but shallow. "Where was it?"

"Eastern Point," Nate said. "Right next to the lighthouse. Young couple out for an evening stroll at the Dog Bar stumbled on him, thinking he was a piece of driftwood until they saw the Grunden's fishing pants on him."

Cross narrowed his eyes, and a smirk crossed his lips as he asked, "Wait, fisherman? Are we sure this is suspicious and not an unfortunate accident? Guy fell overboard and wasn't noticed, maybe?"

"You know, I would've thought that too, but the OOD called me because he suspected you were in the woods, and he said something didn't feel right about it."

"Did he say what part exactly?"

There was a pause as Nate collected his thoughts. "He said Grayson took charge of the case and investigation and is locking him out."

Cross couldn't contain his feelings about this revelation. He growled, "WHAT?"

Nate kept his voice calm. "I know, man. So, what the hell do we do about this?"

It took Cross a moment to bring himself off the rage-filled ledge he was teetering on. After a deep breath, he said, "For now, as much as it pains me, nothing. I'll make some outside inquiries; see if there's something else behind this. For now, not a word about it. Don't put a target on your back by asking too many questions."

"Yeah, buddy. I understand. My lips are sealed."

"Thanks for the update. See you in a couple of days." Cross hung up and looked at Melanie.

"Seriously? What the fuck is it with this guy?"

Melanie placed a tender hand on his shoulder and said, "Let's get home."

Cross turned off the hazards and put the 4Runner in drive. Once he got home, Cross realized he'd have to figure out the story with this supposed drowned fisherman. It couldn't be a coincidence that Grayson had taken it over. Grayson had waved Cross off the first case. His intervention in this second death brought up some questions. It was consistent in the sense that the old man had taken it over. But it was still off protocol and mildly suspicious. He had to call up the chain this time. He would start with Gloucester police and work from there if he had to. He informed Melanie after their return home that he was making a phone call and stepped into the garage. He sat at his workbench, looking up the number for Gloucester PD. Transferring it to Signal, he placed the secure call.

A thick Boston accent answered, "*Glousta* police *depahtment*. How can I help you?"

"Officer, I'm with the US Coast Guard. Got a couple quick questions if you've got a few minutes."

"Shoot."

"I understand there was a drowning victim yesterday, a fishing boat crewmember. Is that right?"

The officer was clearly not in the mood for small talk. He answered, "Yeah, that's right. What do you need to know?"

"Only a couple of questions. First, does this seem entirely

accidental?" Cross wasn't sure what kind of response he would get to this question, so he was trying to sound open-minded.

"I think, but..."

"But what?" Cross suspected he knew what was coming.

"But the vic had a nasty bruise on the back of the head and neck, according to the *coronah*."

"That is strange. Second question, with a part two to follow."

"Okay, go ahead," the officer said. "What have you got?"

"Do you have an ID on the victim?" Cross was not entirely sure what he would find out here.

"Honestly, no. We've got no idea who this guy is."

"Why not," Cross asked. "He's not from around here?"

"He doesn't come up in our system at all," the officer said. "He's like a ghost."

"Who would be able to ID him? Essex, state police?" Cross asked.

"Probably," the officer said. "But we've been *ordah'd* to rule it an accidental drowning to protect the community."

"And who ordered that?"

"Funny thing," the officer said without realizing how unfunny it was. "That was Coast *Gahd*. Station *Glousta's Commanda* Grayson."

"What's the possibility of contacting Essex and state anyway?" Cross asked. "Can you do that?"

"Yeah, sure," the officer said. "Though I don't see why over a drowning."

"Humor me," Cross said. "And call me back at this number when you find out anything." Cross then gave the officer his personal number.

"Okay," the officer said. "We'll be in touch."

The next morning, Cross was in his garage gym early. After a five-mile run at a brisk pace, he settled in for a short kettlebell workout with a sequence of deadlifts, thrusters, swings, and repeated it until he'd done a hundred of each. Melanie joined him as he finished the bodyweight element. They hit the heavy bag and practiced with the karambit for a few minutes to keep their skills sharp. Cross was finishing his stretch when his phone rang through the Signal calling function. He answered the number belonging to the Gloucester PD. "US Coast Guard, how can I help you?" He wasn't going to give his name unless they asked.

"Good *mohnin'*. I was able to track down a name for our dead guy. You ready?"

Cross took a deep breath, hoping it wouldn't be someone he knew again. "Yeah, go ahead."

"Guy's name is Eddie Valero," the officer said. "Name mean anything to you?"

SHIT!

"No, not a thing," Cross lied. "Thanks again for all your help."

"Not a problem," the officer responded. "Have a good one."

Cross paced the garage. Eddie Valero was someone. He recognized the name from case files in the deck back at MSRT. The real bad apples who would start a gunfight if the Coast Guard came their way with intent. Valero was a known gun trafficker, masquerading as a fishing boat crewman. He'd have the captain stop by a boat with supplies, the money already handled through discreet offshore accounts, and their boat would take delivery. Then they would leave the area to transfer the black-market arms to another asset, which would play its part in a shell game to prevent anyone from seeing where the guns ended up once they hit the shoreline. Once they hit the mainland, those guns were flat out gone. These folks were good at what they did.

Melanie broke off her workout and asked, "Honey, what is it?"

"Another of our team deck traffickers just ended up on our dead guy list."

"Who the hell is taking these guys out with such precision?"

The thought caused Cross's gut to tighten at the prospect of targeted eliminations in a beautiful city like Gloucester. "I don't know. But I'm sure as hell going to find out."

7

UNITED STATES COAST GUARD STATION
GLOUCESTER, MASSACHUSETTS, JUNE 2022

CROSS CAME BACK on duty with plenty of new questions in his head that swirled through his mind in disorienting patterns. He had to remain passive because he didn't want to betray his suspicions about his officer-in-charge. Grayson could be involved in something serious, but Cross needed more time to piece everything together without anyone knowing he was digging into it.

That morning, during the section pass-down and early tasking before letting the starboard section off for a couple of days, Nate was uncharacteristically quiet. Cross approached him in the engineering office. Before Cross could say anything, Nate shook his head side to side with a neutral but guarded expression on his face, then said, "Not here, let's step outside."

The two men walked outside of the boat haul-out and toward the split pier used to pull a motor lifeboat from the water for maintenance. "I know you're working this, but something is really not sitting right with me."

"Okay," Cross said. "Hit me, what am I missing?"

"Well, maybe not missing, simply not seeing far enough."

Cross was intrigued, and a slight grin lifted the corner of his mouth. "Keep going."

"I spent some time on an MSST but didn't stay because I preferred turning wrenches to all the internal politics. One thing I picked up there is that when things stack up, there's a reason. Multiple events like this don't happen without a connection. We need to look deeper into Grayson. He's connected to something. He has to be."

"Okay, I'm inclined to agree with you, but how do we dig in without causing suspicion?"

"Shit, that part I'm not sure about yet. But seriously, tell me I'm not crazy here. Two suspicious deaths and Grayson covering both, sidelining the crew?"

"You're not crazy," Cross said with some hesitation as Nate's assessment converged with his suspicions like a slow-motion trainwreck. "I just don't know where to take this yet. I don't know what else I'm not seeing, and I don't want to let on that we're trying to investigate the OIC. That brings heat we won't be able to walk away from. Is this the part where I say that I knew the drowning victim, too?"

"Holy shit! Seriously?"

"Yeah," Cross said. "We were tracking him in Chesapeake."

"This changes the game. We need to act."

"No." Cross was adamant. He wasn't going to act until he knew what was really happening. "If we do anything now, we're going to get buried."

"Gotcha," Nate said, calming down slightly. "I guess this is kind of a hurry-up-and-wait game, huh?"

"Unfortunately, it is. A proper investigation takes time, proper surveillance takes time, and this one's more complex because it needs to be done under the radar."

Nate said with a grin, "I assume you've done this kind of thing before?"

●●●●●

Port of Norfolk, Virginia, 2018

Surveillance was an art form, and Cross found that out when the team had been training on it in their pre-deployment cycle. It was in part to keep their skills fresh, and in part to be able to share these techniques with partnered international agencies during their deployment. This time it was the culmination of their training block on a night so dark it could have come straight from Edgar Allen Poe's mind.

The mission profile had them observing the Port of Norfolk in a specific area of a specific terminal. A team of bad actors was supposed to be involved in loading illegal arms into an unknown shipping crate for transport outside the United States through the black market. The targets were private military contractors playing the part, and the arms were Pelican cases full of inert weapons for defensive tactics training. The team had minimal information: the terminal number, a timeframe, and that the target was a shipping container. The art in it all was that the team, loaded with full assault gear including ballistic helmets and attached NODs, was supposed to stay silently obscured in their boat. They floated far enough out to look like a random recreational boat hanging around the port, fishing at night, and they observed everything out of the ordinary.

Cross had picked it up quickly, and tonight, he was mentally capturing the normal rhythm of everything in and around this section of the port. Jake Harper had recently been cleared to join the pre-deployment work-up, and after a quick crash course on what he had missed, he was attached to the other part of the direct-action team holding station a little further down the terminal on a barge with good lines of sight to the target area.

The plan was simple but effective. Once visual was established with the subjects and cargo, the team would wait for the subjects to be committed to their actions on their objective. The boat would rapidly close to the pier, offload the shooters, and both elements would box the subjects in. The result would be no route of escape for the hostiles other than a gunfight; they would certainly lose. If they never showed up or didn't commit, the teams would back off after recording anything of consequence.

After more than two hours of waiting in the ink-black darkness aided by the eerie green hue of their NODs, Cross suddenly spoke into the all-team radio, "Bravo one, Bravo four. Movement at the container closest to water, far right; might be our HVIs."

"Bravo four, Bravo one. Good eye. Have visual. Alpha one, bravo one, do you have visual?"

"Negative bravo. Standing by for visual. On you for executing order."

The team leader walked to the aft deck of the delivery boat and softly put his hand on Cross's shoulder. "Good eye, Cross. Still have them?"

"Affirm," Cross said, keeping his cheek welded tightly to the riser on the stock of his modified M4 Carbine, looking steadily through his Aimpoint T2 optic, accompanied by a 3X flip-to-side magnifier as he watched the four target individuals walk around the container. He scanned methodically for any indication that someone was aware of their presence.

These guys had no optical advantage and no technical or tactical advantage to exploit. They seemed completely oblivious to the predators lurking in the dark. Cross grinned as he watched the future targets of decisive and violent, albeit simulated, death. His thoughts echoed a brutal sentiment drilled in from months of continuous and arduous training. "Nox Noctis est Nostri," from their unit patch, the message translated to English as: "The night is ours."

Finally, after a short wait, the target individuals worked on opening the shipping container, clearly committed to their objective, thinking no one was going to stop them. Eagle-eyed, aware of everything, Cross called it first. "Bravo one, Bravo four. Targets opening container, call is Pandora." Pandora was the verbal indicator that the illicit action was proceeding. It was the green light for the teams to execute their mission as planned.

"Bravo four, Bravo one. Copy Pandora. Break, break. Alpha one, Bravo one. I pass Pandora, standby for order."

A quick confirmation, "Bravo one, Alpha one standing by to execute."

Both team leaders looked to their teams with a direct thumbs-up confirmation that they were ready to deal death with speed, surprise, and violence of action. The radio crackled to life again as Cross heard his leader speaking once more. "Lasers on once we hit the pier. All teams, execute, execute, execute!"

Cross grabbed the rail and held it tightly as he took a knee. The boat accelerated like it was being propelled by a rocket engine. They closed the distance to the pier in mere seconds and waited a beat as the highly trained delivery operator slid the boat skillfully to the pier like a drift car on hot tires. As if on autopilot, a fraction of a second after contact with the pier, all the operators quickly ascended the pierside ladder. Instantly, a half dozen infrared lasers came to life, pointing up the pier toward the shipping container in question, the beams dancing like skinny fingers in the green illumination of their NODs. The team moved skillfully and quickly toward the objective on soft rubber-soled boots that easily masked the sounds of their feet running along the concrete. As they stacked behind the shipping container next to the target, Cross felt the man behind him squeeze his shoulder, signaling he was ready. Cross passed the signal forward, and a moment later heard, "Alpha one, Bravo one. Stacked and ready to move on objective."

The reply was, "Bravo, Alpha. Stacked and ready. Going hot on your fire."

Bravo's team leader put up a fist, then three fingers from the fist. He closed each finger one at a time. Then he extended his hand with all fingers pointed toward the target container. They all moved in unison; a single stack of seasoned predators ready to strike unsuspecting prey. As briefed, they punched out into a single line abreast, all lasers pointed toward the target. They got in line, and one of the subjects rounded the door from inside the shipping container, immediately drawing a pistol on the approaching team. Before he could raise his weapon, there was a sound like a dozen firecrackers going off in less than a second. A series of splatters sounded as a dozen simunitions, or soap rounds, impacted the chest of the target, and he fell backward onto the ground with a dull thud. His friends inside the container heard him fall, and one tried to run away from the team. He met a similar deadly fate at the hands of the opposing element.

Realizing they were cornered and badly outnumbered, the remaining combatants chose to live rather than die, and they slowly emerged from the container, holding hands in the air. The immediate roars of the team telling the subjects to interlace fingers on top of their heads and drop to their knees filled the chilly night air. The contractors were flex-cuffed when a voice behind Bravo team yelled over a bullhorn, "Endex, endex. Stand down! Nicely done, team!" It was the commanding officer of MSRT-East. No one knew he was on the pier behind a nearby crane, watching his men execute a near-perfect assault on a high-value objective. The team gave fist bumps all around as the CO stepped forward to congratulate each man on the completion of their outstanding surveillance and assault.

Cross and Harper sought each other out after the action died down, and Harper said, "Well shit! That was fun."

"Nicely done, buddy," Cross said, feeling proud of their

skilled surveillance action under less-than-ideal circumstances, which still resulted in a successful mission. "Nice to have people you can rely on."

•••••

Cross and his duty section experienced a highly routine first duty day, almost numbingly boring. Cross took note that the dead fisherman hadn't come up. Cross now observed his environment as keenly as he would if he were on the trail. The silence was deafening. Though someone else might think Grayson was trying to keep the crew from reliving those horrors, Cross was familiar with that eerie quiet on the trail when a predator slips in too close to other wildlife. The silence was speaking; Cross was all ears.

Grayson was still acting like Grayson, appearing to everyone like he was in complete control. As he ate lunch, it occurred to Cross that his first duty day was simply waiting for something else to happen. Would it be another dead body, or something else? There still seemed to be no purpose in any of this death. The only thing Cross knew for certain was that Grayson was stalling or killing investigations into marine deaths, and that the dead were known traffickers. Cross was not a trained investigator and couldn't figure out how any of this was connected. Eventually, Grayson would make another mistake, and the dots would connect, if they were supposed to connect. It was a waiting game, and Cross had the patience.

•••••

The next morning, the crew had their breakfast, the smell of freshly brewed dark roast coffee, bacon, eggs, and potatoes filling the air in the Can-Do Café. As the first of them started bringing their plates to the scullery to be washed, the SAR alarm blared its shrill call, followed by a report of a person in the water near Magnolia Beach. The crew of the 29183 dumped their plates in the scullery bin and then ran to their lockers to gear up.

The crew reached the boat a couple of minutes later, just as Cross was completing a mission record. Engines started, communications were established with the station, and they launched six minutes from the initial call. They had thirty minutes from the call to launch and still be operating in Coast Guard policy, but they never needed that much time.

As the boat cleared the helicopter pad breakwall, Nate hit the blue lights and siren, and Cross yelled, "Coming up!" Then he pushed the throttles to the firewalls as he urged on the 183, "Go baby, go!"

The response boat was on plane and skimming the surface at thirty knots in mere seconds. Cross established the mission parameters with his crew. "Okay, folks. Person in the water off Magnolia; no indication of other distress. The reporting source said they couldn't tell how the person was sitting in the water, so standby to render medical attention. Questions, concerns?"

There were none.

"Call out risk assessment so I can log it with the station and assume lookouts."

The crew called the mission a low-risk, high-gain as they might be saving a life, and Cross readily agreed. He called it into the station for proper documentation. He whipped the boat to port and starboard, dodging lobster pot buoys for the few minutes it took to get to Magnolia Beach. Cody took the time to pull out the aid bag from the gear cutout and did a quick physical inventory of blankets, bandages, and other things that they might need. Cross and his crew were ready for the challenge.

When they arrived at Magnolia, it took a moment for the crew to find what they were looking for. Lauren, with her keen eye, spotted something to their left and called it out. "Small object in the water, port side, three-zero-zero degrees, about a hundred yards," she said with confidence. "Got visual?"

The whole crew shifted their gaze to where Lauren had said she saw the object. Cross noticed something that looked different from the lobster pots. It looked like a small, dark object bobbing in the waves like a cork. "I have it. Good eye. Coming around to approach. Stand by the recess to recover." Cross intended to have his crew assess immediate injuries and pull the person from the cold water as quickly as possible.

Cross pivoted the boat toward the object as quickly as he was able and announced he was making his approach. As they closed the distance to eighty yards, then sixty, then forty, then twenty, it quickly became clear that this was no medical call. That strange feeling Cross had on that first call more than a month earlier instantly returned. His instincts, grounded in experience, screamed at him that something was terribly wrong. As the RBS approached the object, which was now clearly a person, the crew all started getting the same weird feeling about it.

As they closed with the person, Cody spoke up first. "Boats. Am I wrong, or is this one...?"

Cross was devastated. It had been less than a week since the last incident with the other section. "Yeah, Cody." Cross noticed how pale and lifeless this person was. "They look dead." Cross would still need to confer with medical authorities before officially declaring them dead, but this one wouldn't take much.

Cross wondered if the events of the first death they had come across would repeat, but he had no way of knowing without following his procedures. This appeared to be a drowning, but without any indication of anything else, he couldn't assume much. "Station Gloucester, Station Gloucester. Rescue one-eight-three, rescue one-eight-three," Cross started. "We're on scene. Prior report of a medical emergency was inaccurate. This appears to be a drowning. Please notify state and local police to coordinate recovery and investigation. Inform command, over."

The station watchstander confirmed the request, then a few minutes later, everything changed. "One-eight-three, station. Command says local and state are unavailable, we need to recover and coordinate once we can reach them, over."

Cross felt his blood boil, but he forced a calm demeanor in front of his crew. They needed his leadership, not his wrath. "Copy on all, one-eight-three, out."

Cross spoke calmly after a brief round of box breathing to settle his racing heart. "Shift to recovery. Grab the body bag. Let's get this guy on deck. If anyone needs to swap positions, tell me now." Cross was more than ready to take over for anyone who wasn't comfortable hauling a dead body into their boat. He didn't want any further trauma to his crew than they had already dealt with. The problem was that this had happened too many times to them.

Lauren looked like she was going to be sick, and Cody told her to get in the cabin with Cross and get near a window to make sure she was getting enough air. She readily agreed, then stumbled to the port rail and immediately and violently vomited over the side. The rest watched, feeling no less sick about the situation. It wouldn't get any easier by delaying.

Once Lauren had gone into the cabin, Nate and Cody positioned the body bag across the aft deck, then positioned the body to get maximum leverage to bring it onboard and guide it straight to the bag. Gloved and masked, they reached for the shirt and pants of the victim, and on a quick count, pulled the body skillfully over the rail and straight to the body bag. Once they were done, they zipped the bag and told Cross the deck was secure. Cross noted the position with a digital marker on the chart plotter screen for later reference, and then he called Cody in and asked if he could take the sticks for a minute. Cody sounded disheartened but readily agreed and clipped in to drive.

Cross walked to the aft deck, acting on an instinct that he couldn't quite articulate. His past steadied his nerves like tempered steel, guiding his hand like an invisible anchor line. As Nate looked over the side, lost in thought, Cross unzipped the body bag enough to see the face of their apparent drowning victim, and he felt his blood run cold once more. His heart thudded in his chest like a jackhammer as it became abundantly clear he was looking at a third victim he knew by name. He looked up and noticed no one was looking his way as he snapped a quick picture of the new victim, and then he quietly zipped the bag closed.

Cross took a second to consider their next actions. He could play by Grayson's rules and watch this death get buried like the previous ones. It would likely raise no suspicion, but a marine death would be unsolved, and Grayson would continue to do as he pleased.

The other course of action was riskier. Cross could call the Massachusetts State Police, send a picture of the victim to confirm the identity, and hope that they would investigate further. It would likely result in further information about what was likely a suspicious death and could help uncover what was really happening. The problem is, it would almost certainly tip off Grayson that there was someone digging into his actions. That couldn't be helped.

Cross looked at his crew with a keen professional eye. He considered once more whether they were at risk due to Grayson and his departures from policy. He owed it to them to uncover whatever was happening before it went too far. His pulse steadied, and his fists closed tightly. He wasn't going to let this threat keep escalating. His decision was made. He would wait until he was off duty to make a secure call, loop in state police, and ask them to reach out directly with anything further. They were likely still going to contact Grayson, which would tip him off, but there was no other way to get better information. This was the only correct course of action.

The crew took some time to compose themselves and then informed the station that they were en route with the deceased person. As expected, Grayson was on the line moments later, telling the crew he'd meet them on the pier with Gloucester police and an ambulance. Cross knew from his tone what he was about to do, especially since Grayson had already done it twice. He was going to bury this investigation with Gloucester PD and let the public think nothing was amiss.

●●●●●

The conclusion of the case went as expected, with Cross and crew each writing brief statements of what they saw. The chief offered counselors and chaplains again, and Cross completed his post-mission documentation. The following morning, Cross was in the gym, Cody alongside him, working his legs heavily with squats, lunges, and burpees using a weighted vest, then more Krav Maga and some practice with the karambit. He needed a clear head, and this was the one way that always worked for him. He pushed himself hard once again under the glow of the emergency lights, trying to purge all the ugly things from his brain.

As they stretched, Cross said, "Nice job keeping up, Cody. You're in damn good shape."

"Thanks, Boats." Cody smiled briefly, but it disappeared like smoke in a dark room seconds later. "I'm seriously wondering what's going on, though."

"About the cases, you mean?"

"Yes." Cody took a deep breath with his hands behind his head before continuing. "Something just seems so wrong about it all. It just seems like something horrible is going on here, and I'm trying not to jump the gun like you said after the first one."

"Thank you for not going cowboy on this, Cody. I know that's a hard thing to embrace. It's also the mark of a good leader, which I know you already are."

"Thank you. I'm just wondering what we're missing here."

"Have you seen or heard anything I haven't?"

"Well, I walked by Grayson's office right after we got back from recovering that guy, and he was on the phone with someone. I couldn't tell who, but it sounded serious."

"Cody... how serious?" Cross was all ears. He suspected Cody had just stumbled onto a significant detail.

"If I'm being honest, it sounded like Grayson was getting his ass handed to him. He kept pausing mid-sentence."

"Cody, thank you for keeping an ear out. I don't know what it means yet. As I said, I'm working through the details. We'll figure it out soon enough. Just stay sharp, and please let me know if you need any help, would you?"

"I will, Boats. Thank you for hearing me out and not judging me."

After showering and getting into his uniform, Cross met the incoming starboard section OOD for an early pass-down, cleaned the station sooner than normal, and then logged onto a computer to make sure his case documentation had been accepted. When he checked the online database, he found his narrative, but something was different. The description of a potentially suspicious marine death was gone, and his narrative had been edited to read more like a normal discovery of a person who swam out too far from the beach and drowned due to lack of experience in the waters off Cape Ann.

Cross had no answers, and asking about it now would raise too many red flags about what he was doing. The smartest way to play this was the great chess game that the whole mystery had become. A covert move to cover up ill intent would be met with a subtle dismissal of that action by Cross to uncover further information from a different angle. Cross was locked in a game of wits with people who had likely been playing this game as long as he had, if not longer. Making too bold a move now would cost him. It was time for Cross to improve his fighting position and attempt to gain the upper hand.

8

BEVERLY, MASSACHUSETTS, JUNE 2022

CROSS WALKED in the door to find Melanie doing some light house cleaning and interrupted her with a hug. They kissed, and then Cross jumped in to help her with the cleaning. She was immediately interested in knowing how things were going.

"Well, after the dead fisherman," Cross started. "We got called to a person in the water that turned out to be another dead guy. That's three now."

"And you don't believe it's a coincidence? Do you?"

"No." He hesitated briefly before answering. "I don't."

"There's something else, isn't there?"

Cross thought about his response. Melanie had lived a life of secrecy before and would easily be able to keep the secret if asked. "Yeah, and this is going to sound crazy, but I know all three victims. Well, by reputation anyway."

"Oh, God! Seriously? So, who are they?"

"They're all known traffickers of drugs and weapons," Cross said. "All East Coast threats we were tracking through intelligence while I was on the team."

"Are these deaths related?"

"I know they're related," Cross said. "But I can't figure out how yet. To that end, I have a call to make."

He stepped out to his garage, and Cross first texted Harper on Signal to relay the now three names and one new picture he had. He hoped Harper could continue doing a quiet dig to see if anyone at a higher level knew of something bigger going on that would tie all these deaths together. It was Tony Rivetti, Eddie Valero, and now Frank Lombardi. Lombardi was an associate of the Philly mob, known for trafficking in black-market arms. There was little chance that these three deaths were isolated events. Cross remembered that Harper said he might have something that could help, so he wondered if the new information would play into what Harper already knew. He would need to wait on Harper to tie those threads together.

The second step was a call to the Massachusetts State Police Troop A barracks in Danvers. Cross knew he was straddling a very dangerous line, making this call. It was like reaching a hand into a shark tank and hoping not to lose the hand. Whatever was going on, he would likely put a target on his back when this got back to Grayson. The more he thought about it logically, the more he realized Grayson had already been informed that he had someone investigating him. Why it had thus far gone unanswered was something Cross could not yet figure out. Either way, this step was likely the definition of kicking a hornet's nest. There was no chance of this going unanswered as state police conducted their investigation. Cross would need to prepare for fallout on the back end of this call if it went accordingly.

He punched in the saved number on Signal and connected the call. After ringing twice, a female voice answered, "Massachusetts State Police, Trooper Mendez."

"Good morning," Cross said, trying to be as friendly but professional as possible. "This is Petty Officer Cross with the United States Coast Guard. How are you today, ma'am?"

"Can't complain," Mendez replied. "And yourself?"

"Not too bad," Cross lied. "But I need to run something up the flagpole here."

"Well," Mendez said with an obviously sarcastic tone. "This should be good."

"You won't be disappointed," Cross said with a slight edge to his voice that he didn't quite intend. "Did you hear about a couple of drownings off Cape Ann in the last week?"

"Can't say I have, I assume that's what this is about?"

"Fair assumption, Trooper Mendez. And I'm not surprised you haven't heard about either one. I'm beginning to wonder if these are more suspicious than they seem on the surface."

"What makes you say that? Got something I can run with, or just a weird fuzzy feeling?"

Changing his tone to reflect his experience and instinct for the ugly side of human nature, Cross said, "Well, having hunted men far more dangerous than these victims before, it's not a hunch."

Suddenly, there was a stunned silence on the other end of the line.

"Okay," Trooper Mendez responded calmly and professionally. "I apologize for any assumptions. Let's talk through what you have."

"Thank you. Before I go on, I need to ask a favor. Can we make sure this doesn't go anywhere for now, until we figure out where it's pointed?"

"You mean quiet digging until we turn up more?" Trooper Mendez was catching on quickly.

"Exactly, you get it."

Cross knew the investigation wouldn't stay silent for long, but maybe it would buy him enough time to get more information developed on the situation as it now stood. "If this leaks to the press, my command, the city of Gloucester, it's going to get really messy, real fast, and that's bad for everyone."

"I agree," Trooper Mendez said with trepidation. "But I have a feeling your command will know before too long that we're digging into a pair of drownings as suspicious."

"I know. Just try to keep it under the radar as long as you can. Inform me directly if you find anything significant. Can you do that? In the name of interagency cooperation?"

"I think I can work with that. So, what are you working with?"

Cross paused, putting his thoughts in a coherent order. "First, you're aware of the murder over a month ago, south of Great Misery?"

"Yes," Mendez said cautiously. "Was that the first?"

"Yes, I called about that after it first happened," Cross said, recalling the other trooper's stunned reaction at a murder that state police never knew about. "And your office was never informed."

"Thanks for that. Sounds like we gave Station Gloucester a real hard time about that."

Cross could now say with certainty that Grayson was aware of the inquiries into the death of Tony Rivetti.

"Like I said, interagency cooperation. The next was less than a week ago. A fisherman drowned right off Eastern Point Lighthouse. Got buried by Station Gloucester when they informed Gloucester PD it was a simple drowning and should stay with them to protect the community, if you can believe that."

"That sounds fishy," Mendez said with a dry chuckle. "Pardon the pun."

Cross chuckled a little at that, too. "Okay, and when I talked to GPD on that, the desk officer said the ME found a large bruise on the head and neck that seemed to have no bearing on a drowning. It sounded like they weren't sure where that would have come from."

"And the plot thickens," Mendez said ominously. "And what about the third?"

"That's where it gets really interesting, because that one screams normal run-of-the-mill drowning in almost every way."

Cross could nearly hear the switch flipping to the detective side of Mendez's persona. "Almost?"

She caught that part immediately.

"Yes, Trooper Mendez, almost. Bear with me here. Two drownings, two investigations, buried by our officer-in-charge. At least, probably, with the second one. I haven't spoken with GPD to find out if it went the same direction as the first drowning. It's more than likely it did, considering who was responsible."

"Okay," Mendez said. "Now, back up a second. I can see drowning investigations stopping in their tracks, but why the murder? I never heard why that stalled out."

"Because the vic was a pusher, an interstate drug trafficker."

"And how exactly would you know that?" Mendez was dumbstruck by the direct assertion, but she was about to find out the hard way that this was all skimming the surface.

"Are you sitting down so I know you won't injure yourself?"

"Yes," Mendez said with a dry chuckle. "Go ahead."

"Because I know all three victims, at least by name, photo, and reputation."

"Whoa! That's heavy. Say that again more slowly, so I know I wasn't hallucinating."

"I know all three victims." Cross felt weird repeating himself, but he had to figure this mess out.

"And how is that?" Mendez sounded like she was in shock, almost as if she wasn't sure she wanted the answer to the question she had just asked.

"Remember, I said I've hunted more dangerous men than these three?" Cross felt his past flood him with memories of his most dangerous missions, the bullets meant for him that missed, the high-risk takedowns of violent extremists and criminals, killing people with automatic weapons fire and his karambit. "I meant every word of that."

"So why these three?" Mendez asked, still too shocked to conceal it. "What do they have in common?"

"They're all traffickers," Cross said. "They dealt in drugs and black-market weapons. These were all guys my team was tracking, that is, if they got a case of the dumbs and decided to play on our turf."

"Okay," Mendez said finally. "We can't keep doing this over the phone. Are you in the area? Can you come in and speak with me privately?"

"Still good with keeping it on the low-low, or are we on different pages?"

"Why do you think I'm asking for a face-to-face?" Mendez had the picture on this, and Cross felt he could trust her.

"How's twenty minutes?" He was maybe fifteen minutes away, but he was always one for an early arrival, ever since he was a kid.

"Sounds good to me," Mendez said. "I'll be waiting."

Cross stepped back into the house and told Melanie where he was going and why, but he said to keep it quiet for now. She agreed, kissed him before telling him to be careful, and watched as he quickly jumped in the 4Runner in civilian clothes that somewhat masked his muscular build.

● ● ● ● ●

Massachusetts State Police Troop A Barracks, Danvers, Massachusetts

When Cross arrived at the state police headquarters, he parked the SUV at the side of the road, waiting to see if anyone parked close by. There was little likelihood he was being followed, but he wasn't going to take any chances. He subtly scanned the area, looking for anyone sitting in a vehicle, but he found nothing out of the ordinary and walked inside. Trooper Mendez was waiting for him. Her name plaque was proudly displayed on her neatly pressed uniform. She was about what Cross had expected. She was five-feet-seven-inches slim and muscular with dark brown hair pulled into a high and tight bun. Her tanned face revealed hours outdoors during her off-duty time.

She extended a hand with a locked-out arm, which gave Cross the impression that she took pride in her appearance. She was no stranger to a gym.

"You must be Cross," she said with genuine enthusiasm. "I'm Trooper Mendez, nice to meet you! Now, let's find an isolated room to talk."

They retreated to a back corner of the station adorned with memorabilia of the many years of honorable service Troop A had under its collective duty belt. They finally entered what looked like an interrogation room, complete with a one-way glass pane that made Cross's pulse quicken as though he was under investigation for something himself. "No recording, right?"

"What you've told me so far is intriguing, and I have no intention of seeing it blown before it can see the light of day in the right way."

"Call me Logan. I'm only Cross with my crew."

"Stephanie. Nice to meet you the right way, Logan."

What followed was an hour-long discussion over coffee during which Cross detailed his operations on MSRT, his time to date in the Coast Guard, his relationship with Harper, and all the facts and suspicions he held on the three cases that had already occurred. Mendez was a good listener, taking a small handful of scribbled notes that only she could decipher. She even asked about Cross's private life and Melanie, so she had a full picture of the man she was dealing with. Mendez quickly found herself impressed.

The problem, as they discussed the details of the three deaths, was simple. There wasn't anything more than circumstantial evidence that Grayson was up to anything specific. He was stalling legitimate investigations into these deaths, but no one could figure out why. As the conversation ended, Mendez made it clear that while this would likely reach his command as the investigation slowly unfolded, Cross could trust her to use her utmost discretion to start pulling on the loose threads. She finally urged him to be careful, because if there really was something bigger at play, the target on his back would grow larger the more he tried to uncover this mystery. From Mendez's time in the Army, she equated it to digging a foxhole in a minefield, and Cross took her meaning. Mendez gave Cross her card with her work cellphone number in case he ran across anything else that might help, but she urged him to keep a low profile otherwise and expect fallout.

•••••

After the conversation with Mendez, Cross filled Melanie in. Melanie expressed her overwhelming concern about the "expect fallout" part, and Cross agreed. His refined senses from years of combat spoke up, quietly suggesting more weapons practice. They drove out of town for range time after a candid conversation about how to handle what came next.

The scent of gunpowder hung in the air as Cross adjusted his stance, raising his Sig-Sauer P365XL toward the target downrange. Beside him, Melanie held her own Sig-Sauer P365 X-Comp, chosen for the recoil management. Her fingers were steady on the grip, and her eyes narrowed in concentration. The indoor range was quiet except for the rhythmic crack of gunfire, muffled slightly by their ear protection.

Cross squeezed the trigger smoothly and evenly, landing a controlled pair in the center mass of the target. Melanie followed suit, her shots grouping tightly in the upper chest. She exhaled, lowering her pistol slightly as she turned to him.

"Not bad," Cross said with an affectionate smile and approving nod. He lowered his weapon to a safe position. "You still overcompensate a little when you fire fast, though."

Melanie smirked. "Yeah? Maybe I'd do better if someone let me train more often."

Cross chuckled, "You know I'd have you out here every weekend if we weren't always running around, dealing with... everything else."

Melanie tucked a stray strand of hair behind her ear. "Speaking of which." She paused, glancing at him with a cautious smile. "You've got what, four years left on this tour?"

Cross's expression sobered slightly as he ejected his magazine and checked his pistol. "Yeah. I'll be home for a while. No sudden ops, no last-minute deployments."

Melanie studied him for a moment before setting her gun on the bench. "Then maybe we start talking about the next step."

Cross arched a brow, but his lips arced into a small smile. "You mean?"

She nodded. "A family, Logan. We've talked about it in passing, but I think it's time we seriously consider it. I don't want to wait until the 'perfect' time, because let's be honest, that doesn't exist for us."

Cross exhaled slowly, leaning against the bench. He looked at her, settling on her beautiful brown eyes, and felt the weight of everything they'd been through together. The deployments, the near misses, the long nights of uncertainty. Yet, here they were, still standing. The future was the only thing that mattered in this moment, and the impact of it hit him like an uppercut from Harper.

"You're right. It's never going to be perfect, but maybe that doesn't matter. Maybe what matters is that we're ready to face whatever comes, together."

Melanie's eyes softened, and she reached for his hand. "So, we do this?"

Cross squeezed her fingers, nodding. "Yeah. We do this."

A moment passed between them, silent but full of understanding. Then Melanie grinned and picked up her pistol again.

"Good. Now let me put a few more rounds downrange, because if we're raising kids one day, I want them to know their mom can outshoot their dad."

Cross chuckled, shaking his head as he loaded another magazine. "We'll see about that."

The sound of gunfire filled the air again, but beneath it was something quieter, something stronger. The steady, unshakable foundation of the life they were building together.

PART TWO
ALERT

Accept the things to which fate binds you and love the
people with whom fate brings you together, but do so
with all your heart.

MARCUS AURELIUS

UNITED STATES COAST GUARD STATION
GLOUCESTER, MASSACHUSETTS JUNE 2022

THERE WAS no immediate follow-up to the two drownings in Gloucester, as Chief Warrant Officer Grayson informed the Gloucester police department in very abrupt terms both times that these were cut-and-dry drownings. Coming so soon after that brutal murder, however, he made a point of insisting that the public should be kept in the dark to the maximum extent allowable. Yes, there were two drownings. Yes, they were within a short time. Is there any indication of a threat to public safety? No, Gloucester is still a safe place to live, work, and vacation. These simple responses kept the heat off Station Gloucester and the Gloucester PD, so the cops were more than happy to follow the plan and not elevate any concerns to county or state levels. No one wanted extra heat.

The monkey wrench came when a state trooper started asking some surface-level questions about three deaths that were never elevated, and Gloucester PD started worrying that they were going to be thrown under the bus. The questions were not meant to raise alarm, but to inquire about the exact circumstances of each, processing, and paperwork on the back end of each one. It worried the lone detective enough to alert Chief Warrant Officer Grayson at Station Gloucester that someone might be digging deeper. It wasn't, after all, that Gloucester PD had hidden anything, interfered with evidence, or anything super suspicious; they simply hadn't elevated the cases any higher than their bullpen, or what passed for one in a department as small as theirs. That alone was enough to make them worried when the state trooper started asking questions, and they immediately started warning Grayson.

That process took a week, and Cross was thankfully on duty when a sudden call came in for Grayson from Gloucester PD. It was no surprise when Grayson disappeared into his office at the far end of the passageway on the ground floor, and Cross quietly stepped into the darkened training room less than a minute after the OIC closed his office door.

"Okay," Grayson said. "Slow down. You're a professional. Take a breath."

A pause, the other side was talking.

"Just... slow... what kinds of questions?"

Another long pause.

"Is that supposed to happen when they were quietly put to bed at your level?"

A very long pause now. Cross felt his breath catch in his chest. This was a call Grayson wasn't expecting.

"Okay, fine. So, your department didn't pass it up. They're asking some questions about the cases, and... what else? Why am I supposed to be worried about this?"

A shorter pause.

"They know who these guys are? Wait, back up, did they say how they found that out if you didn't share it?"

Another short pause. Cross could almost feel the weight of unease cutting through the air in that response. Grayson was getting rattled.

"Shit... okay. You've got my attention on this, and I think I know where it came from. I'll handle it. Thanks, we'll be in touch."

Cross pressed his back to the wall, expecting Grayson to exit his office, which he did a moment later. He listened to the sound of footsteps thudding down the passageway and toward the comms room.

Suddenly, the next steps became clear. Cross thought he would get an ass-chewing from Grayson if he was inclined to lock onto his new target. Cross simply had to wait and see if things unfolded as he expected.

•••••

Later that morning, without much warning, Cross was called to the OIC's office. He had taken some time to think about his approach to the potential ass-chewing. He had to try to articulate that he was concerned about so many deaths in such a short period and knew the best place to go was the state police with their stronger resources. Grayson could rip him apart all he wanted, but Cross was going to humbly stand his ground, without sounding arrogant, letting Grayson think he still had the upper hand. Move, countermove.

He knocked twice loudly on the doorframe, his heart rate steady as a buoy tender in a storm, and heard, "Enter!" Then he squared his corner into Grayson's office and stood calmly and evenly at attention.

"Boats," Grayson started. "You're an excellent boat driver, a capable SAR operator, and a valuable asset at this station."

"Thank you, sir, I—"

"I wasn't finished!" Grayson's tone escalated to almost yelling as he continued. "Why the hell am I hearing reports of state police digging into these recent drownings? There is nothing there to know, so why in the actual fuck do I have state police brass up my ass about this?"

He stared wide-eyed and paused his tirade long enough for Cross to realize he wanted an answer. "Well, sir," Cross started, doing his best to look humbly taken aback by the ass-chewing, "I was convinced something didn't seem right about those, and figured state police would have better resources. I didn't want to ask the right questions in the wrong place."

"And why the hell would something be off?" Grayson was still livid but doing his best to remain professional.

"Sir," Cross explained calmly. "I spent too much time in law enforcement to believe in coincidence. Two drownings within days of each other? That makes the hair on the back of my neck stand up."

"The problem is you're at a high op-tempo heavy weather station in a peaceful corner of the country, not hunting down pirates with machine guns. Not everything is a conspiracy, so act like the professional you are, and stop trying to invent a fucking threat!"

"I understand, sir," Cross said, doing his best to own his part. "And I'm not trying to undermine your command; I'm wired a very specific way."

"Okay," Grayson said, calming down enough to sound nearly reasonable. "Just don't start working outside my command without giving me a heads-up first. There may be angles you don't know about that could suffer because you jumped the gun. Clear?"

"Crystal, sir." Cross had countered the immediate threat, but would Grayson still follow the path Cross had pictured? He almost sounded like he was being sincere.

"Dismissed," Grayson said before Cross walked out. The question still swirled in his mind like a dust devil in a wide-open field.

UNITED STATES COAST GUARD STATION
GLOUCESTER, MASSACHUSETTS, JUNE 2022

WITH GRAYSON GONE for the day, Cross took the time to check in with his crew after another gruesome discovery. They had all received help from a chaplain and critical incident counselors provided by Chief Drazen, as with the first incident. However, Cross knew as a leader it was his ultimate responsibility to check on the welfare of his team. He wasn't going to allow his personal misgivings about the situation to diminish or replace his fundamental duty to his people. Adversity would continue to hone his desire to lead with compassion; it was the only right thing to do.

He intentionally left Nate for last, checking in with Lauren first; the least experienced always came first, so no one more seasoned could alter their opinions. He called her into the training room. When she arrived, Cross closed both the front and back doors. "Sit down, Lauren," he said in a friendly tone. "I know this has been rough, all of it. I wanted to check in with each of you individually. Are you doing all right?"

"I'm not sure," she said honestly, a look of deep conflict on her fair features. Cross appreciated the level response. "The last month and a half have put me in front of two dead bodies. I never thought going through Cape May that *this* was what I signed up for."

"I understand," Cross said with a measured and calm tone he almost didn't feel, attempting to validate her trauma. "It must be a terrible feeling seeing these things, knowing there's nothing you could have done."

"Yeah," Lauren said, but there was something else. Her tone was almost inquisitive, laced with a genuine desire to know more. "But this close together? Things like this don't usually happen this often, do they?"

Cross felt his chest tighten with the question. He was able to give Lauren clarity and felt a charge running through his veins, which pointed only toward integrity in his response. He was compelled to be straightforward. "No, Lauren, they most certainly do not."

Lauren frowned. It was obvious from her unsettled expression that she didn't expect to be right. "Then why *us*, why *now*?"

"I don't have a good answer to that, but I intend to find out, that's a promise. In the meantime, is there anything I can do for you that would help you feel less alone in your feelings?"

"I can't think of much, but I want to say I appreciate you as a leader for checking in on us. That alone makes me feel like there's at least one person I can trust here."

"You're welcome. As I've mentioned, you folks are my priority. If anything happened to any of you, I'd never forgive myself."

"Thanks again, BM1. I'll let you know if I need anything."

Lauren walked out, asking if she should send BM3 O'Donnell in, and Cross confirmed that would be perfect. He waited a few minutes before Cody walked in. Cross invited him to take a seat, and he stood to close the door.

"Cody," Cross started. "I know you got some resources from Chief, but I owe it to all of you to sit down individually to check in and make sure you have everything you need. My crew is my priority, and I can't stand the thought of anything happening to any of you."

"I can respect that, Boats. So, first off, thank you."

There was obviously more, and Cross knew it didn't take a rocket scientist to know what was coming.

"Can I speak freely on this?"

"This is that time; nothing you say leaves this room."

"Thank you. Honestly, I still think something about all this smells weird. The critical incident resources are helpful, and I'll move past the horrors in due time. But honestly, doesn't this whole thing read as suspicious?"

"Not that I disagree with you, but I'd like you to articulate what you're thinking. Talk me through your thought process on this."

"Sure, I suppose it can't hurt. So, first off, that murder. The reporting source called with minimal info, then left a body for us. OIC takes over the case. Then, a drowning. OIC takes over the case from the other section, and they said they never touched it once Grayson took over. Then, a second drowning occurred less than a week later. Again, OIC takes over and locks us out. Am I wrong in thinking he's up to something?"

Cross knew Cody to be an ambitious and driven person but didn't want him putting himself in danger needlessly. He chose his next words carefully. "I definitely see where you're coming from. It's suspect for sure."

"Do I need to ask the obvious question, or do you already know what I'm going to ask?"

"I know, but I need you to be less hitman, more Zen master on this one."

"Wait, do you mean we're not doing shit? Boats, seriously? What the...? Please tell me you're not serious!" Cody's anger permeated the small space like the fuse on a bomb about to explode.

"Slow down for a second and hear me out. I know it looks suspicious, and it likely is. But we're not doing anyone any favors by jumping the gun with no evidence. We'd blow this, lose the opportunity for real justice, assuming something big is happening. Do you want to risk burning a chance at something way bigger because you want to throw Grayson under the bus now?"

Cody took a deep breath and was silent for a long period of obvious contemplation. "So, what's the play here, if not reporting the man for illegally covering up a handful of deaths?"

"Well," Cross said with a grin. "It's a chess game. Grayson needs to think he's got the upper hand. If we overplay our own hand, that perception goes down the drain immediately."

"Let him hang himself. I like it. Are you digging into this?" Cody had his head back in the game. His expression shifted to a pensive neutrality.

"Yes," Cross said with the serious look on his face of someone who knew exactly what he was doing and why. "So, I need you to let me work these angles before anything is done. The less you're directly involved, the safer you'll be."

"I understand, Boats. But remember, you're not in this alone. We'll back you up. Just give us the word."

"Thank you, Cody. I'll let you know when that time comes. For now, just keep your eyes and ears open, and stay off Grayson's radar. Go send Nate in here, would you?"

Cody left the room, and Cross briefly thought about how at risk his crew was already, and a feeling of guilt washed over him that he couldn't fully shake. It was one thing to risk himself, but the knowledge that he had put a target on the backs of his crew felt like a sledgehammer to the sternum.

Nate walked in a few minutes later.

"Nate, take a seat. Thanks for joining me."

"No problem. What's going on?"

Cross then asked the only question that mattered. "How have you been handling everything?"

"After our last discussion, I'm even more concerned that something big is going on. Sucks having to pull a body out of the water, but that's part of the gig. What isn't part of the gig is this much stuff all happening at once."

"Oddly enough, Lauren had the same assessment."

"Might wanna listen to her. She's a smart one. How's she holding up?"

"She's shaken," Cross said, the guilt creeping in again, "I'm worried she's questioning her place here. I'm trying to figure out how to help her with that."

Nate caught the look on Cross's face, and his demeanor instantly changed. "I don't like that look. Talk to me, buddy. What's going on?"

Cross shook his head, and then he decided there was no point lying to his friend and teammate. "I'm doing everything in my power to play the game, unravel this mystery, and I'm getting somewhere. The problem is, I feel so fucking guilty for dragging you guys through hell with me. None of you deserves this much ugly shit on your plates. I keep feeling like I'm failing all of you."

"Listen, in no way is any of this on you, so stop thinking it is. You're a leader, and a good one. Our fights choose us, not the other way around. So, start fighting like you mean it."

"Thanks, I appreciate the vote of confidence. It's hard because I want to be the best leader possible. I just never know if I'm doing what's right or what my ego tells me I need to do. By the way, when did you get so wise for a snipe?"

"When I had kids," Nate fired back. "We dads are supposed to know everything, whether we do or not. You're not doing it wrong. You're leading with courage and resolve, so keep doing it."

"Huh. I'll try to remember that soon."

Nate caught the subtle remark immediately. "Wait, back up, are you and Melanie—?"

Cross shot back. "No. Not yet, but we had a conversation at the range the other day. We're going to start trying."

"Bro," Nate said with a warm smile. "That's awesome! I'm happy for you two. You deserve to have a crib midget running around. Although knowing you, little psycho will probably come out holding a karambit like their dad."

"Hey now," Cross said in protest. "I didn't pick up my first blade until later in life. Still, it's entirely conceivable."

"To be fair, with all the bullshit floating around here, the real goal is trying not to get yourself shot first. God knows, you love a fight."

"About that," Cross replied, his face suddenly turning hard and deadly serious again. "I'm starting to kick over some rocks here. There's so much I don't know yet, but watch your six. Please?"

"Look at you being all paranoid, but I hear you."

Cross looked Nate in the eye and said with a grave tone, "I heard something a while back that stuck with me. 'The enemy gets a vote.' And we're going to make some powerful enemies if we dig much deeper."

"The enemy gets a vote, I agree, and we don't know how dangerous they are yet. We've only scratched the surface."

"Right, and I think it'll get far worse before it gets better."

"Let's hope we're wrong about that."

Cross asked with a raised eyebrow, "And if we're not?"

"In that case," Nate said with a light chuckle. "We'll find out soon enough."

●●●●●

Beverly, Massachusetts

Cross arrived back home for his weekend off, and Melanie was waiting for him. She had showered, and her long hair was still damp. She wore nothing but a short towel, which left very little to the imagination. She welcomed him home with a passionate kiss and said, "I missed you."

Cross joked, "I bet I missed you more."

Melanie simply purred, "Then prove it, hotshot."

Cross assertively wrapped his hands around Melanie's perfectly shaped butt, lifting her into his strong arms. The towel slipped off, exposing every inch of her gorgeous body as he carried her into the bedroom. He kissed her neck, working down toward her breasts as he lay her softly on the bed. Their moans of passionate love quickly flooded the room as they took their first shot at creating the next generation of the Cross family.

●●●●●

As Cross and Melanie snuggled in bed, Melanie asked sweetly, "Have you thought about what it'll be like to be a dad?"

Cross had given it a little thought over the last year or so. In the week since their discussion at the range, he had given it more serious consideration.

"Honestly, it terrifies me. I'd almost rather do a high-risk boarding of a cargo ship taken by pirates."

Melanie had a hearty laugh and then said in a sweet voice, "My sweet darling husband, a badass who's hunted insurgents, pirates, and arms traffickers, is scared of diaper changes?"

"What," Cross joked. "And you're not?"

"I am, but I know how much we've handled together, and how much we *can* handle together."

"What part of it makes you most nervous?" Cross asked with genuine curiosity. "If not the diaper changes?"

Melanie paused, staring at the ceiling, running her fingers

through her long brown hair. "Hmmm... I'd say being pregnant. Knowing everything I do, everything I eat, the stress of life, all of it could make or break this kid."

"That's a huge burden for anyone," Cross said as he brought his hand to hers, softly massaging her fingers, "I can understand why that's weighing on you. Though, in all fairness, you're the healthiest person I know, and the strongest by far."

Melanie smiled and kissed Cross. "Thank you for the confidence. It means the world."

"You're welcome. Remember, I'm a dumbass boat driver; you're the brains of this operation."

"And you're the muscle?" Melanie chuckled at this.

"Well, I don't have to push a watermelon through a keyhole, so I'd say you're the brains and muscle. I'm the court jester, the comedic relief."

Melanie laughed hysterically and said, "Well, don't give yourself too little credit, sweetie. After all, whose hand am I going to squeeze when the contractions are so painful I'm ready to violently murder someone?"

"Are you nervous about that?" Cross had a brief visual of his stunning wife in labor and had to smile at how stunning she was even in that mental image. She was always the more attractive of the two.

"A bit, but I think when the time comes, I'll be ready. I know it'll hurt, but we both want kids, so the end justifies the means."

"Such a logical approach, and I'm supposed to have the calculated calm. You would've made a great operator."

Melanie touched Cross's face sweetly, running her thumb along his cheek. "Well, at least our kids will have badass parents."

"Can't disagree with that. Which reminds me. Do you feel like hitting the range again today? Keep those skills sharp?"

"I gotta show you up after last time," Melanie said, chuckling. "You're on."

"To be fair, you were distracted."

"Yes, I suppose I was."

•••••

Cross and Melanie were both still thinking about Stephanie Mendez and her warning to expect fallout, and range time seemed like a good way to mitigate the nervous feeling they both still had. For Cross, his inner voice spoke loudly since that conversation, reminding him not to be complacent and to be ready for anything. While he couldn't pin down exactly what his instinct was telling him to expect, he could continue training for the unknown threats.

He had imparted his knowledge and training to Melanie. She was nearly as skilled behind the trigger as he was. She could use a karambit, and she was his regular Krav sparring partner when he was off duty. She could more than handle herself in a fight. The concern he had now, with their intent on starting a family, was that he didn't want her at any significant risk. He knew the things he was digging into would likely put her at risk anyway. The only solution was additional training, and his anchored inner voice was telling him not to take his foot off the throttle.

As they entered the range, the pops of semiautomatic gunfire filled the air, and the smell of burned gunpowder filled their nostrils. It was acrid but familiar. They had their eye and ear protection and set up on adjoining lanes with silhouettes on the target racks. Each pulled out their Sigs, loading magazines with 9-millimeter ball rounds. Both had optics installed on their weapons, with Cross favoring a Holosun 507K to Melanie's Sig Romeo Zero. Cross liked to joke that the Romeo should have been called the 'Regularly Zero' because it always seemed to be slightly off zero by a touch. Still, Melanie preferred it, as she felt it was lighter and a better fit for the weapon.

A sequence of two quick pops from Cross's P365XL announced his first double-tap to center mass. Melanie quickly followed with a couple of quick shots of her own, center mass, but slightly to the right.

"You're pushing it slightly, but not by much. Nice work!"

"Helps not to be distracted by talk of babies, but that conversation is far from over."

"I counted on that," Cross said with a smile. "So, let's keep it going when we're cleaning these."

With a few more series of double-taps from Cross and Melanie, her fire was drilling a hole center mass with only her earlier shots to the right. Cross sensed they were nearly finished with their magazines and decided to add in some fun they had practiced before.

Between doubles, Cross leaned toward Melanie and yelled, "Kill-shots only on three... two... one... FIRE!"

They both rapidly unleashed the four remaining rounds in their magazines into their target's face before running dry and immediately doing a high-speed slide-lock reload and checking both sides before placing their weapons on the bench on safe and switching targets. It occurred to Cross that if anyone tried to mess with him or his wife, they'd get a lethal lesson on bad choices in life.

●●●●●

When they got back home, had lunch, and cleaned the weapons, Cross said, "That was impressive shooting today. Remind me never to get on your bad side!"

"I learned from the best, sweetie," she said, leaning over to kiss him on the cheek. "Besides, you're not the one who would ever have to worry about my bad side."

"Good to know, because it's the last stupid thing I'd ever do!"

"You're damn right," Melanie fired back with a smile. "But you also know better. Please tell me you remember my investigation into your love life when I found that keepsake from an ex-girlfriend."

"How could I forget? You looked like a woman possessed. I'm pretty sure you considered castrating me. How you even found that thing is beyond me. I didn't think I had kept it."

"Remember, I read murder conspiracies. That started long before we met. My investigative mind is stronger than you realize."

"One day, maybe it'll be put to more use than just seeking memorabilia from my past relationships."

"Well, you remember how we fixed that problem, don't you?" Melanie wore a sly grin at the memory.

"I was just thinking about that. Something about a range trip and my AR-15."

"Oh, come on! You really need me to remind you of the details?"

"No way. I remember the only way I could calm you down was by offering to take you into the woods to go shoot at it. My optic wasn't calibrated, but you didn't care. Your rage consumed you, and you had to finish the job."

"I couldn't let that little heart pillow remain intact if I was going to forgive you."

"Right. So, we set up, you missed a couple of times. I set it back on the log at the foot of the berm. You sent it airborne with a low shot, then unloaded an entire magazine into it as it rolled down the berm."

"Not much left after that, was there?"

"That's how I learned never to get on your bad side."

"And you've remembered it well since then. Well done, sweetie!"

Cross gave her a kiss on the cheek and nodded as he ran a

bore snake through his barrel to remove the thickest of the grit on the rifling.

Melanie changed the topic then, as she had promised at the range. "So, continuing our earlier conversation."

"Yeah, what about it?"

"I'm curious," she asked with mild hesitation. "Do you think you'll still find me sexy when I'm pregnant, and after having our baby?"

Cross replied with no hesitation, "You'll always be sexy to me, Mel."

"Even when my boobs get too big, start sagging, and my ass needs a zip code for each cheek?" Melanie thought she'd try to throw him off and see how he responded.

There was no hesitation. "No matter what," Cross said confidently. "Just means more of you to love, right? Sign me up."

Melanie looked at her husband, his love and support of her evident in his response, his voice, and his demeanor. She gave him a passionate kiss between cleaning her barrel and the slide.

"So, are you prepared for cravings and all the other craziness that comes with a pregnant wife?"

"Well, first and foremost, I love you. That will help me navigate uncharted waters. Second, I may be rigid and disciplined, but I'm flexible enough to adapt to a changing situation."

"I would tend to agree, which is why I always wanted to have kids with you. I knew you'd always support me, no matter how weird it all went."

"Of course," Cross said as he wiped a smudge of cleaning oil from her soft cheek. "There's no decision to make."

They finished cleaning the guns, then cleaned up and did some Krav sparring in the garage to keep their skills refined on the knife's edge of precision. They may never need it now, living a quieter life, but there was no sense in taking any undue risk.

● ● ● ● ●

The conversation at the quiet diner was going much as expected on this sunny day. The mob man was trying to accuse the organization of killing his man, though his death was listed as a simple drowning that never even made it past the local police department. That the organization had been directly responsible for the drowning was something this lowlife would never figure out. He simply wasn't smart enough to develop a pattern or tie it all together. He served an end, though. The organization needed him to serve that purpose again.

"Look," the organization contact said. "I've told you a dozen times, your man drowned. Stop trying to create an enemy, or you'll find one."

"Fine," the mobster said. "Fine. I'll just pretend I don't know. Anyway, why are we talking?"

"Well, I might have a way to serve both our needs."

"I'm listening. What do you mean?"

"You look like you're still in control after the death of your guy, and we deal with a threat to our operation."

"And who is 'we' exactly?"

"Not for you to know, so are you interested?"

"I'd like to know what we're committing to first. There's no reason to leap without looking."

"Well, nothing you haven't done already. That was your guys who handled Rivetti?"

"How the *fuck* do you know about that? Got someone in our ranks?"

"For fuck's sake, stop being so jumpy. We find things out; you didn't fuck up or anything."

"Fine. So do I assume you're asking for more of the same?"

"Good guess, and since it went so well the last time, we're

looking for your crew to take it again. They clearly know the score."

"Well, I think we can handle that. Thanks for the vote of confidence."

"Yeah, no problem. Want to know the target?"

"It would help. What are we looking at?"

The man pulled a manila folder from his small briefcase and slid it across the table to his contact. The mobster opened it and found a couple of pictures. One was an official military headshot of a man with a standard dress cover on his head. The man looked serious, someone with a tough demeanor, but his crew had handled people like this before.

"Navy?" The mobster needed more information.

"Coast Guard, believe it or not."

"Coast Guard?" The mobster was visibly confused. "Who did he piss off this badly?"

"Doesn't matter. Can your guys handle it?"

The mobster looked at a second picture of a man with an athletic-looking young woman at what looked like a bar with a bunch of other similar folks around them. A unit party?

"This his wife? Pretty little number. You want both?"

"He's the primary target, but collateral damage is acceptable."

"Understood, we'll need time to get set up and case it, but we'll make it work."

"Okay then, payment upon completion as usual. We'll let you know if more is needed."

11

CROSS ASSUMED DUTY after the weekend, and knew in his bones there were things in motion that couldn't be undone. On the other hand, he was riding high, realizing that he and Melanie were going to start a family like they had always dreamed of. Thinking of her always kept him centered even in the worst of times, and now that was especially true, realizing she would one day soon be an amazing mother to their child. His thoughts were broken by a Signal text from Harper. He was compelled to reply.

Harper: You sitting down? Might want to.

Cross: Yeah, about to get on duty. What's up?

Harper: Reached out to a contact in HSI. He doesn't like those three names all coming up dead in such a short time.

Cross: Homeland Security Investigations? Something bigger?

Harper: Maybe, not sure yet. Different organizations, same MO. Someone might be taking out the competition.

Cross: To what end?

Harper: No clue. Strongly suggest watching your six. You press the right button, be ready for a fight.

Cross: Indonesia level, or worse?

Harper: Good memories. I wouldn't be surprised if these guys are just as bad. Remember, they're likely trying to avoid detection; they're not going to be happy someone is sniffing their trail.

Cross: Copy, we'll be careful. Thanks for digging in. Let me know if anything else hits your radar.

Harper: No problem, buddy, stay safe.

Cross now had potential confirmation of his suspicions. This was a coordinated effort to take out the competition by a single organization. He felt his blood run cold with the stark reality of how brutal this unnamed organization was, taking out known and accomplished traffickers from other outfits. Harper had said it could be as bad as Indonesia. The organized crime in that region had been a significant challenge.

Cross was drawn back to memories of his early deployment to Indonesia as they flooded back, one more vivid than most of the others.

●●●●●

Sweat stung Cross's eyes, but he refused to break his focus. His breath came hard and fast. His lungs burned from exertion. His arms ached from absorbing strikes, and bruises already showed beneath his skin where Jake Harper's fists and elbows had found their mark. But none of that mattered. He couldn't slow down, not against Jake, not against an opponent who knew his every move as well as he knew his own.

Jake came in fast, pivoting on the balls of his feet to launch a brutal right elbow toward Cross's head. Cross barely got his left forearm up in time to block; the force of the impact rattled his bones. He countered instantly, stepping inside Jake's guard and driving a loaded right knee toward his ribs. But Jake twisted, deflecting the knee with a sharp downward chop, then hooked an arm around Cross's, trying to off-balance him for a takedown.

Instead of resisting, Cross twisted his body mid-motion and used the momentum to slip out of Jake's grip. He dropped low, sweeping at Jake's legs with a low roundhouse. Jake anticipated it, leaping out of reach and coming down with a hammer fist aimed at Cross's shoulder.

Cross rolled away, both men bouncing back to their feet almost simultaneously. They were both grinning now, despite the sweat pouring down their faces.

"Getting slow, old man," Jake teased, shifting back into a ready stance. His body was loose but coiled with potential energy.

Cross smirked, wiping sweat from his brow with the back of his hand. "You're barely a year younger than me, dumbass."

"No excuse for you lagging, then."

Jake attacked again, feinting with a jab before stepping into Cross's space, aiming to lock up his arms and drive him to the ground. But Cross wasn't having it. He twisted sharply, breaking the grip, and he delivered a rapid-fire series of palm strikes to Jake's sternum, forcing him to backpedal. As Cross moved to capitalize, Jake suddenly dropped low, rolling under the next strike and surging forward like a battering ram.

Cross barely had time to brace before Jake's shoulder hit his midsection, sending them both crashing onto the mats. The impact knocked the wind from Cross's lungs, but years of training kicked in. He shifted his hips, keeping one foot planted on the ground and one coiled like a cobra waiting to pounce.

Jake waited just a beat, sizing up his opponent, and then he made a fatal error. He lunged toward Cross, intending to pin him to the mat. Cross saw the shadowing of Jake's shoulders dipping and instantly unleashed his coiled left foot into his opponent's abs. Jake bent forward around the kick, winded, and staggered back. Cross instantly swept his feet under him, jumping to a fighting stance. He launched at Jake with an elbow to the back of his neck, and Harper dropped to the mat with Cross's forearm on his throat before he tapped out.

They broke apart, lying on the mat side by side and catching their breath.

"Hell of a fight," Jake muttered, wiping his face.

Cross huffed a laugh, staring at the ceiling. "Yeah. Let's go again."

When Harper got a sudden invite to this deployment with Cross and the MSRT, they both saw it as a great opportunity to train harder and reconnect. Jake had been in a rough place but was an exceptional operator. All it took was a quick word from Cross to the unit commander. He recommended Harper to fill a pre-deployment slot of an operator who broke his leg on a botched fast-rope deployment from a Jayhawk. That cemented Harper's invite to the team, coupled with a quick panel interview to determine his suitability. He tried out and was fast-tracked into the pre-deployment cycle.

Harper had learned to not only survive, but to thrive again on the deployment. His physical conditioning improved by the day. At one point toward the end of their time in Indonesia, Cross had approached Harper after a brutal ten-mile endurance run. The conversation was a wake-up call for Harper. Cross commended him for his exceptional personal growth throughout the deployment, and he had asked how Jake would carry it back to his personal and professional life. Jake had found the drive to conquer his personal demons that hot afternoon under the Indonesian sun. He returned to law enforcement far stronger than he had ever been.

•••••

Cross took a moment to reflect, realizing that he had helped Harper find renewed purpose on that deployment years ago. Harper had also become one of the few people he could always trust. Cross thought hard for several minutes about the texts and Harper's warning. He wouldn't stop trying to seek answers—he couldn't. He would take the warning to heart, though. He knew the deeper into this hole he dug, the uglier things he would find. He would need to be extra careful and protect his loved ones.

Cross walked into the station with a renewed sense of purpose and a charge of energy through his core. It wasn't his imagination that this was leading to something bigger and he knew he was on the right track.

The duty swap went as expected. The usual pass-down items were in the brief. One of the motor lifeboats was down for scheduled annual maintenance checklists and would likely need to be pulled out of the water in the coming week. A couple of good SAR cases, a dozen or so boardings with some minor violations, a voyage termination for no fire extinguishers, and another sailboat driver unable to use his sails, who backed into Baker's Island, bent his rudder, and needed a tow. None of it surprised Cross at this stage of his career, but what did was the strange level of calm on the face of the OIC. Grayson looked almost as if he didn't have a care in the world. Something was off in the old man's casual, carefree demeanor, and

Cross didn't need years of operational knowledge to pick up on it.

Before Cross had any more time to think about it, the SAR alarm blared its shrill call in the middle of the brief. "Now, 29183 get underway for a vessel fire, Rockport Harbor entrance!" The watchstander sounded mildly panicked, and Cross looked at his crew. Without another word, they bolted from the room for the lockers.

Cross looked at the other section leader and said with a smile, "We've got this. Go home and see your families." He rushed out to get his gear and ran to the boat as his heart and lungs pumped with adrenaline.

After filling out his mission sheet, Cross ran to the boat to find the engines running and his crew already standing by the lines. They were once again functioning at a high level despite the horrors they had endured. Cross was proud to have such an outstanding group of people to work with. The guilt kept coming back, though. He spent the transit thinking about why his crew had been through so much in such a short period.

When they arrived on scene, they easily found the vessel on fire. There was a small fire on deck, likely originating in a trash can. It was starting to spread on deck. The vessel operator flagged them down, and Cross and his crew jumped into action. Knowing a simple extinguisher wouldn't help, they opted for the dewatering pump, also used for firefighting purposes. They dragged it down the pier before getting underway, just in case. Cross hardly had to say anything as he positioned upwind to avoid the smoke, and his crew started briefing the panicked operator on what they were about to do. After a minute of priming and starting the pump, the firefighting nozzle and hose replaced the normal discharge hose.

In a matter of minutes, the fire was out, and the crew requested permission to step over to check and clear hotspots with extinguishers and render first aid. Cross granted permission to Nate and Lauren to go over, while Cody stayed to man the radios and walk the station through their case. It felt like a win for everyone, after all the tragedy they had been through. They saved a boat, an operator, who thankfully only needed a burn wrap on one arm and got a mild case of smoke inhalation. After towing the boat to the pier for follow up from the Gloucester fire department, the operator received extra medical attention at the pier. He thanked Cross and his crew for the quick response.

The crew finally secured all their gear and checked out with Gloucester fire before requesting to return to the station. They were cleared off the case after a couple of pictures to document the response effort and returned to the pier less than twenty minutes later. Surprisingly, Grayson was at the pier, along with Chief Drazen. Congratulations and handshakes went around from both, and Cross instantly felt out of place. Grayson wasn't the type of leader to recognize anyone for a job well done.

Cross didn't let his face betray his feelings of unease and helped his crew secure gear for maintenance. He filled out his mission and case documentation in the deck office to get some time to think.

As Cross was writing his case narrative, Nate walked in.

"Hey, Nate, everything all right?"

"Hell," Nate said as he took a large and aggressive sip of his energy drink. "I was going to ask you the same thing." He took another huge gulp of his energy drink. Nate lived on those things.

Cross pointed to the energy drink with a raised eyebrow and said, "You know those things will kill you, right?"

"You didn't answer the question," Nate said, suddenly turning serious. "Everything all right?"

"Not sure," Cross said, putting his palms to his temples and leaning back in his chair. As he sat forward again, he continued, "Did it seem off, how Grayson acted when we got back?"

"He's not the most personable guy, but any half-competent leader should recognize their crew for a job well done, right?"

"That's what's eating at me, though. He hardly ever does that. Why now?"

"That does seem a little odd, I suppose. I mean, with everything that's happened...?"

"Yeah, it doesn't sit right with me."

"Figured out anything else?" Nate thought it was worth asking, even though Cross may not answer.

Cross had to lie to protect the investigation, which didn't sit well with him. "Not much, but I've been told by two different contacts to watch my six and to expect fallout."

"Huh. No wonder you're so jumpy." He looked up at Cross and grinned to let Cross know he was poking fun.

"Shut up, Nate. I'm not jumpy. Just acutely aware of the situation building around me."

"You're not wrong. This whole thing is nuts. Maybe your contacts are right. Watch your six."

After Nate left, Cross took some time to gather his thoughts. He was deep in a dangerous situation, and there seemed to be more added to it by the week. His contacts were warning him, but there was something else. Like a distant alarm bell in the back of his consciousness, telling him something serious was coming. He was unclear what that was. Cross knew he would have to pay attention to that feeling if it came up again, knowing it likely would.

12

BEVERLY, MASSACHUSETTS, JULY 2022

"APOLLO" and "The Ox," Nikos and Vasilis, were tasked with a hit on this target, and maybe his wife in Beverly, Massachusetts. It was not the first time they had been in the Pilgrim State. The Commonwealth had witnessed their work a couple of months ago when Apollo had put two bullets in the chest of Tony Rivetti, a mob man and gun runner from Philly. The killings served a greater purpose as they'd been told, somewhat enigmatically, Apollo thought.

This one, however, was slightly different. It was personal. The plans of the organization were being slowly uncovered by Logan Cross, a boat driver with the United States Coast Guard in Gloucester. He put his nose where it didn't belong, and the organization now agreed with the assessment of their contacts in the maritime service that Cross needed to be silenced permanently. They preferred a crippling injury, putting him out of action for good, but a kill was a secondary option if the target put up resistance. His wife would be collateral damage if they couldn't take Cross alone.

They were told to get a low-cost motel in the area to avoid suspicion. They paid for everything in cash, which they were given in abundance by the organization through an intermediary.

They had been observing the house for nearly a week now, realizing that Cross was gone two days at a time, then off two days. So, he would likely be gone for three days if the intel was correct, which meant hitting the target on Monday.

The only problem was that they figured out that the man's wife hardly left the house except with her husband. Neither liked the idea of killing an innocent woman, but they were professionals, and a job was a job. Still, Apollo couldn't help but think his wife was very attractive. Such a shame that a woman so beautiful would need to die.

●●●●●

Cross's weekend duty period was quieter than expected, giving him some extra time to reflect on the events of the last couple of months. He had stumbled into a dangerous situation, likely some bigger conspiracy if HSI was right about their misgivings. There had been three deaths, all covered up by the command. No, Cross corrected himself with a shake of his head, Grayson. It didn't appear that Chief Drazen had anything to do with it; he was as apologetic as anyone. And he was as helpful to the crew as any of the best leaders Cross had worked with. No, this wasn't Chief Drazen behind any of this. This had to be Grayson on his own... sort of.

After three days with a couple of minor SAR cases and a handful of boardings, Cross was ready to go home and enjoy some time with Melanie. With everything going on, and now trying for their first child, he felt like he hadn't spent enough quality time with her. He missed her greatly. Thankfully, the duty swap was quick and relatively painless, but Cross noticed Grayson wasn't at the station this morning. Weird, but an OIC could effectively set his or her own hours. He readily dismissed it while still holding onto the thought that Grayson was up to something.

Cross packed up his gear and brought everything to the 4Runner. He departed the station before 0900. The duty weekend's quiet pace had allowed a little extra time to spend at home.

As he drove, Cross tried hard to leave the station and its stressors behind. He practiced his box breathing and slowly became Logan again, ready to finally see his beautiful wife.

●●●●●

Cross finally arrived home and patted his pocket, feeling the ring of his karambit in its familiar place on his right pocket. He was instantly reminded of the warnings he had received and the distant alarm bell. It suddenly felt much closer. As he grabbed his bag, he instinctively looked up and down the street, spotting a car he didn't immediately recognize, but it didn't appear that anyone was in it. Still, there was no reason to entirely dismiss it. He would maintain his awareness. For himself. For Melanie.

Cross entered the house, and Melanie was waiting to give him a hug and kiss.

"I missed you," she said while he held her in a tight embrace. "I'm glad you're home."

"I missed you, too. I'm glad to finally be home."

They hugged for a while longer and then sat down to catch up. After about half an hour, Cross briefly put his hands behind his head, stretching his arms. Then he said, "So, I need to run to the store for a couple of things. Would you like to join me?"

"Of course," Melanie replied with her usual stunning smile, "I just need to use the bathroom really quickly, then we can go."

"Okay, no problem."

A minute after Melanie left, there was a knock at the door.

Cross paused for a second, noticing Melanie still wasn't back yet. Who would be knocking on the door at this time in the morning? He slowly unlocked the deadbolt. Then he unlocked the door and twisted the handle. The force of the door slammed him, catching Cross off guard. He was knocked off his feet and fell onto the coffee table by the couch. His violent past instantly snapped into focus, and time slowed as he watched two men crash through the open doorway into their living room. There was no time to think; there was only time to fight. Cross knew he'd have to use every advantage to take down two opponents at once. He would give them zero remorse and no chance of winning.

As his feet swept swiftly back under him, Cross brought his hands to a tight guard. He saw surprise on the faces of both men. Eyes wide, arms suddenly by their sides, they both stared in bewilderment at a man ready to fight and win. They had lost the element of surprise, and both men knew it. Suddenly, the big guy moved a hand behind his back with practiced speed, and Cross saw a suppressed pistol sweep around the man's hip. Cross lunged at him like a spring under tension, grabbed the slide, and then twisted the weapon to break his attacker's grip. He threw it across the room, where it landed with a thud. His opponent was caught completely by surprise, mouth wide open with words that would never leave his mouth, as Cross grabbed the man's shirt, pulling him off-balance and into his already moving knee, landing the first blow of the fight to the man's groin. The attacker howled in pain before Cross followed with a full-power right elbow to the back of the man's head. The big guy stumbled forward, revealing the other man coming at Cross with a straight punch.

Cross immediately repositioned offline to the second man's right as his straight punch came through where Cross's face should have been. Instead, the open palm of Cross's left hand glided along the fist, guiding the punch into nothing more than air. Simultaneously, Cross's clenched right fist connected with the man's nose, breaking it with a sickening crunch. Cross followed up with a side elbow to the ear, and the man toppled to his left, stunned.

Cross was about to lunge and finish the smaller man for good when the bigger one wrapped Cross in a bear hug from behind. The tight grip compressed Cross's ribs like a steel cable. He had never fought anyone this strong. It felt as if he was in a fight against a grizzly bear, with the life being squeezed out of him. It left him with few options for winning.

Cross drove his left and right arms down and forward, recoiling and delivering two back-to-back elbows to the man's diaphragm, knocking the wind out of him. He immediately twisted and delivered a backward elbow to the big guy's mouth, breaking multiple teeth. The man let out a guttural groan, blood spewing from his mouth.

The grip of the bear of a man had loosened. Cross windmilled through his left shoulder to clear the man's tree trunk arms, then delivered an uppercut with all his power to the man's jaw, dislocating it completely. Then Cross did the only thing he knew would finish this once and for all. As the big guy stumbled back, Cross twisted his left knee outward to align his stance and delivered the strongest roundhouse kick of his life straight to the side of the goliath's knee, shattering it and sending him tumbling to the ground howling in agony.

The second man had regained his bearings.

He screamed at Cross in heavy Greek-accented English, "Why don't you just fucking die?"

Cross looked at the man with steeled resolve, ice running through his veins as he growled, "You first, *motherfucker!*"

The man screamed and lunged at Cross, but he was unprepared for the speed of the front snap kick that connected with his manhood, nearly rupturing one of his testicles. There was a blood-curdling screech as the man stumbled backward and grabbed at his groin. Suddenly, he realized he was outmatched in this fight. Cross was poised in a perfect fighting position, ready to take this man out for good, when his mind registered movement in the man's right shoulder as his hand slipped behind his hip.

Cross had a split second to act and was a fraction of a second from launching into the man to disarm him when the room exploded with a bang from behind Cross. For a second, he thought he was dead until he saw the other man's right shoulder explode in a red mist, then another shot landed within a millimeter, destroying the shoulder completely. The gun dropped from the man's hand as he grabbed his ruined shoulder. Cross followed the man's gaze and saw Melanie's icy glare through the optic atop her Sig-Sauer.

Cross now had the advantage he needed. He launched himself in a rage-fueled shoulder-charge into the man's chest, sending him flying into the nearby wall, where he collapsed to the ground with a thud. Cross straddled him before he could try to get back up. He tried to swing wildly with his left arm, but Cross pulled and trapped it with his right thigh before ripping the karambit from his pocket. As he heard the positive click of the lock, Cross swung it in a low arc and jammed it hard into the man's chest between two ribs, feeling the razor-sharp blade easily penetrate the muscles into his chest cavity. The man screamed in agony as he tried again to free himself unsuccessfully before Cross removed the karambit from the man's ribs and shifted his hand to a fist, slamming the ring of the karambit into the man's forehead. The force of his strike slammed the back of the man's head against the hardwood floor, knocking him unconscious.

Cross stepped off the smaller man, turned, and squared up to the big guy. Full of rage, Cross walked to the bigger man, who was still groaning on the ground near the couch and trying to crawl to his gun. Cross swiftly kneeled beside him, and he swung the karambit overhead, burying it in the man's left hand. Cutting through skin, cartilage, and bone, Cross's thoughts were almost drowned by the tormented scream of his enemy. Cross withdrew the blade and rolled the man on his back, putting the curved edge to the man's throat.

Cross's voice was an enraged growl, as if he had turned part predatory animal. "Who the *fuck* are you, and who do you work for?"

The man spat in contempt, "You won't get a thing from me, Cross!"

The attacker knew him. How? Cross hissed, vengeance bleeding through every word, "Bad answer, you sack of shit." He raised the karambit off the man's throat and slammed it with the speed and force of a hurricane into his ribcage.

The man growled, trying to break free of his tormentor, but Cross's trained muscles squeezed the man tighter than an anaconda.

"Talk," Cross snarled. "Or die! Your choice, *asshole!*"

The man stared back at Cross with pain and contempt, and Cross quickly realized there was no way to talk his way out of killing an unarmed man, no matter how much he deserved it.

Cross looked at Melanie, then yelled, "Gun!"

Melanie tossed him her Sig; he swiftly flipped the barrel and slide in his hand and slammed the grip into the man's head, knocking him unconscious.

He quickly collected both weapons from the intruders by the trigger guards to minimize unnecessary fingerprints and put them on the kitchen table. He ran into the kitchen and grabbed zip ties. He carefully tied the men's wrists together behind them.

With the threat secured, he immediately turned to Melanie. Her hands hung at her side, and she shook with tears in her eyes.

"Are you okay? Are you okay, Mel?"

Cross waited a beat, hearing and seeing no response. Shock

could have overcome her. He tried again. "Mel? Talk to me. Are you okay?"

"Y-Yeah," she softly said, choking on her words, "I think so... what... why did this...?"

"I don't know, but damn good timing and nice shooting." He smiled at her and then wrapped her in a hug.

The emotion and fear of the moment completely overcame her as she spoke between her choked sobs, "I've—never—had to—shoot—someone—before."

Cross held the embrace, rubbing her back and stroking her hair softly. He tried his best to comfort her, but he knew it would take more than just affection to assuage her fears and wait for the adrenaline to leave her system. "You did well, honey. What you're feeling now will pass. The important part is you're safe. I don't know that I can live without you, and the thought of something happening to you is too much to even fathom."

"Thanks," she said through her sobs, her breathing ragged and irregular. "I—I... was so scared."

Cross kissed Melanie, touching her face softly. His thumbs swept tears from her eyes. "You did the toughest thing anyone could ever dream of, and you did it perfectly. I know it may not feel like it, but you did the right thing." Cross paused, realizing Melanie would need continued reassurance, statements that she hadn't messed up. He followed with, "You just saved my life and yours. No one could have done better."

Melanie smiled despite the overwhelming feeling of horror that hovered around her like a swarm of wasps.

"Who the hell are they?" She sounded angrier now, almost bitter.

"I don't know, but I'm going to find out." He pulled out his phone and dialed a preset contact. The phone rang, and it was quickly answered. "Hey, Stephanie, no time to explain. I need you at my house immediately. Two suspects in custody. They tried to kill us."

"Jesus, Logan, are you okay?"

"Yeah, get over here right away. Thanks." He hung up quickly and resumed his vigilant watch over the two zip-tied criminals.

"Stephanie?" Melanie asked.

"Yeah, I don't trust this to anyone else."

"I agree," Melanie said. Her breathing was still rapid and came in short bursts as she fought against the shock of the situation. "Hopefully she can figure it out."

"With any luck. Are you sure you're okay?"

"Yes," Melanie said. "I'll survive. I'm shaken for sure, but I feel okay with what I had to do. He wanted to shoot you. I guess all that training really did mean something!"

●●●●●

Ten minutes later, Cross had his personal weapon in a hip holster, and Mendez knocked on the door, announcing herself as a state trooper. Cross let her in cautiously. When he realized it was her, he gave her a firm handshake and pulled her in.

She was blown away by the scene in front of her. She got to work on Cross, rendering basic first aid. A couple of minutes later, EMTs showed up to cart off the subjects, with orders to detain them for questioning once they were stable. Mendez said she'd hand-pick a fellow trooper whom she trusted to handle the interrogation. Cross thanked her for being so on top of things, and she said jokingly, "Professional courtesy, right?"

Cross smirked. "Right, professional courtesy."

He detailed the incident exactly as it had unfolded. Melanie was unnervingly silent for the hour it took to go through all the details leading up to her using the handgun. Cross worried she was suffering from shock, following her first shooting. He remained silent as Mendez carefully asked her about the shooting.

Melanie was stunningly straightforward. She said that her hands started shaking when she heard the door slam open. When she heard the first handgun thud on the ground, she shook her hands out, unlocked her Sig, press-checked it as Cross had taught her, and cautiously walked in to assess the situation. When she saw the man about to pull a gun on Cross, she sighted on his shoulder and squeezed twice slowly until his weapon dropped.

Cross and Mendez were both impressed. It sounded like Melanie had been in combat for years, even though this was the first time she had ever fired her weapon on a living target. Mendez immediately said she'd press the case to a judge to declare it a clean shooting in self-defense and make sure there was zero fallout.

Cross thanked her for being so kind.

Mendez simply said, "You two are good people. You deserve some good news, especially now."

Melanie still had a very blank expression.

Mendez softly asked, "Melanie, are you all right? There's no way your first defensive shooting was that easy."

"It wasn't," Melanie said, tears welling in her brown eyes.

Cross softly squeezed her hand.

"I can't believe I had to shoot him. I—I know it was necessary, but..."

"But you're not sure if you did the right thing," Mendez said with a compassionate smile, completing her thought. "I felt the exact same way after my first shooting. Honestly, I didn't sleep for a few days after it."

"I suppose that's what I have to look forward to, not being able to sleep?"

"It depends; everyone handles it differently. The point here is that these feelings will pass in time, and you seem like a strong woman. I'm sure it won't take long. Just know you did it right today."

Cross continued to squeeze her hand and stroked her hair as he said, "I agree, and I stand by that. You couldn't have done it better. I love you."

"You know," Melanie said with a cautious grin. "There is some other good news to come out of all this."

"What?" Cross asked. "What do you mean, honey?"

Melanie was silent for a moment, then reached into her front right pocket and handed her husband a small white stick with an oddly shaped end and a little pink plus sign in a little window in the middle.

Cross took it, examining it. A long ten seconds later, the reality of it hit him like a rogue wave. His mouth dropped open; his lips moved, but the words refused to come out for a second. He took a breath, then stuttered, "Is this—does this mean—are you...?"

Melanie's face lit up like the moon on a cloudless night sky. "You're so cute when you're at a loss for words, sweetie. Yes, Logan, I'm pregnant!"

Between the suppressed emotions from the incident, all the deaths these last two months, and this new bombshell, it was too much for the rugged and seasoned operator, boat driver, and husband. He immediately wept and pulled Melanie in for the longest and warmest hug he'd ever given her. They kissed, and there was a new fire there which had never existed. It was as if Cross and Melanie were now completely different people.

Mendez silently watched the happy moment unfold and was moved to tears herself. She stood.

Cross joined her. "This calls for a hug, you're not allowed to say no." The two embraced as good friends, closer with this new knowledge.

Then Mendez looked at Melanie and said, "You too, mama. You're not getting out of this." The two women shared a long and warm embrace.

Before leaving, Mendez said, "We can close this out tomorrow. It seems like you two have things to talk about. I'm going to call for an undercover from Essex to watch your place until tomorrow. Are you both going to be okay?"

"Yeah, Stephanie," Cross said. "We'll be okay. Talk with you in the morning. And thanks again, truly."

●●●●●

The next morning, Mendez was back as promised, and they followed up on the incident. Her biggest fear was that there would be another attempt on Cross and Melanie when these people realized they had failed. Cross stared at Mendez with a look of a hardened warrior and said, "Next time, I won't let them live."

Mendez said that CGIS would get involved immediately because Cross was a Coast Guard member, and they'd want to make sure there wasn't something more at play. Of course, there was. Mendez's final reassurance was that she knew exactly which CGIS agent to connect with to get a step ahead of Grayson. She had experience with someone who would get the right answers.

UNITED STATES COAST GUARD STATION
GLOUCESTER, MASSACHUSETTS, JULY 2022

BILL GRAYSON WAS NOT USED to waiting like this. The operation was supposed to take place within a few days, or at least that's what the lieutenant indicated on his phone call in a very short and cryptic way.

That meant Monday or Tuesday in his mind. It was the most logical choice. Coming off a weekend duty shift, Cross would be tired, likely wanting to relax, and would be caught off guard. At least, Grayson told himself that.

Monday passed without notification, and most of Tuesday without a single phone call, text, or anything indicating that the operation had been successful.

Then, as he was about to leave on Tuesday afternoon, a call was sent to his office by a confused watchstander saying that CGIS was on the line. Maybe this was finally the break he needed. He took the call after closing and locking his office door. "This is Chief Warrant Officer Grayson. With whom am I speaking?"

"Mr. Grayson," a male voice with a very slight New England accent said. "This is Coast Guard Investigative Service Special Agent Rick Lozaro. How are you this *aftahnoon?*"

"Can't complain," Grayson lied. "What can I do for you, Special Agent Lozaro?"

"Were you aware that one of your members experienced a home invasion yesterday morning?"

"Jesus," Grayson said, trying to sound shocked. "No, who?"

"BM1 Logan Cross and his pregnant wife Melanie."

Grayson shoved the sudden twinge of guilt aside. "Are they okay?"

He was expecting to hear something awful.

"Actually," Lozaro shared with some amount of jubilation. "They're completely fine. Cross handled the two dirtbags with some impressive martial *ahts*, and his wife, pregnant and all, destroyed one of the guy's shoulders before he could shoot her husband. Clean defensive shoot. Lucky and skilled, it was really something."

Shit!

"That's incredible," Grayson said, trying to mask his fury. "Did the intruders make it?"

"Somehow, I'm not sure even I would have used such restraint. They're in custody, and we're working with Mass State Police and the FBI to build a case against them. With any luck, we can figure out who's behind this. Not sure it was a coincidence based on my phone interview with Logan and Melanie."

Fuck!

"Okay," Grayson responded with as much calm as he could muster, trying to sound like a concerned father figure. "Thank you for the help, Special Agent Lozaro. I think I'll reach out to Cross now and see if he needs anything."

"Might not be a bad idea, sir. He's not very happy, and I can't blame him."

The line went dead, and Grayson called Chief Drazen into his office for a closed-door meeting.

● ● ● ● ●

Beverly, Massachusetts

The phone call surprised Cross. He was sitting on the couch with Melanie, starting a baby registry early. Checking his phone, the caller ID showed, "XPO – Personal", and Cross was inclined to answer. He still wasn't quite sure who he could trust now, but nothing indicated that Chief Drazen was involved.

"This is BM1 Cross." His voice held a dark but professional tone.

"Logan, it's Chief. Bosun told me what happened after CGIS Agent Lozaro gave him the rundown. Are you okay?"

"*We're fine*," Cross said with an equally heavy tone. "Both of us."

"Shit," Drazen said apologetically. "I meant to ask how are the two of you—three of you? Congratulations, by the way!"

"Oh, yeah, thanks, Chief. She was taking the pregnancy test when those two clowns busted open the door."

Chief Drazen chuckled. "Melanie must have been pissed that they ruined the moment."

"Pretty sure that's why she shot the one guy twice in the shoulder. She blew it away completely." Cross smiled, remembering how determined Melanie had looked after firing on the guy.

Chief Drazen had a good chuckle and said, "Remind me never to get on her bad side!"

"I remind myself of that daily. Chief, quick question."

"Of course, Logan, anything."

"Why are you calling me and not him?" Cross was referring to Grayson.

"Honestly, it sounded like he was pretty shaken and needed time to process it all."

"Chief, can you stop by my place in Beverly for a few? There's something we need to discuss."

"No problem, Logan. My evening is on hold. Shoot me the address and I'll swing by now."

●●●●●

Cross remained armed. His Sig was in a Blackpoint concealed holster on his right hip. He wasn't going to take any more chances, not after the fight he had encountered. There was a knock at the door twenty-five minutes later. Cross's hand instinctively moved to the grip of the Sig and motioned for Melanie to stay behind him, ready to move to the bedroom. He kept his hand wrapped tightly around the grip as he slowly unlocked the door and peered out to see his chief at the door. He motioned the chief inside.

Drazen eyed Cross's hand still gripping the Sig at his hip. He jokingly said, "It's just me, Logan."

"Sorry, Chief, force of habit. I'm not sure who I can trust right now."

"Call me John. I figured this must be serious if you wanted to talk in person."

"It means I'd like to think I can trust you. But, John, my trust is limited to those who don't try to have me and my pregnant wife murdered."

"Hi," Melanie said, stepping from around the corner. "I'm Melanie, the nearly murdered pregnant wife." She extended a hand.

Drazen moved in and gave her a warm hug instead.

"I'm so sorry you had to go through this," Drazen said with sincere sadness. "You don't deserve this. And congratulations, by the way!"

"Thank you. We found out as it happened." She waved to the living room. There was a blood stain still evident on the floor.

Drazen stared at the large red stain for a moment and said, "Serves the idiot right for ruining your moment."

Melanie giggled and then said, "I never thought about that part. But yeah, I guess he did."

"You're in good spirits after having shot a man. Are you doing okay?"

"Well, I'm lucky I have a husband who's been through this before. We're unraveling it, but carefully enough to process it the right way."

"He's a good one. Which brings me back to the elephant in the room."

"Why you're here," Cross said.

"You said you wanted to think you could trust me, with what exactly?"

Melanie brought three glasses of water as Cross invited Drazen to sit down on their couch.

Over the next hour, Cross and Melanie took turns explaining parts of the story in turn. Drazen listened intently and asked a few clarifying questions. When they were done, he gave a long sigh and said, "Jesus, this is really something. Now, here's the real question. Do we know for sure Grayson's behind it?"

"That's the problem," Cross said. "So far, it's only circumstantial. He's left no trail of evidence—nothing tying him to any of it. There's a suspicious action here and there, some odd absences which could mean jack, and a single suspicious conversation. He's playing this like a chess game, and whoever he's working with always seems to be a step ahead of us. Our only hope now is that these clowns who attacked us start singing like canaries."

"Okay, but you're leaving something out. Your buddy Harper said that HSI thinks this is suspicious, too, right?"

"Yeah, but even they don't have any leads. This is a cold, dark trail to nowhere."

"Shit, I'm inclined to believe you, but without direct evidence of a crime, no leads, it's going to be hard to get additional scrutiny on the old man, let alone increased area presence if something is going down. What's your plan from here?"

"He's playing a chess game. We read our opponent and wait for mistakes. Note it for reference and capitalize on it if we can. In the meantime, I need you to coordinate with HSI to see if they're turning up anything that matters. I'll stay on state; I'm working with Trooper Mendez to turn our attackers into an asset."

"You've done this before," Drazen said. "So, I'll follow your lead. We quietly develop a pattern, notes, and wait for something we can use. I think telling you to watch your six is pointless but be careful. There will be demons under every rock you kick over going forward."

Cross looked at Drazen with a face that showed pure professional determination. "Copy, Chief." Cross suddenly remembered a name he was once given on MSRT, a fitting moniker that was suddenly making a comeback. His inner warrior was coming back into focus and was starting his warm-up stretch.

●●●●●

Chesapeake, Virginia, July 2021

The morning started as usual. It was a sunny day in Virginia with a light breeze blowing through the trees on the base. A team workout full of kettlebells, pushups, pull-ups with weighted vests, a long run, and some combatives after... just for fun. Cross was at the peak of his game, smoking the workout and motivating everyone to dig deep for that little bit of extra reserve they all possessed. It was why they were here as operators instead of others who wanted it equally badly. They were the superior operatives, the ones who didn't hesitate to get their hands dirty, grind harder than anyone around them, and then smile after getting smoked and ask for more. They were conquerors in a circle of go-getters.

The team had knocked off, showered, and dressed in their multicam uniforms. They walked together for a big lunch after a rough-and-tumble morning.

While the team was away, a call reached the operations center, their TOC, at approximately 1300 local. There was a cargo carrier experiencing a hostage situation. A group of pirates had seized the ship off the coast of Nova Scotia, which was a bit odd for the usual pattern of hijackings.

The team received the call less than half an hour later and acknowledged orders to start mission prep for immediate deployment. There wouldn't be much time for an intelligence brief, building a mission plan, and then launching. Based on the current location, the speed of the tanker, and the lack of an available Navy asset on such short notice, the Coast Guard Air Station Elizabeth City HC-130J Super Hercules would likely need about two hours to ferry them over 400 miles to Coast Guard Air Station Cape Cod.

The plan they quickly developed would see them do a hot transfer, fully geared up, into a topped-off MH-60T Jayhawk whose crew would already have the rotor turning. They would lift off the moment they were belted in. The Jayhawk would then drop the team on the deck of the *National Security Cutter Joshua James*, where the crew would be prepped to brief a "lights-out" approach to the tanker's bow using their over-the-horizon small boat, or OTH, to provide the least visible approach angle.

Airborne time would be four-and-a-half hours. Time to insertion would be another half hour on top of that. With the only statement from the hijackers that they would kill their first hostage at midnight, it left the team barely five hours to plan, brief, gear up, and drive to E-City to make their bird.

Cross quickly texted Melanie on Signal to keep her in the loop.

> Cross: Bellringer, short notice, let you know when secure. I love you!

> Melanie: Be safe, kick ass. I love you!

Time to dial up the ninja energy. Nox Noctis est Nostri.

Cross and the team rallied for an intelligence brief, which told them only that the hijackers had a team between five and eight. They would take the full complement of shooters on Bravo team. The hostages were being held in the galley, a confined space with windows to the outside and multiple ingress/egress options. Quiet weapons were a must with such a confined space, so they opted for their M4s, sacrificing size and agility for noise suppression and stopping power. All were fitted with the best electronic optics that US Government money could buy. With the briefing and planning phase complete, they selected and packed all their gear into watertight Pelican deployment cases, loaded plate carriers with extra M4 and Sig pistol magazines, and tested radio headset encryption and operations. With a few quick buddy checks, they were out the door ahead of schedule in three hours instead of the four they had allowed. E-City was notified in advance to have the bird start spooling engines and prepare for immediate departure once the team was loaded.

The team arrived in their op gear, checked in at the gate, and were directed to the tarmac. The sweltering heat radiated off the pavement, making an eighty-five-degree day feel like a solid hundred. A young ensign took the keys from the chief, who was driving the van, and he told him it would be waiting for them on their return. The chief saluted the ensign as he turned to walk to the Herky bird, thanking him for the assist on such short notice. The team rapidly secured gear, sweating heavily from the exertion, and were airborne for Cape Cod twelve minutes later, surrounded by the loud and aggressive hum of the six-bladed propellers on each of the four massive turboprop engines.

The landing was smooth, considering Otis Air National Guard base was built for fighter jets that could get in the air a lot faster than a giant Hercules. The aircrew had to do a short-field approach with flaps down and engines running at barely above stall speed to avoid running off the end of the runway on touchdown. Once down, they spotted the Coast Guard hangars and a lone Jayhawk getting a hot top-off its external fuel tanks.

The Hercules taxied faster than the team thought it would, leaned heavily on each turn, and braked hard until it finally rolled to a very fast and shuddering stop about a hundred yards from the Jayhawk. True to their word, AIRSTA Cape Cod had the Jayhawk's rotor spinning. Hot exhaust gas billowed down toward the tarmac as it awaited the team of operators to depart for the *James*, 130 miles and two and a half hours away. The crew loaded their Pelican cases into the Jayhawk nearly at a sprint, wasting no time lashing them down for transit before belting in and yelling to the pilot-in-command, a seasoned commander, that they were ready to go wheels-up. The commander turned to his co-pilot, an expert female lieutenant commander, and mouthed, "Watch this shit!"

Barely a second later, a grin from the lieutenant commander caused the operators to suddenly look terrified. The Jayhawk launched itself into the air like the old Slingshot amusement park ride. Cross yelled to the lieutenant commander, "Ma'am, was that for our benefit?"

The lieutenant commander grinned like a flight-suit-clad

demon and said, "Always nice to scare you strap-hanging knuckle-draggers!"

"BM2 Logan Cross, strap-hanging knuckle-dragger," Cross introduced himself with a grin of his own. "What's your name, rotorhead?"

Matthews gave a hearty chuckle and replied, "Lieutenant Commander Alicia Matthews, decorated rotorhead!"

"Thanks for the lift, ma'am. I'll sit my ass down and shut up now, so you don't accidentally kill us all crashing into the ocean."

Cross watched as Lieutenant Commander Matthews turned back to her controls and shook her head with an easy smile as darkness enveloped the coastline.

The transit was uneventful, other than the landing. Matthews was given the sticks as the commander took his hands off and called the *James*, directing their landing approach. Cross thought he heard, "Co-pilot's aircraft."

Two minutes later, the Jayhawk, under the night vision-aided control of Lieutenant Commander Matthews, cranked into a hard banking descent to port in the low illumination of a waning crescent moon as the operators all grabbed whatever handholds they could find. A few seconds later, they were centered on the glowing iridescent approach line running the length of the flight deck, up the face of the flight operations window, and super-structure.

They edged toward the cutter several meters at a time, faster than any of them thought was possible or safe, and a minute later they bumped softly against the non-skid flight deck of WMSL-754, *United States Coast Guard Cutter Joshua James*. As the skilled flight deck crew scrambled to secure the Jayhawk to the deck pad-eyes as fast as a Formula One pit crew, Cross leaned toward Matthews. "Fancy flying, ma'am. Remind me to look you up next time we need a lift!"

"Thanks, Cross. We're going to top off and get a little R&R

while you're kicking doors in. Don't get shot out there! Stay safe, would ya?"

"Roger that, ma'am. See you soon! Enjoy the R&R for all of us. Maybe the wardroom has a good movie on!"

"Good thinking, Cross. Maybe you're not just a knuckle-dragger after all!"

Cross remembered every time an officer accused a boatswain's mate of being a dumb deck ape. He fired back a ready comedic response. "I *are* boatswain's mate!" He walked away into the chilly night air of the North Atlantic, grinning to a howling laugh from Matthews.

He checked his Luminox on the way to the bridge with the team. The blacked-out dial stood out with a green, tritium glow at each of the hour marks, with the hands in a contrasting orange. It was 2220, just over an hour and a half until an innocent person would die. They had time on their side, and Cross knew they would do it right. They would mock the plan in the ship's hangar and set up a floor plan using shoring timbers from the *James's* damage control locker. They would walk through the entire boarding and execution from top to bottom, including contingencies, at least three times, depending on the mission clock. The boat crew briefed their part first, entering the risk assessment in the ship's computer logbook. They preemptively signed out the OTH for a 2330 launch, though they would likely launch sooner. The deck department had been tasked with readying the OTH and standing by the boat davit controls to start the evolution at a moment's notice.

The team expected there would be extensive delays to set up the mock galley. On arriving at the hangar, the mockup was fully assembled with shoring, marking the appropriate walls and doors of what the tanker galley should look like. Cross was surprised, along with everyone else on the team, and asked the nearest damage control petty officer who had told them to set up ahead.

"Commander Matthews. Her brother serves with Maersk, knows the layout by heart."

Cross owed Matthews for thinking so far ahead of the mission's needs.

Under the dim glow of the hangar floodlights, the team ran through multiple simulated scenarios, including a team injury both before and during execution, loss of comms, and weapons malfunction. In forty minutes of rehearsals, they proved to themselves and everyone else watching, including the *James's* commanding officer, that this would be a perfectly executed operation.

With a little less than an hour until the deadline, the team informed the commanding officer they were ready to launch, and everyone geared up, buddy-checked each other, and the team moved to the boat deck. With NODs perched on their helmets and weapons at the low ready, they looked like they were about to make life miserable for some savages who thought it was acceptable to take over a US-flagged cargo ship for fun. Less than ten minutes later, they were in the OTH making maximum speed in total darkness toward the bow of the tanker through the freezing sea spray. As a courtesy with the time they were given to prepare, deck force had painted the normally orange sponson of the OTH matte black, which they assured the executive officer could be easily removed after the op. The team, in their blacked-out boat with no lights, was about as invisible as they could ever hope for.

As they approached the tanker, there was no Jacob's Ladder to climb. One of the team, "Hooker," nicknamed for his ability to hook any ship in any sea state at any place, anytime, loudly said, "Got a shot!"

The chief tapped the OTH driver, who gave permission, and the chief pointed at a perfect spot and replied, "Take it. Aft corner by that vent."

Hooker did his usual amazing work, putting the hook forward

of the vent with a louder than expected *CLUNK*, and pulling tight to lock it under the gunwale of the tanker. He signaled he was climbing, and then ascended the rope and over the side of the ship, disappearing for a moment. He then gave a thumbs-up to the rest of the team to ascend. "Bull" and "Taters" followed per the plan, with Cross and the chief close behind. Then the last three followed. They inventoried people and gear before the chief said, "Bull, take us topside, watch for any sentries."

Bull replied with his usual focused calm, "Copy, moving."

The team silently ascended to the nearest exterior door leading toward the galley. Their breathing was the only visible marker of their clandestine presence. The cold air turned their exhalations into clouds in front of them.

As they all stepped inside, Taters quietly dogged the door shut, and Bull said, "Still got the element of surprise. Time to ruin their night."

"Copy," the chief said. "Bull, Cross, you're leading entry as briefed. Flash and enter; watch your fire in there. Zero casualties other than hostile. Weapons free."

Calls of "Copy" came from each member of the team before they all stacked on the primary door into the galley, with Bull to port and Cross to starboard. Once all were set, shoulder squeezes went from farthest back to the door, then Bull silently counted from three with a raised fist as Cross quietly undogged the door and opened it a sliver. Two flashbang grenades left the hands of Cross and Bull simultaneously before Cross closed the door slightly to minimize flash impact to the team.

WHOOSH-WHOOSH

Both flashbang grenades exploded, muffled behind the heavy door, and Bull slammed the door open to enter. The acrid smell of the smoke from the grenades filled the air around them. The whole team's optics and NODs, even their radios, suddenly and simultaneously went dead with frightening finality. They were literally and figuratively in the dark in a tanker galley surrounded by hostiles, who were only incapacitated for a few more seconds.

Cross, second in the room, button-hooking to starboard, saw his world go black and instinctively threw his NODs to the vertical position. It had to be an EMP, but there was no time to think about that.

As Cross flipped his NODs to the vertical, his left hand moved from the vertical grip of his M4 with lightning speed to the attached backup iron sights, flipping both up in milliseconds. Cross returned his hand to the handguard barely in time to see the first hijacker coming to his senses and raising an FN Herstal FAL automatic rifle toward the rest of the team.

With zero hesitation, quickly adapting to the low-light environment, Cross smoothly brought his M4 back online. He aimed using the iron sights indexed in the frame of his now dead EO Tech holographic sight and smoothly squeezed his trigger as his weapon erupted with a blast of five rounds to the first man's face, dropping him like a bag of bricks. His eye caught movement to the right, and his body automatically responded, pivoting and changing direction toward a second target, bringing an FNC rifle up. The pirate's head also erupted in a burst of rounds from Cross and his M4. Quickly losing the element of surprise, another man brought his FAL up and squeezed a few rounds wide of Cross as he pivoted left. He swiftly dropped to a knee and sent the man to the afterlife with another hushed bark from his M4. Half a magazine empty, Cross heard the rest of the team catch up to him, and two, then three, then four M4s barked. Four more hijackers met a brutal and bloody end at the hands of the US Coast Guard's most elite counterterrorism force. Cross mentally noted seven down, scanning the room for further threats in the low-light environment. Calls of "Clear" echoed throughout the darkened space.

As Cross started repeating the call, the word barely left his mouth. He was tackled without warning, stumbling forward onto the deck. The final hijacker climbed onto Cross's back; he was about to put a bullet in his head with a pistol from behind. Cross was pissed and wasn't going to die this way. He was caught by surprise by this asshole. He wasn't out of the fight.

Using his knees, Cross violently pushed up, throwing the man off-balance and forward. As the man stumbled forward, he attempted to turn to his side. The attacker's pistol was still in his hand, and he hurriedly scrambled to angle for a shot.

Cross leaped forward, wrapping the slide with his gloved hand, wrenching it and the subject's hand to the right, breaking the wrist and multiple fingers in the process. The man screamed in pain, but he still tried to throw a punch with his uninjured left hand. Cross held the upper hand in top mount, and he deflected the wild punch.

The man reached to take Cross's handgun out of its drop-holster, and Cross lost his last measure of composure. He trapped the man's arm to his chest with an elbow to his sternum, then launched a series of palm strikes to the man's jaw before swiftly drawing his karambit from his pocket, swinging it in a low overhead arc, and opening the man's throat from ear to ear. He remained on top of the man, watching the blood spew from his throat. He stood up, shocked but alive, to see his team and all the hostages staring at him like he was the Grim Reaper. He slowly exhaled and held, inhaled and held, until his heart rate returned mostly to normal.

Bull stared at Cross in staggered disbelief as he wiped the blood from the karambit on a dead hijacker's shirt. "You've earned your nickname, kid. You're officially 'Iron Cross.' I've seen nothing like that. Thanks for saving our keisters."

The chief added, "Expect some good things out of this, and seriously, nice job. They had us on the ropes; you seriously saved our asses."

Everyone congratulated Cross.

Never seeking credit or accolades, Cross said, "It's part of the job."

After securing the tanker, photographing and bagging the bodies for transfer to the *James* and further processing, the team quietly extracted to the small boat by the ship's Jacob's Ladder, then returned to the cutter so the *James* could retrieve the eight body bags. The *James's* corpsman was dispatched to check the medical condition of the tanker crew to determine whether they could still safely operate their vessel after their harrowing ordeal.

As they got on board, Lieutenant Commander Matthews watched from the bridge wing. She signaled for Cross to join her, and he told the team he'd rejoin them for the debrief in a few minutes. He slung his M4 across his back and then walked up the ladder to the bridge wing, where he saluted Matthews. She returned the salute and walked with him out of earshot of the others on the deck. "Cross, Chief called the CO while you guys were securing the crew. He told the skipper what you did. I want you to know I already called your CO to recommend you for some awards. Chief told me you refused to take credit, but that kind of quick thinking deserves recognition. If you ever need anything, you can reach out anytime. I'll drop everything to help you."

"Thank you, Commander. You didn't have to do that." Cross was trying not to look stunned, but he failed miserably.

"You're welcome, and I disagree. I felt compelled to lift someone who saved that many lives despite the odds. You've got a hell of a career ahead of you, make it count."

"Copy that, Commander," Cross said, confidently shaking her hand. "I will."

UNITED STATES COAST GUARD STATION
GLOUCESTER, MASSACHUSETTS, JULY 2022

CHIEF DRAZEN OFFERED to let Cross sit out the next duty period to get his head straight and spend time with his wife after their ordeal. He thought about it at length but chose to continue duty as normal. The deal was that the chief would contact a cleaner on Friday to come out and clean the blood stains. Melanie spent the next couple of days with Cross in his duty room. The cats were set up on automatic feeders, and she packed some belongings. She was able to work remotely, so she logged into the station's WiFi and continued to live life as normally as she could, considering the unusual lodging situation.

When the SAR alarm went off the first time after she arrived, she nearly jumped out of her skin. She watched as her husband's crew ran to their boat, followed by Cross, who gave her a brief kiss on the way to rescue a crewmember on a survey boat who had a seizure. There were undue delays when the helicopter was grounded by a mechanical failure. Sector Boston insisted on waiting for its air option. Cross played hardball and told Chief Drazen he was saving a life and would prep for the court-martial later. The man was quickly stabilized and evacuated for further medical attention.

Melanie was lucky enough to have a brief opportunity

afforded by Chief Drazen to listen over the radio to her husband in his element as a highly skilled boat driver and SAR operator. She earned a new appreciation for him and realized he was at home as much with her as he was behind the wheel of a boat or the trigger of a weapon.

She also had the opportunity to sit down with Chief Drazen a few times and learned that he had used his handgun in a fight before, been shot at, and he helped her further come to terms with her situation. It was nice to talk to someone with similar experiences other than Cross. It was helpful to have another perspective on the incident and truly find peace with what she had done.

As Thursday ended, Cross stopped in to see Chief Drazen, closing the door. "Chief, has Grayson been in at all these last two days?"

"No, he hasn't. He told me he has command meetings at Sector, and he asked me to handle all critical business on his behalf."

Cross's response came across clipped and flat. It betrayed his strong feelings on the matter. "Uh-huh. Do you believe that?"

"Not quite sure I do at this rate," Drazen replied honestly. "But it doesn't paint a picture either. Like you said, it's a cold, dark path to nowhere."

"Right," Cross said, putting his finger to his lip in contemplation. "We need more."

"Do you have something in mind? I'm thinking it's not a good idea to just confront him and ask."

"Well, do you think he's paranoid enough to keep a paper trail?"

"If he is working with others, and it's a big if, he's likely the little fish in the pond. He wouldn't want to be eaten by the next bigger fish when they think he's screwed up too many times. I suppose it's possible."

"How about we take a casual peek?" Cross was confident there had to be something.

"Good chance he's not back until tomorrow at least," Drazen said with a restrained grin. "No time like the present for treason."

The pair walked to Grayson's office, which was thankfully unlocked. The smell of the hardwood furniture and the aging carpet, and the lingering cologne of their unit commander made both feel almost guilty. The thought quickly passed. They closed and locked the door, keeping the lights off to prevent anyone from thinking the office was occupied. They agreed to one item at a time, careful SSE, or sensitive site exploitation, as Cross had done many times on a counterterrorism op. If you disturbed too much at once, it was difficult to impossible to put everything back where it belonged. They didn't want to tip off someone that they were looking for something.

They had gone through the office looking for hidden panels, careful not to disturb any sitting dust. They found nothing. Then they looked through each desk drawer and cabinet, even more careful to leave the contents of each exactly as they were found. Cross worked on the bookshelves with no luck. They were almost done and about to give up when Cross saw the personal protective equipment logbook on Grayson's desk. The impropriety of the discovery ground in his brain like a busted gearshift. It was as out of place here as a circus clown at a funeral. And yet, they had nearly missed it, hiding in plain sight.

Cross stopped suddenly enough that Drazen noticed and turned toward him. "What is it?"

Cross had a look of stunned determination on his face that chilled Drazen. It felt like the air temperature in the room spontaneously dropped ten degrees. "Maybe it's just me," Cross said suspiciously. "But why would an OIC need the PPE log in the middle of summer?"

"Holy shit, you're right." Drazen's fists tightened.

Cross carefully picked up the standard hardcover green logbook. Then he opened the front cover, looking for anything out of place. These things were at every station and cutter he'd ever been to, and if something was off, it should stand out like rust on the white paint of a pristine National Security Cutter. That was when he noticed the evidence he sought. It stared at him like a taunt. The paper seal on the inside of the back cover looked like it had been removed and reattached. He held it up so Drazen could see, and he held a finger up, pulling his iPhone out to take a picture of the cover liner and the logbook itself.

Cross pulled the edge of the liner with his finger, and it peeled up a little too easily. He shot a glance at Drazen, who looked like he was ready to throw something through the wall. The liner peeled upward, and Cross finally got a look at the inside. His blood chilled, and his muscles tightened. It felt like the walls were closing in on him.

There were three dates, each a few days after each of the deaths around Gloucester in the last couple of months. Each one had "$9,000" written next to the names. They had to be payments for each of the deaths. No one would think of looking in an everyday log for a payoff record. Then Cross looked at the last line and instantly became enraged. It was Monday's date. There was no dollar amount written next to it... yet. Cross recalled what happened a couple of days ago. Grayson was paid to sit by while Cross and his pregnant wife were attacked in their home. His face was red with anger. He turned the book to Drazen so he could see, and after taking a picture, he examined the lines.

"Jesus, they're payoffs to look the other way. But what's that last one?"

"What happened a couple of days ago? You're telling me you don't recognize why it's blank?" Cross felt his face flushed and his hands balled into tight fists.

"Jesus fucking Christ, the failed attack on you and Melanie."

"I'm going to fucking kill him," Cross said. The rage built in him like an over-pressurized fuel tank. "I'm going to cut his fucking heart out."

Pain. Anger. Rage. Suffering. Death. Cross could no longer control the savage feelings that boiled deep in his soul like a dormant volcano suddenly ready to destroy its surroundings.

Drazen stepped up to Cross and put a friendly hand on his shoulder, attempting to help his subordinate dial back the rage and clear his head. "No, we need time to build this case. This is the first factual evidence we've found of his involvement, but it's not enough. You kill him, and he's out of the picture. But what did we miss?"

"I don't give a *flying fuck*, Chief!" The rage spilled over, and he unintentionally targeted Drazen with its venom. "He tried to murder me, my wife, our unborn child! I'm going to find him and put my karambit right through his fucking eye socket, then cut his fucking throat. One less threat."

"Damnit, Logan. I get it, I'm on your side, but think! Use your fucking head for a second! Control yourself! There's more to this than just him!" Drazen took a deep breath and tried to calm the situation down. "He's a tiny piece of this puzzle, and if he dies now, you've lost your shot at figuring out what the bigger threat is."

Cross took a deep breath and then responded coldly, "Fine, he's being paid off to look away, and those assholes have an objective. We take him down, they still win. Copy, Chief. Now what? The guy gets away with nearly murdering an entire family?"

"For now," Drazen said with a raised palm, a final suggestion toward a more level approach. "Yes. We need him alive and working to prove he's still connected to whatever the hell this is. It's your playbook, Cross. I'm not telling you what you don't already know."

"I know, I get it, Chief. I'm sorry for lashing out at you. I hate that he's getting away with it."

"Oh, I don't like it either, but he won't get away with it for long. We need him in the picture long enough to connect the dots and figure out who's paying him off and why."

"Yeah, agreed. I hope our home intruders sing, or we won't have anywhere to go with this."

●●●●●

Trooper Stephanie Mendez picked Trooper Caleb Knight to help her with the interrogation of the two subjects who had attacked the Cross family. Knight was a younger Trooper and had been part of a Marine Force Recon unit in Iraq that had performed some daring nighttime raids on high-value insurgent targets; he still couldn't say anything about it. He knew how to play the game. He understood quiet discretion for the sake of operational security, and he brought that level of expertise to the troopers he worked with.

Troopers Mendez and Knight would need to work carefully to get any information out of the two hardened criminals; they would not break easily. Their rap sheets included ties to the mob, which meant they would be trained to resist interrogation efforts. The troopers knew there was a clock on their efforts. Whoever was really behind the deaths of Rivetti, Valero, and Lombardi wouldn't stop. A live asset would be of great value. A dead asset couldn't reveal secrets.

Mendez and Knight agreed to start with Apollo, knowing he'd be the smarter of the two; he was likely the more savvy of the two. The Ox would likely put up a wall, unless he knew Apollo had surrendered something willingly. The seasoned interrogators would capitalize on the relationship and the leverage to get something out of the two. It also helped that they would be recovering from surgery and post-anesthesia, which should make them a little more compliant; both Knight and Mendez hoped the upper hand would get a lead.

When they entered Apollo's room, a nurse was adjusting his IV. Dressed in plainclothes, Mendez and Knight waited until she was done before calmly asking, "Could we have the room, please? Official police business."

The nurse replied calmly, "I understand. He might not be totally with it, so try to exercise a little restraint."

"Of course, ma'am," Knight lied, smiling as charmingly as he could, knowing how far he would likely need to push this thug. "We'll be careful."

As the door closed, Mendez grabbed a chair, quietly jamming it under the doorknob. This would take time, and they didn't want to be disturbed. Their actions tonight would be off-reservation and off-record.

Knight leaned in and quietly said to Mendez with a grin, "Just so we're on the same page. We can't Mirandize him in his state. Nothing will stick. Not that I don't have your back, I just want to make sure we're not just putting a target on our backs for no reason."

Mendez looked at Knight with a quietly confident expression, eyes narrow, jaw set. "I know. We're going to take some fire on this. I chose you because you know how to push the limits enough to get things done. All I can tell you is there may be something much bigger at play. If we don't get Apollo to cooperate quickly, he and The Ox are both dead. If that happens, we can kiss our only lead goodbye."

"So," Knight said as he connected his service history to that of Mendez, "how do we keep ourselves from getting thrown in the brig for this?"

Mendez smiled broadly at the reference, then her smile faded into that of a confident and serious professional. "This is straightforward. We're blatantly breaching protocol today, so that part will muddy the waters. It can't be on record, or we're toast. We can clean it up with the DA by getting Apollo to land on a proffer agreement. He needs to believe we're his only shot at staying alive long enough for protection, and he needs to cooperate with us. If he agrees to moving forward, we don't need to worry about blowback. The DA and the attorney can legitimize it with any officer on scene to work with him in better condition, and he gets to start singing like a canary with full protection in paper form."

"Okay," Knight said, staring at the floor for a moment. "Good cop, bad cop?"

Mendez chuckled softly and said, "It's an oldie, but a goodie. Let's do it. You're the bad cop."

Knight smiled mischievously. "Of course, I am."

This was bigger than both their careers, and they both agreed they would take the heat to uncover whatever nasty plot was underway.

"Nikos 'Apollo' Karousos," Knight said as he strolled up to Apollo's bedside. "How are you feeling, pal?"

"Been better," Apollo replied groggily. "What the fuck do you want?"

"I wish that young lady had blown your brains out," Knight said with a devious grin. "But since that didn't happen, I want to know why you and your oversized buddy were in that house."

"You..." Apollo said, losing focus temporarily. "You already know why."

"Funny," Knight said, grinning. "You must think this is a joke." He reached for Apollo's bandaged shoulder and thumped it with a closed fist, causing Apollo to groan.

"Fuck, Knight," Mendez said, pushing him aside. "Back off! Let's try again."

Stephanie Mendez's warm smile glowed across her gorgeous, tanned complexion. "I'm Stephanie. What my partner meant to ask was who sent you there. This wasn't random. If you give us anything, anything at all, we can make a case for reduced sentences."

Knight leaned in from behind Mendez. "Remember, boss. No deal, need the DA proffer."

Mendez acknowledged with a subtle nod.

"You need to cooperate with us," Mendez said calmly. "We can only help if you give us something that will aid in our investigation. If you stay silent, whatever happens next is on you."

"You can gamble on the idea that those above you in the food chain aren't looking at you as a liability and aren't currently planning a way to cut you to pieces before you compromise them. Personally...," Knight flashed his practiced Marine Corps interrogator charming smile. "I wouldn't play Vegas on the odds they're going to let it go."

"Why the hell?" Apollo asked as the pain toyed with his ability to remain conscious. "Why the hell would I help cops?"

Knight looked at Apollo with contempt. "Because we're your only way out of this if you want to keep breathing."

"We've done this before." Mendez offered with a compassionate smile. "We can get your attorney in here to talk with the DA. They can provide a deal for protection in exchange for information. But if you give us nothing, we're not going to bother asking."

Apollo fired back, "Why should I trust you?"

"Because we believe in justice," Knight said. "Even for a scumbag like you."

Apollo softly chuckled. "What if I tell you that you're full of shit? What if I tell you to fuck off?"

Knight grinned and then looked at Mendez. He stared at Apollo again. "Okay. It's your funeral. See you in the afterlife, asshole."

Mendez and Knight pivoted and started walking to the door.

"What? Wait, shit! Hold on!"

The panic in his voice was overwhelming. It was music to Knight's ears.

Knight turned his head over his shoulder without breaking stride. "Wait for... what? You already said you didn't want to talk. Good luck not getting a bullet to the face."

"Wait, what if I changed my mind? STOP!"

"Bingo," Knight said to himself.

Mendez was grinning at the psychological seesaw effect they were having on the seasoned hitman.

"Okay," Knight offered to Apollo. "What is it you have to say?"

"I—I don't know if I should. These people, they're so violent."

"You're stalling," Knight said bluntly. "Stop dicking us around, or we'll leave for good. If that happens, you're a dead man and you know it."

"I hate to say it," Mendez added as she approached Apollo's bed, softly stroking the man's arm like a sad lover. "But my partner is right. Knowing your associates, they've already decided you need to die for your failure, so you're not long for this world. Maybe return the favor for that disloyalty?"

Apollo slipped to the edge of consciousness from the recent pain and release. He groggily asked in his Greek-accented drawl, "After all we do for them?"

"What do you mean? Do you mean you've done too much for them to target you?" Mendez urged.

"Yeah," Apollo said with an obvious edge of pride in his voice, cutting through the anesthesia-induced fog. "Rivetti... was us."

Mendez signaled to Knight to write it down, which he promptly did. Apollo was breaking. It was time to give him some hope and let him spill his guts.

"So, wait, you killed Tony Rivetti? Wait, before you answer, I need to say something. You've already sealed your fate with those who sent you. We can't offer much here and now. But we can set up the resources responsible for providing that kind of deal. You just need to cooperate with us first."

Apollo sighed, realizing he didn't want to die for these people when they'd effectively written him off for all his loyalty. The icy look in his eyes and the firm lines on his face surprised both Mendez and Knight as he said, "Fine, protection for both of us, and we tell what we know?"

"Not to us. But we can provide short-term protection until that deal can be made by those above us. It's your best shot at staying alive. All we need to know is that there's more to tell."

"Okay, what do you want to know?"

"Who are you working for, and why did they want this couple dead?"

"We were hired by, go-between, so the short answer could be anyone. They need to die for some personal reason for those who ordered it. Not sure why."

It wasn't much, but it was something. Mendez needed more, though. "Anything else you've done for them recently other than the Rivetti murder?"

"Only one thing comes to mind," Apollo said, scratching his cheek with a finger. "We were asked to look at a boat on the way to Rivetti."

Mendez realized she might have just uncovered the first real break in this case. "Which boat?"

BEVERLY, MASSACHUSETTS, JULY 2022

CHIEF DRAZEN LET Cross off duty early Friday morning to meet the cleaners who would remove the bloodstain on their floor and make the home normal again. It would provide a small sense of closure to this awful event in their lives. Knowing his wife was safe in a home that had been rendered whole again would hopefully allow Cross to continue serving with distinction.

More than anything, Cross realized he and Melanie needed time away. While the cleaner was at work, the couple planned an overnight hike to the section of the Appalachian Trail that they had enjoyed so much the last time. They both felt it would be a good way to unwind and to escape the violent disruption to their otherwise quiet lives. As they packed their bags, Cross got a call from Stephanie Mendez. He answered right away, "This is Cross."

"We broke Apollo, the leader of the two who broke into your place."

Cross responded, "That's good news. Any indicators that he was leading you in the wrong direction?"

"No, he's sincere. And he's cooperative. He also cased a boat in Salem on the way out of killing Rivetti."

Cross felt a weight lift off his shoulders with the knowledge that the intruders would cooperate and hopefully reveal more about this threat. "Okay, it's something, but we'll need to run it up the flagpole. I suggest getting Rick on it and see if he can tap federal resources to dig up anything else."

"Right. The two of them will be getting a proffer deal with the DA later today. We had to go off the books on it to get that to happen. We'll take some heat, but it'll still come across the DA's desk in a legitimate way. Logan, that boat may be a key element in all of this. We just don't know anything more yet."

"Okay. Good work. Thanks for staying on top of it. We'll be in touch."

Cross waited for the cleaner to write up paperwork but found out the bill had already been paid by Chief Drazen. He had become quite an ally.

They finally walked out the door and loaded their bags in the 4Runner for the drive. They had a good time, changed into boots, and took a casual pace to the same campsite they had found the last time. They set up camp the same way they had before. Cross once again built a fire, and they sat down to talk alone for the first time in what felt like ages.

"Do you have any names in mind?" Melanie asked with a soft, inquisitive tone. "Any that are a must, or any that are a no-go?"

"You know, with everything that's happened, I haven't really thought about it. Do you have any?"

"Some I've had for a while," Melanie said with a smile that belied the fact that she had wanted kids her entire life. "James for a boy, Alicia for a girl."

Cross smiled, remembering his early exchanges with then-Lieutenant Commander Alicia Matthews. Then he said, "I love Alicia, got a good friend by that name. She's a badass. James is good, too. Although we have plenty of time to make those decisions."

"You're not wrong," Melanie giggled playfully. "But nothing wrong with thinking ahead, right?"

"No way, I'm all for it. The more we figure out now, the less we need to scramble later. Leaves minor adjustments only, which is fine."

Melanie sighed and leaned back in her chair. A sense of satisfaction flooded her as she spoke again. "I'm honestly relieved we got pregnant on the first try, because I wasn't prepared for months of frustration."

"I've heard it can take a toll, but I'm glad we don't have to deal with that. I still can't believe you're pregnant. It all seems so surreal."

"I know, but it won't be for long. Once the morning sickness kicks in, it'll be very damn real."

Cross laughed hard and then said, "Sorry, I don't mean to laugh, but your delivery was amazing on that."

"Uh-huh, I'll remember that when I get some strange craving at three in the morning." She glared at Cross and then broke into a beaming smile. This was a happy time for both, and the humor in it was natural, born of love.

"My biggest concern now is protecting you both."

Melanie softly touched Cross's arm as she said, "You've done an incredible job so far. I'm not worried."

"Thank you. I need all this to be over. The threat is too big."

"I agree, but you've got a good group of people helping you. Let them work their angles on it, and the path will reveal itself."

"Did pregnancy turn you into a philosopher?" Cross gave Melanie a funny grin.

"I guess it did, who knew? Though pregnancy brain might eliminate that entirely."

They talked and relaxed for a little while longer before having dinner. They made love under the stars again, fueled by the high of knowing they were going to be parents for the first time.

●●●●●

Cross arrived back on duty Monday morning after spending a relaxing and recuperative weekend with Melanie. He showered her with praise and affection, and he continued to look for signs of her guilt from the shooting creeping back in. It seemed like it was going away for good, but he knew how insidious that level of remorse was; it could easily come back in a heartbeat.

When he finally left home Monday morning, he made sure Melanie had everything she needed and could reach her weapon and his in a hurry. He advised her to keep the doors locked, keep a low profile, and call if something seemed even remotely off. She reassured him that she would be completely fine, and he finally left for duty.

Cross noticed that Grayson had returned to the office, but his commanding officer was again no different from before. It occurred to Cross how good the old man was at masking his involvement in everything that had transpired. There was no change in his expression or overall demeanor; it was like nothing was wrong.

As he was getting into his uniform, Cross thought about how difficult it was going to be getting Grayson to make mistakes enough to figure out what he was really involved in. He would need to do something truly awful again for there to be a connection to this plot that Cross and everyone else involved seemed to believe existed. The problem they all faced was that they each had one tiny little piece of the puzzle, not enough to act on, and nowhere near a full picture of any larger threat.

Cross grabbed his karambit off the bed and unfolded it, examining the blade and its deadly sharp edge. He remembered the tanker mission where he had first earned the moniker "Iron Cross" and how deadly he became to deal with the threat in that moment. He had protected his team and the hostages with automatic and decisive action. He recalled his actions with the karambit that dark night off the coast of Nova Scotia and thought briefly about the upcoming threat. Would he need to return fully to his prior life and his deadly persona? If he did, would it meet or exceed the threat, and would he be able to stop what was coming? As unclear as the endgame was at this point, Cross realized he was more than up to the task, which was why the universe was putting this on his shoulders. He would have to continue playing the game and see it through to the end.

●●●●●

The next morning after the ceremonial raising of colors and boat checks, word came down that the station was short on boardings and needed a good push on numbers to make Sector happy.

Cross heard the rumblings and stopped in to talk with Chief Drazen before drawing up a plan.

"Chief, what's the word?"

Chief Drazen stared at his computer screen with a look of disbelief. He took a moment and then replied, "Honestly, I'm a little confused."

"How so? The numbers?"

"No," Drazen said sternly. "The area."

"Which one?" The confusion on Drazen's face caused Cross to pause.

"Baker's Island, Great Mis," Drazen said, scratching his chin. "The same place you found that murder a couple of months ago."

"Why there, why now?"

"I wish I knew. I mean, it's a slightly high-traffic area, but not like the harbor and near-shore zones. We'd have better luck with numbers right outside Ten Pound."

"I agree, but they're insisting on targeting this area. No wiggle room?"

"That's how it sounds, and the OIC confirmed a conversation with Sector Enforcement to that effect when I asked."

"Huh. Any chance this is another play?"

"Not likely. Sector has been up our asses for numbers. We've been slow with everything that happened."

Cross grinned, then asked, "Assuming they don't care why?"

Chief chuckled and then replied, "Does that sound like the Sector Boston you know and love?"

"Yeah," Cross said, shaking his head. "What have you done for me lately?"

"This is why I like you, Cross," Drazen said with a smirk that betrayed how nonsensical he knew this was. "Because you get it."

"Well, I guess it's time to go get some."

"Copy that," Drazen said, smiling at his subordinate on his way out the door. "Stay safe out there. No more gunfights."

Cross shook his head and said, "No way, Chief. I don't need more of those in my life."

•••••

Cross had the 29183 underway about fifteen minutes later to conduct a day full of boardings. Nate, Cody, and Cross had gunned up, with Lauren wearing only body armor as she hadn't earned a boarding team member certification yet. She had been working hard at it and would soon be ready for an exam board, but she wasn't quite there yet.

As they began the transit out of Gloucester Harbor, Lauren cleared the fenders off the forward rail and came into the cabin.

She stopped cautiously as she got to the forward seats. Nate and Cody were still on the aft deck discussing boarding plans.

She spoke as hesitantly as she had approached. "Boats, I just wanted to share something."

"Go for it, Lauren. What's on your mind?"

"These last couple of months nearly convinced me to leave, but I've decided to stay."

"Oh yeah, so what changed?"

Lauren smiled positively and said, "These are extraordinary circumstances, and we've all survived. It has me convinced that a good crew can weather any storm, and it makes me want to be the driving force of good for other crews I work with later."

"I'm really happy to hear you say that," Cross replied, smiling while still watching the water for obstacles. "Because I think you have an outstanding future, and I was hoping these last couple of months wouldn't tarnish that for you. Also, with all the craziness lately, I needed some good news. So, thank you."

Lauren looked slightly stunned by the compliment. "You're welcome. Glad I could help."

"Ready to get some more boardings done?"

"Absolutely," Lauren replied confidently. "Let's get after it."

The crew started the boardings in the vicinity of Great Misery Island a few minutes later. The bright summer sun warmed every surface of the boat. It gave the crew the energy they needed to keep going despite the horrors they had faced. The first few boardings were completed quickly, with only a couple of small warnings for small items, but nothing extraordinary. As they were pushing off from their third boarding, though, a small center console sailed by them at high speed, way too close for comfort. Cross barely had time to yell, "Wake!" The heavy wake from the other boat rocked them hard, but thankfully, everyone was holding the boat. No one fell overboard.

Cross quickly yelled, "Coming up!"

He pushed the throttles to the firewall, saying to himself, "Go, baby, go!"

The RBS came up on plane quickly with the twin Honda outboards screaming, skimming the water as Cross hit the blue lights and siren. It took a little too long for the offending boat operator to realize the Coast Guard had quickly gained on him and was directly off his stern. The driver finally brought his throttle down, and Cross followed suit, turning off the sirens and calling Nate up.

"Nate," Cross said. The distant alarm bell rang loudly in his head again. "Eyes on a swivel. Watch yourself with this guy."

"You got it, boss," Nate said with a purposeful stride out the door. "Initiating contact."

As Cross maneuvered the RBS along the port side of the center console, he caught a look at the vessel's hull number, MA 648 AZD, and wrote it on the windscreen. Cody did the same on the report of the boarding form. Cody then walked back to Nate to assist him in checking off safety equipment. Nate asked if they had any weapons on board, to which they answered that they did not.

Two people were on board, the operator facing Nate, and the passenger sitting on the opposite side bench, turned away. Cross heard the alarm bell in his head ring again, closer this time. He turned toward the other vessel fully, and something caught his eye as Nate asked for the owner's license and boat registration card. The operator glanced at Nate and Cody nervously, which often happened when they approached with guns on their hips. Then he turned partially toward the other occupant after he handed his license over.

Cross had a knack for observing behaviors and analyzing threats quickly. The operator was acting evasively and suspiciously. Every alarm bell in his head started going off at once as he said, "Guys, why don't you—"

Before he finished his statement, there was a sudden bright flash and a pair of deafening bangs as the occupant fired rounds at his crew. All three simultaneously jumped down to the deck. Cross was dumped into combat mode and screamed, "Stay down!"

There was a momentary hesitation as the RBS ground through the forward detent, then accelerated as fast as it would go. Cross mashed the throttles forward until the levers nearly broke off, and they were clear of the other boat in seconds as more bullets flew in their direction, but all missed their mark. Cross let the boat fully accelerate, steering back toward Station Gloucester as he quickly worked his way to max speed. Only once he'd covered more than a quarter mile from the other boat did he look back toward his crew. They were off the deck. He saw Cody and Lauren. He couldn't see Nate, and the thought caused his chest to constrict as if there was an elephant on it.

"Guys," he called over the roar of the twin Honda engines now screaming at their max design power. "Status report, now!"

A moment later, Cody edged into the cabin as he said, "Boats, Nate is hit in his shoulder and upper thigh. He's bleeding badly. We need to get him medical attention quickly!" His voice wavered. His hands were covered in blood, and sweat soaked his face. Lauren put pressure on Nate's leg wound using her uniform top, which she had removed from under her body armor. Cody resumed holding pressure on the shoulder wound with his own uniform top.

"Returning," Cross said abruptly. His hands shook violently from the shock of the situation. He had a blinding rage that nearly consumed his senses. "I'll have EMTs meet us at the pier."

As the 183 glanced over the water, trimmed for maximum possible speed, sirens and lights on, Cross kept glancing back at his crew. Cody and Lauren desperately tried to keep Nate from bleeding out on deck. He was conscious but looked pale. Cross knew he needed help quickly if he was going to survive.

"Station Gloucester, Station Gloucester, two-nine-one-eight-three, two-nine-one-eight-three. Working channel secure. Shots fired from a rec boat. We are returning to base with one wounded, GSW, need EMTs waiting at station pier before we arrive, over!" Cross tried not to let the shock of a wounded crew member and the rage he was feeling take over, but he was failing miserably.

The XPO's voice came over the radio a moment later, "One-eight-three, Gloucester. EMTs are en route. ETA five minutes to station, over."

"Roger Gloucester," Cross responded with the tension obvious in his voice. "We're seven mikes from station. Request line handlers, over."

Drazen responded, "Roger, one-eight-three. They're on their way to the pier now, over."

Cross simply acknowledged in a stone-cold tone, "Roger, out."

As the 183 rounded the break wall of the helicopter pad, multiple station personnel and a few EMTs were waiting at the pier. Cross skillfully slid the 183 to the pier, where the lines were tightened. EMTs got to work assessing and putting Nate on a gurney.

Cross staggered over to Nate's side after they had put him in the gurney. He was barely conscious. Cross leaned in and said, "I'm so sorry. This is on me." Tears welled in his eyes.

Nate said in a hushed voice as he grabbed Cross's hand, "Don't blame yourself. Just make it right." He let go, and Cross realized he had the other boat operator's driver's license in his hand. Nate had held onto it the whole time. His courage broke Cross completely.

As the gurney rolled up the gangway to the station parking lot and the waiting ambulance, Cross stared out onto the pristine shimmering waters of Gloucester Harbor. Remorse and shock overwhelmed his senses. He still had to somehow find a way to stop what was coming.

PART THREE
DISTRESS

He who fights with monsters should look to it that he himself does not become a monster. And if you gaze long into an abyss, the abyss also gazes into you.

FRIEDRICH NIETZSCHE

UNITED STATES COAST GUARD STATION
GLOUCESTER, MASSACHUSETTS, JULY 2022

WITH NATE gravely wounded and Cody and Lauren traumatized from having to render lifesaving first aid to their boat crew engineer, Cross's boat crew was broken and ineffective. Chief Drazen approached Cross to inform him that the boat crew was on stand down until further action could be taken to determine exactly how this had happened.

Cross barely heard a word. His engineer, his friend, a good husband, father, and Coast Guardsman had been shot by some asshole on a recreational safety boarding for seemingly no reason. His responsibility was his boat crew's safety before anything else, and he had utterly failed. Cross wasn't sure whether Nate would survive with all the blood loss, but even if he did, it couldn't remove the crippling remorse he was feeling with the enormity of his error in judgment. He couldn't help but feel like he should have seen the attack coming a mile away and stopped it.

There were no clear indications why this would be premeditated, but Cross felt it in his bones. It was the kind of certainty that resulted from years in a combat role—years of reading people and environments. This wasn't an accident. That feeling was what pulled him out of the depths of his remorse long enough to call Mendez. She answered in one ring, "Logan, I heard some rumors. What the hell happened?"

"A guy on a rec boat fired on us unprovoked. He hit my engineer twice. I'm not sure if he'll make it." Cross sounded dead inside, even to himself.

"Logan," Mendez asked compassionately, "what do you need?"

"I need time to feel like I'm not going to crawl into a hole. I also need you to get Rick on this."

Mendez knew why. "Right. CGIS is required to investigate any use-of-force situations, but Grayson would find someone to say you were at fault. Rick knows you, knows what's been happening. I'll get to him before they can and make sure he takes it."

"Thank you," Cross said as he rubbed his temples as if it would make the horrors go away. "I appreciate it, Stephanie."

"Are you sure you don't need anything else? No other loose ends?"

"Actually, yes," Cross said, his tone shifting slightly as his eyes narrowed and he swallowed hard against the horrible lump in his throat. "Can you run a name and hull number for me?"

Beverly, Massachusetts

Cross made it home to Melanie after leaving the station late Tuesday evening. Chief Drazen told Cross that his crew was no longer on duty rotation until they could be properly debriefed. CGIS would conduct a proper investigation. He was assured it wouldn't take too long, and he would have to stand by at home until there was some forward movement.

When Cross stumbled in the door, his defeat was immediately evident. He looked like he was completely dead inside.

Melanie walked toward him and wrapped him in a tight hug. The moment she put her arms around him, he nearly collapsed with grief, sobbing uncontrollably.

The letdown, the "First Responder's Curse," was the worst Cross had ever experienced. He literally felt like it was suffocating him, sucking the air right out of his lungs.

After being lost in the grief for nearly ten minutes, he finally composed himself enough to share what had happened. "Melanie," Cross started, trying hard not to break down again, the tears still wet on his cheeks. "We went on boardings this morning. On our fourth one, the passenger in this boat opened fire on us and put two bullets in Nate."

"Oh, God," Melanie said, her eyes wide as saucers. Her hands shook. "Is he going to be okay?"

"I don't know yet," Cross said honestly, fighting back more tears. "We got him to the EMTs at the station. They took him from there, but he didn't look good. One bullet went through his shoulder, and one stopped in his leg. He lost a lot of blood. I don't know."

"Is John going to let you know when he finds out more?"

"Yes, that's what he told me. I assume probably soon."

Cross sat down at the dining room table, staring at the grain of the wood. He was unable to comprehend where to go with this. He would have to wait until Mendez came back with anything and would hopefully hear about Nate soon.

Melanie sat silently with him for a moment.

"I was thinking," she said as she massaged his forearm with her soft fingers. "I'm not sure if it's the right time, but is Grayson behind this, too?"

"What?" Cross had been lost in his thoughts. Melanie's words sounded like they had been spoken underwater.

Her words became crystal clear as she spoke again. "Yeah, I feel like this could make sense. He fails to get you here, and his goons are in police custody. He may feel desperate to throw you off."

"Keep going. The investigative side of you is coming out," Cross said as his tone changed to one of intrigue. The feeling briefly subdued his grief as his eyes locked on hers. "I already have deep suspicions of the man, but I'd like to hear what you think. What else?"

Melanie clasped her hands together briefly and then started placing all the details with her hands in mid-air as she went on. It was almost as if she were placing the thoughts on a shelf. "Well, it seems like this is bigger than some random killings. They're all traffickers. And Grayson was behind the attack on us. At least he was paid to let it play out. Those guys looked at a boat in Salem. What's that all about? It seems like something else is in the works. So, wouldn't Grayson's people want to keep that hidden? What better way to do that than by burying the guy who is hot on their trail?"

Cross lowered his head slowly, eyes fixed on the floor for a minute, and then exclaimed, "Honey, thank you! I was too lost in the grief to think straight." Then he pulled out his phone and texted Chief Drazen.

> Cross: Look for another entry in the log in a few days.

> Drazen: Already planned on it. Call you in a minute or two.

Then Cross's phone rang through Signal showing 'XPO,' and he answered on the first ring, "Hey, Chief."

"How are you holding up? I shouldn't be worried about you, right?"

"No, Chief. I'm not going to suck-start my Sig, if that's what you're asking."

"That's exactly what I'm asking. I'm glad to hear I don't have to worry, but I have some news."

"What's that?"

"Nate is banged up. The doctors acknowledged how much your crew did, but..." Drazen trailed off.

Cross felt the need to press him. "Chief. What is it?"

"God, I don't know how to say this. With all the blood loss, they were worried about brain damage. They had to put him into a medically induced coma."

Cross felt the air sucked out of his lungs once again. "Dammit, Chief. That's not what I needed to hear."

"I know. Me neither. The good news is he's alive. I believe your crew is entirely responsible for that, and so did the doctors. The problem is we don't know if he's going to pull out of it."

Cross was devastated, and his next words sounded far more broken than he had intended. "I wasn't sure he was going to make it to begin with, Chief."

"I didn't either, but he's a strong guy. I don't think we're getting rid of him that easily."

Cross felt his chest tighten all over again with the guilt. He had failed Nate, and now he was in a coma that should have been avoidable. "I appreciate your optimism. I'm not sure I know how to forgive myself for what happened to him."

"Tell me about it. That reminds me," Drazen asked with a perfectly timed and skillful deflection away from his subordinate's overwhelming remorse. "What did Nate pass to you at the pier?"

"I'm surprised you noticed that. It was the ID of that operator. Nate held onto it while he was bleeding out on the aft deck."

"What in the hell? Why?"

"Chief," Cross said with an assertiveness he hadn't felt since before their day of boardings began that morning. "Nate was thoroughly convinced that Grayson was up to something seriously wrong. I had to talk him down from taking immediate action and told him I'd handle it. He told me when he passed me the ID to make it right. There's a bigger threat that we're not seeing yet."

A heavy sigh escaped Drazen's lips. "The more I see, the more I'm convinced of that. As I said, I'm planning on checking the log in a few days. If there's another entry with a date in the next week, we'll at least know he's still involved with someone who keeps paying him for his services. Then we need to figure out who and to what end... carefully."

"I've got a state trooper working that end now. She interrogated our home intruders and is looking up the boat and operator."

"Smart move, as long as she keeps it quiet. Let me run what I can on my end, too."

"Perfect. She's also prepared CGIS Special Agent Rick Lozaro to take the shooting investigation, so Grayson can't accidentally bury me."

"You've got this handled. Nice work. And did your state trooper get anything out of those dirtbags?"

"It took a while. The smaller of the two, likely the leader, broke down after a lengthy interrogation. Trooper Mendez said they secured the pair a proffer deal with their attorney and the DA. The leader mentioned they cased a boat in Salem."

Cross noted Chief Drazen's as he collected his thoughts, which he was prone to do when there was this much information to process. "Okay. Did she say which one?"

"The vessel name is 'Second Chance.' Does that mean anything to you?"

"Not immediately, but... let me dig into it a little. I'll let you know."

"Thanks, Chief. I might visit Nate tomorrow if they'll let me."

"You should. He'll be recovering from surgery tonight. It's likely they'll let you see him tomorrow as long as he's stable. Enjoy your time with Melanie. Give her my best, and I'll let you know the next steps as soon as CGIS gets in the game."

"Thanks again, Chief. Talk with you soon."

BEVERLY, MASSACHUSETTS, JULY 2022

CROSS AND MELANIE woke up the next morning as soft summer light streamed through the blinds and birds chirped outside. As they snuggled in bed, Cross caressed Melanie's soft belly. She smiled and said, "You're ready to be a dad, I can tell."

Cross inhaled deeply and let out a sigh. "I feel like I am, but right now I'm trying to focus on the light in my life, which is you and our unborn child. There's a storm brewing, and I'm going to need all the light I can get if I'm going to make it through this in one piece."

"I'm curious. Has it helped in the past, thinking of me?"

Cross had to clarify. "You mean like when I was on the team?"

"Yeah. When things got scary, dangerous, and dicey. During those times, did thoughts of me help or hurt?"

"It's funny, because I don't know that we've talked about that until now."

"I know, silly," Melanie said with a giggle. She gave Cross a soft tap on the shoulder. "That's why I'm asking."

A small grin crossed his lips. "Fair point. Honestly, I always struggled with leaving you, but I knew how strong you were, still are, and I knew you'd survive. When things got super dangerous, the missions where we got shot at, or got in a hazardous insertion, my thoughts went a couple of places. First, I thought about how you'd feel if you lost me. The immediate follow up to that thought was how I absolutely would not let that happen. I'd go full berserker rage mode and kill everyone myself if it meant I made it home to you."

"I was almost afraid to ask. I worried that you'd say you tried not to think about me or something."

"No way," Cross said as his slight grin was replaced with a broad smile. "You're the light in my dark world."

Melanie smiled with tears in her eyes and said, "And what about now?"

"I'd kill for you and our child, but I'd also find a way not to. You're my grounding force now, the one thing that keeps me from slitting Grayson's throat tomorrow morning."

"I'm glad to hear you say that." Melanie massaged little circles into Cross's palms. "Because this whole thing may lead you down a very dark path, and I want my husband here in truest form when it's all over."

"Yes, ma'am. Copy that."

Melanie punched Cross's arm. "You're a goofball."

"Takes one to know one, honey."

"Okay, you're not wrong. Now, have you thought more about what I said? Regarding Grayson?"

"Honestly, yes. I trust your investigative instincts more than my own. You've got a degree in forensic psychology, and I don't. Do you think he's flagging anything that would make him a suspect?"

Melanie stared at the ceiling for a moment. "You mentioned those payments. That part could be a major red flag, but only for what has already happened. Unless there's something else, he doesn't scream criminal mastermind."

"I agree. He may be part of something bigger. But without

knowing anything more concrete, it's hard to see a giant target on his back."

Melanie paused before she gave Cross a knowing look. "What would Jake Harper say about this?"

Cross grinned at how Jake would react to the present situation, knowing how determined he was in seeking justice and answers. "He'd say to keep pushing buttons. He'd say giving up was not a choice."

"Then I think you know where to go with Grayson, don't you?"

Cross's grin shifted into a determined stare at the floor. There was no way he would back down.

They showered together and got dressed for the day. They had a trip to make.

●●●●●

Boston Medical Center, Boston, Massachusetts

After a long drive with substantial traffic, Cross and Melanie exited the 4Runner and stretched their legs. Cross locked his weapon in an installed lockbox he had bolted in the trunk. He was under enough scrutiny, and though he was trying to be extra cautious with a pregnant wife and a friend hospitalized with gunshot wounds, he also wasn't looking to get arrested for being armed where he shouldn't be. He kept the karambit in his pocket and would default to his Krav if anything went down. However, he felt that this environment would be safe enough. Instinctively, he checked the parking lot systematically as they entered, aware of anything out of the ordinary, which, thankfully, there didn't seem to be.

They finally reached the lobby and gave their names and who they were there to visit. They were directed to the appropriate floor and wing. When they arrived at Nate's room, Cross stopped short of the door. He again felt the crippling remorse of having failed to protect Nate from the evil lurking around them. He needed to take a moment and compose himself.

Melanie reached for his hand affectionately. "It's okay," she said. "You're here for him now. He'll be okay, and so will you."

"Thank you," Cross said, his breathing surprisingly controlled despite the raw emotional energy that he hadn't yet come to terms with. "I know. I'm just not sure I know what to say."

"It'll come to you; that's never been your problem."

They entered the room together and found Nate's wife, Lindsay, in a chair next to his bed. She was slouched over, hugging her knees to her chest and looking completely shattered. Their three kids were notably absent. When she saw Cross and Melanie, Lindsay dropped her legs and used an arm to wipe the fresh tears from her face. She approached her friends to give them both a hug.

"I'm so sorry, Lindsay," Cross said, feeling the lead weight in his chest all over again. "I don't even know what else to say."

"It's okay," Lindsay said, her voice hollow and eyes filled with heart-wrenching gloom. "The risk was always there; it didn't seem real until now."

"It's my fault. I should have—"

Lindsay cut him off and said, "Logan, it's not your fault. Nate would've followed you into hell. There's no way you were responsible." She paused and took a long breath. "I'll tell you, though, for him, for our kids, I want to know who really is responsible. He didn't deserve this, and neither do you."

Lindsay's courage caused Cross to choke up. The raw vulnerability of the moment was too much for the rugged operator, and his next words caught in his throat. Tears welled in his eyes as he tried to control his breathing. "Lindsay, I can't fathom how you're feeling right now. You said I didn't deserve this, but I put him at risk. He wouldn't be in this situation if I'd been more aware. It would be wrong if you didn't blame me."

Lindsay's tears flowed freely down her cheeks again. "Logan, I can't blame you. You're the one leader Nate has always put full faith in. I can't remember any other Coastie that Nate trusted more." She took another deep breath and paused. "What I want to know is who the hell would have done something like this, and why."

Cross paused before responding, realizing that if he said too much, he would put more innocent lives at risk. "I'm working on that," he replied. His breathing was ragged and barely controlled. The rage in him burned beneath his words. "I'm going to figure it out, I promise. And when I do, they'll pay for it dearly."

"They told me only that it was an unprovoked shooting. What does that mean exactly?"

"It means someone probably wanted it to happen, and Nate already gave me a critical piece to figure out who that is. I won't rest until I find them."

Lindsay sniffled, wiped the tears from her eyes, and then locked eyes with Cross. "I know you. I know your inner nature, which is why I know you're telling the truth."

Cross looked at Nate, who was hooked up to machines beside his bed. The soft sounds of the hospital beeped and clicked from the IVs and monitors that were hooked up to read his vitals. He suddenly remembered the last time he had been in this situation, helplessly watching as a friend recovered from grave wounds. Cross felt his self-doubt squeezing around him as if Jake Harper had him in a headlock. Though he had promised Lindsay answers, he wasn't sure how he could move forward.

Raleigh, North Carolina, August 2021

Cross sat in the dim light of the hospital room, the smell of mechanically sterilized air overwhelming his senses. He occupied this chair for several hours, waiting for the patient to wake up. He was informed about an hour earlier that the patient in this case would make it, but he stayed by her side since they brought her in. Commander Matthews had been his pilot-in-charge on this mission that had taken a turn for the worse. She was severely wounded. An enemy combatant's bullet went through her shoulder. Cross thought she likely should have been dead. She had simply gotten lucky. Cross dismissed his own part in saving her life.

●●●●●

Six Hours Earlier, Atlantic Coast, East of Elizabeth City

The mission came up as a last-minute, late-evening call. Navy assets were unavailable due to prior commitments. BM1 Cross and the team geared up, were briefed, and Cross called Matthews in advance, asking for a last-minute air assist. She readily agreed, spooling up her duty air crew and making command notifications for a hot deployment with the MSRT.

Less than two hours later, the heavily armed team was assembled, consisting of Cross, Bull, Taters, and Hooker, along with a team sniper, "Donkey," who was named for the Shrek character. He never seemed to know when to shut up. They jumped on board Matthews's running Jayhawk. They were tasked with an interdiction mission against a suspected go-fast loaded with materials for a possible high-yield conventional explosive device for use against a domestic high-value target.

As they got airborne, Cross gave Matthews a tap on the

shoulder and thanked her for the short-notice assist. Matthews leaned back from her controls and said, "I trust you, Logan. I know you wouldn't have asked if it weren't serious. Standby to get some!"

The target's last known location would ensure that the Jayhawk would be in the go-fast boat's likely path about ten minutes ahead. They would loiter, standing by to intercept it, shoot out the engines, and fast-rope to secure the target if a deadly force encounter didn't follow the initial engagement. If it did, the team would go weapons hot and lay waste to the boat and crew before they had a chance to escape.

Inside of eight minutes, as the Jayhawk performed a covert loop of the area, Bull spotted the boat in his NODs, calling it to the team and aircrew. "TOI spotted, lights out, our three o'clock, three hundred yards, estimated sixty knots surface speed."

Matthews replied immediately. "Visual on your target, lights out. Going dark and swinging around their port side." She flipped the navigational lights and beacon lights off to make the Jayhawk as close to invisible as possible.

"Copy," Cross said. "Be careful, ma'am. These guys are no joke."

"That's why I have you," Matthews joked as her eyes rapidly scanned the target vessel. "Just don't miss."

The Jayhawk pulled tightly around the port side of the vessel before the crew suddenly noticed a giant helicopter matching their speed. Donkey kept talking about hoping these guys didn't decide to go full stupid, and Bull kept telling him to shut up and be ready to neutralize the targets.

Suddenly, Matthews came over the loudhailer saying, "US Coast Guard, stop your vessel!"

No change in the crew on the go-fast, but Cross could now see three of them tucked low in the cabin, trying to stay protected from the wind and spray of the frigid Atlantic.

Matthews clicked the button for the loudhailer again. The muffled warble came over the megaphone, indicating it was ready. Before she could say another word, Cross caught movement. Time stood still for him as the normal turned to abnormal in the blink of an eye, and he suddenly saw the unmistakable rounded front sight and slanted muzzle of an AK-47 coming up from the deck, aiming straight for Commander Matthews's helmeted head. Instinct born in the crucible of combat came to the forefront of Cross's consciousness. The whipping of the air, the salty smell of the ocean, and the team's chatter all faded to a dull hum as his combat-tested reflexes shoved everything else aside. Without a fraction of a second's thought, Cross sent five high-velocity 5.56x45mm rounds soaring from his M4, watching the man's head explode before shifting his rifle to cover the next man. The team caught up then, Bull and Donkey each taking down one of the remaining men, then putting a few rounds through the engine and deck to scuttle the boat.

Once the threat was neutralized, Cross lowered his rifle and then heard anguished moaning from the front. Blood was splattered near the pilot's seat, and the co-pilot's panicked screams filled the cabin. "Matthews is hit!"

Cross leaped from his position against the side door frame. The bullet had pierced the panel right behind his head, missing him by inches, but he didn't care about that. His friend was hit, and he immediately assessed her wounds. She had taken a bullet to the right shoulder, which ricocheted off the bone and exited out the front, embedding itself in the aircraft's console. She would likely survive, but Cross knew she needed immediate medical attention. He attended to her wound as he yelled at the co-pilot to find the nearest trauma center with a helicopter landing pad. As the situation stabilized and Matthews was brought in for emergency surgery, Cross thought long and hard about how close they both had come to death.

Boston Medical Center, Boston, Massachusetts, July 2022

Cross's vision from the past was brought to a halt by his phone buzzing with a Signal text from Chief Drazen. Cross opened his phone and read it.

> Drazen: New entry in the log, as expected.

Then his phone buzzed again with a Signal text from Mendez.

> Mendez: Your guy is an invisible man; we've got nothing on him.

> Cross: Copy, I'll run him from another angle.

Cross felt his jaw clench and knew he would have to use the CGIS investigation to his advantage. They would be able to track this invisible man down, but only if they trusted Cross first.

UNITED STATES COAST GUARD STATION
GLOUCESTER, MASSACHUSETTS, JULY 2022

TWO DAYS after Nate's shooting, Chief Drazen finally let Cross know that CGIS wanted him to come in and interview about the incident. Special Agent Lozaro had taken the case out of courtesy to his superiors, largely because there was already a slew of other cases that needed attention. He wanted to take this one to keep it off everyone else's hands. Also, he had recent exposure to Gloucester, so there was a connection there that could be useful in getting the real story.

Cross arrived dressed in jeans, a T-shirt, and a light jacket with a fitted ball cap. He hadn't shaved since leaving the station, so his face had a razor-thin layer of stubble. Most of the crew hardly recognized him as he was directed toward a private office on the second deck. The room was set up for a one-on-one interview with zero chance of intrusion or interruption.

He waited for a few minutes, doubtless because Special Agent Lozaro had not yet arrived. Finally, after what seemed like an eternity, there was a knock at the door. Rick Lozaro entered the room with a purposeful stride.

Cross stood to greet him, shaking his hand. By the firm but not aggressive handshake alone, Rick Lozaro could be clocked as a man of action and not one to waste time on meaningless chatter. He was five-foot-ten, fit but not muscular, and had a full head of black wavy hair parted precisely in a way that screamed prior law enforcement.

"Good to finally meet you in person, Petty Officer Cross, though it would be nice if it were under better circumstances. I'm sorry to hear about what happened to Petty Officer Sutter."

"Thank you, Special Agent Lozaro," Cross said, somewhat guarded. "And yes, that would be nice, but here we are."

"Yes, here we are. Call me Rick, by the way. How's your wife doing? Melanie, was it?"

"Got it, Rick. Call me Logan. And she's doing better, thank you."

"Okay, Logan. Let's get into it, shall we?"

Cross spoke as directly as possible to clear the air about his intention to cooperate. "Yes, let's not drag it out."

"First, a couple of procedural questions. This interview is to ascertain the events that led to the wounding of Petty Officer Sutter on Tuesday morning. Is that your under-standing?"

"That's correct."

"And before we go on record, it is my understanding you asked me to take this investigation. Is there a reason for that?"

"Simple." Cross said without reservation. "There's more to this, and I don't trust anyone with it. Trooper Stephanie Mendez looped you in. She holds you in high regard and suggested I should, too. That's enough for me."

"Copy that. We'll get to it all as we can. If you need to go off-record, give me a thumbs down, and I'll temporarily cease record-ing. Clear on that?"

"Affirmative," Cross said as he settled into his seat with his feet squared and hands on his lap like a professional operator. "Ready when you are."

"Okay. Recording on a quiet count." Then he mouthed, "Three, two, one." He hit the button on his recording device.

"This is Coast Guard Investigative Service Special Agent Rick Lozaro, and this is an official investigation into the events of Tuesday, July 12, during which Coast Guard Station Gloucester personnel participated in a law enforcement boarding in which a recreational boater opened fire on the boarding team, wounding a team member."

Cross was silent, replaying events in his mind, and the alarm bell he should have acknowledged sooner. He remembered the familiar ringing in his ears after a close-quarters gunfight. The adrenaline always caused his hands to shake a little after a brush with death.

"I have with me Boatswain's Mate First Class Logan Cross. For the record, Petty Officer Cross, can you confirm your identity?"

"Yes, sir. Boatswain's Mate First Class Logan Cross, United States Coast Guard Station Gloucester, Massachusetts."

"Thank you, Petty Officer Cross. Now, let's begin. Take me back to before the mission started, that morning. Walk me through your planning process."

Cross proceeded with a detailed accounting of every notification they had received about the need for additional boardings, the supposed call with Sector Enforcement requesting the crew target a specific area, and the lengthy conversation with Chief Drazen about why that area should not have made sense. Lozaro listened intently, writing down one or two things on a notepad and asking only a couple of clarification questions.

"Thank you, Petty Officer Cross. Now, if you don't mind, take me through the mission from underway time."

Cross explained everything in exact chronological order, from their normal risk assessment for every mission, navigating the minefield of lobster pots, lookouts, and even the positive conversation with Lauren. He tried his best to keep every single detail in the narrative.

"Now, it is my understanding from the command discussion prior to this meeting that the boarding in question was your fourth of the day. Can you confirm that?"

"Yes, that's correct. Three normal boardings with no significant issues, and then this one."

"Understood. Please tell me about how this fourth boarding went."

Cross was silent for a moment, picturing the blood on deck, Nate lying there getting closer to death with each passing minute, and Lauren and Cody trying in vain to stop the bleeding from two bullet wounds. He remembered his hands shaking as he pushed the RBS out of the area at max speed. The trauma was so fresh, he had trouble removing himself from it, thinking objectively, and talking through it. He wished Melanie was there. He wished he could hold her hand through this to keep from losing control. He thought about Lindsay in her chair at Nate's side, broken, having nearly lost her husband because of a threat Cross should have seen sooner. The rage and remorse twisted around in his soul like a ball bearing in a pinball machine, bouncing off every exposed nerve, forcing him to relive every horrible moment of the boarding and everything following it.

"Petty Officer Cross... Petty Officer Cross?" Lozaro's voice suddenly cut through the fog of his thoughts, bringing him back to the present situation, where he would need to relive the trauma all over again.

"Sorry," Cross said, shaking his head. "It's a bit fresh."

"We can—" Lozaro started.

"No," Cross said, his eyes narrowing and jaw clenching. "We need to continue."

"Very well. Tell me about the boarding."

"When we approached, we noticed two persons on board.

Nate asked the normal weapons question; they hadn't been boarded by the Coast Guard before. That's when things started going off the rails."

Lozaro paused briefly to allow a mental gap for notetaking later. Then he asked, "What do you mean by off the rails?"

"The operator looked like he was nervous, which, as you know, can be for many different reasons. At first, nothing seemed off about it. Then he looked back at the passenger on his boat about the time he handed Nate his driver's license."

"Okay. He looked back at his passenger, and what happened then?"

"Two shots immediately rang out before I even had time to process that there was a gun."

"Completely unprovoked?" Lozaro asked in disbelief, his eyes wide with shock. "No warning at all?"

"That's the weird part. I spent some time with MSRT. I was shot at more times than I can count. I never got caught off guard like that, and from a recreational boater? I'm at a loss for how the guy got the drop on us like that." He did know, of course, but was trying to test Agent Lozaro to see if he would pick up on how suspicious it all sounded. Then he gave a quick thumbs down.

Lozaro immediately pushed the stop-recording button. "What is it?"

Cross paused to plan his next words for a moment before he continued. "I need to ask, one professional to another, knowing what you know of my background, our boat crew's skill. Do you think it's weird that a rec boater was able to get the drop on us like he did?"

Lozaro looked like he had been asked to weigh in on a major philosophical debate as he paused to collect his thoughts before answering. "Honestly, I've seen gunfights start during boardings for any number of reasons. That would otherwise be almost normal, but this? Unprovoked gunfire taking down a crewmember before you even had time to react? I don't know. Without speculating too much, something doesn't smell right."

"And that's why you're here, because you see the big picture. On that topic, before we continue, there's something you need to see."

Lozaro looked understandably confused. "Okay?"

Cross produced a driver's license that was not his own and slid it slowly across the table to Lozaro.

"Is this...?" Lozaro thought he already knew the answer, but he had to confirm.

"Yes, this belongs to the operator of the other boat. Nate held onto it until he got back to the station. While on the gurney, he told me to make it right."

"Jesus," Lozaro said, his shoulders sinking with the weight of the revelation. "What courage. Have you run this through state police?"

"Invisible man. That's why I'm giving it to you. If the state is stumped, that means something."

"I agree, I'll dig into it. In the meantime, what's next?"

"We continue the interview in a way that doesn't get me kicked out for negligence on a premeditated shooting. Also, I have a favor to ask."

"What is that?"

"I need you to quietly look into someone's background."

"And who are we looking into?" Lozaro barely looked up from his notes.

Cross's face portrayed the look of a man seeking true justice. Eyes cold, jaw set, hands in tight fists on the table. Then he answered in a voice on edge with razor-sharp purpose. "Chief Warrant Officer Bill Grayson."

Lozaro's head shot up toward Cross, his eyes wide with the gravity of the request. "Excuse me? Your officer-in-charge?"

"Yes," Cross said. "I want to know what's driving him."

"That's a tall order. And it can't be undone," Lozaro said sternly. "What are you hoping to find?"

Cross looked down at the table as his eyes narrowed with intense focus for a moment. Then he lifted his gaze and looked Lozaro directly in the eye before he gave the only response he could think of. "Answers."

UNITED STATES COAST GUARD STATION
GLOUCESTER, MASSACHUSETTS JULY 2022

THE CGIS INVESTIGATION resulted in Cross being cleared of wrongdoing and an immediate return to duty. Grayson immediately called the lieutenant, branding Cross a rogue loose cannon and CGIS a bunch of hacks. This was supposed to bury Cross, and it seemingly only worked in his favor. The lieutenant was less than helpful, telling Grayson he should grow a pair and deal with his subordinate before someone else had to. He was forced to re-examine his approach to the problem. If he could catch Cross off guard, tear him down for his inability to protect his crew, try to rattle him, force him to go one step too far in dealing with the problem, then he could bury Cross under the weight of a captain's mast. It was a stretch, but it might work.

●●●●●

Cross returned to duty that Friday a little rattled. He felt off, but he was still insistent on getting back to work. He still couldn't forgive himself for his lack of awareness. He wasn't sure how he would cover Nate's position, but maybe the engineering department already had a plan for that. He would need to ask them first thing and hopefully come up with a short-term solution to the problem until Nate recovered.

As Cross brought his gear into his duty room, the looks he got were a little disconcerting. It was almost as if everyone thought he was the reason Nate was wounded and recovering in a hospital bed. They were not yet told that Nate was in a coma. Even though CGIS had cleared Cross for duty, the crew acted as though he should have done more. Part of him still wanted to agree that he should have done more. But what? He forced himself to put the looks and his demons aside for the time being. He had to compartmentalize his grief and lead his crew. He had done it before, and it was the only way forward now.

At the morning brief, the crew seemed sullen without Nate there to crack a joke about what deck force was going to break for him today, or which boat driver in training was going to nearly make him take a swim in Gloucester Harbor during tow practice. Nate's absence was felt, and the looks on everyone's faces confirmed that the crew wasn't the same without him. Cross would visit him when duty was over, but now he felt remorse. The rage crept up in him until he was shaken from it by the engineering department head, Chief Matt Halverson. Five-foot-nine, small in frame, bald but quick with a kind word, Chief Halverson could tell Cross wasn't in a good place. He put a kind hand to Cross's shoulder. "Hey, Boats. Still with us?"

Cross was terribly unconvincing in his response. His distraction was evident in his vacant eyes, his sunken shoulders, and his whole demeanor. "Yeah—yes, Chief. Sorry. I'm still lost in what happened with Nate. Not sure I'll ever forgive myself on that."

"I get it, but even CGIS said it wasn't your fault."

Cross still couldn't quite see it the same way. "Then why do I feel like the crew still feels like it is?"

"Well, they've been hearing the old man griping about it. It might be steering their thoughts. But if you ask me, he should be keeping that shit to himself. The crew doesn't need to hear those thoughts."

"Grayson? He actually cares at all?"

"Probably not, he's probably pissed about the paperwork. Look, the point is it's not your fault. It was unprovoked. There's nothing you could have done. Your crew's luck was up on that one, and Nate drew the short straw. I know it sounds callous, but you can't keep lingering on self-doubt. Wrong place, wrong time. Still, it would be nice if we knew who those assholes were so we could get some justice for Nate." Halverson had learned over a long career to fully compartmentalize anything bad that happened to his crew, and that calm confidence radiated in his words.

"I know, I want to find out more too." Cross appreciated Halverson's composure, but he wouldn't reveal the extent of his investigation into the matter. He wasn't willing to trust anyone else.

"Anyway, I'm giving you MK3 Alcott. He's a solid guy, a good engineer, and a dedicated boarding officer. He'll fill your crew in on Nate's absence."

"Thank you, Chief. And thanks for the insight."

Cross barely had time to finish the conversation before he was called to Chief Drazen's office. He walked there immediately.

"Sit down," Drazen said firmly. "We need to talk."

Surprisingly, Drazen turned on the desk radio in his office to a weather report and turned the volume up. It was an obvious masking technique, and Cross was suddenly intrigued by the approach.

Drazen spoke just barely over the hum of the weather radio. "First, Grayson still has it in for you. Whatever CGIS told him pissed him off good. So, watch your six. Next, *Second Chance* is a mega yacht ported at Pickering Wharf in Salem. It belongs to the attorney general."

Cross folded his arms across his chest in disbelief. "Jesus, the United States attorney general? They cased his boat?"

"It would seem so. But to what end?"

"There's not enough information to know why. I'll have to run it to other levels and see if anyone's picking up anything that might help." Cross had resources, but it would take time to chase more information down.

"You run it on your end. I might have a few leads I can chase down myself."

"We need to figure this out. These deaths aren't random, the home invasion, the shooting. It's all connected."

"I know, and that's what has me worried," Drazen said with a subtle shake of his head. "Now the attorney general's yacht is in the picture. I don't feel like that's a coincidence. The problem is we don't have a target. Nothing we can use, and no path to follow."

"If the attorney general is part of this, is he part of the conspiracy, or is he a target?"

"I don't know. We need to push our resources to see if they can turn anything. It's our only shot at solving this one."

"I completely agree, Chief. I've got Special Agent Lozaro doing a deep dive on our invisible man from the rec boat. I'm hoping we get something there we can use." Cross had intentionally left out his request of Lozaro to dig into Grayson's background. The less Drazen knew about that, the more insulated he would be.

"I sure hope so, because I'm running out of ideas."

"I might have a few up my sleeve," Cross said with a subtle grin. "Let me make some calls."

●●●●●

Bull answered on the first ring, loudly saying, "Holy shit, Cross. What kind of fucked up situation are you gettin' yourself into up there at the station?"

"Hello to you, too! Yeah, it's a bit fucked up. You're not wrong."

"What's going on exactly, and why are you calling me about it?"

"Perceptive as ever, Bull. We've had a bunch of killings, all known traffickers that we tracked on the deck. I started digging, and Melanie and I got attacked at home. That didn't deter me, so they attacked my crew unprovoked during a boarding. They shot my engineer; he's in a medically induced coma. This is the short version, in case you wondered."

"Holy shit," Bull answered with shock in his voice. "Are you and Melanie okay?"

"We're okay, and pregnant."

"No shit! Congrats, brother! Is the kid going to come out holding a karambit?"

Cross had to smile despite the serious tone of the conversation. "Funny enough, you're the second person to suggest that."

Bull had a hearty chuckle. "It's probably not far off. So, how's this involve us?"

"Well, a couple of us here are convinced there's something bigger in play. I can't seem to find a thread to pull. The only thing we know is from an interrogation of our home intruders by state police. On the way to the first murder, they cased the attorney general's mega yacht in Salem."

"Well, shit! Not small-time crooks we're looking at here. That's some major league shit."

"Tell me about it. So, I need some help."

"Logan, you saved our asses more times than I can count. Name your ask, anytime, anywhere, we'll find a way."

"Thanks, Bull. I appreciate it. From intelligence sources, do you guys have any indication of a new criminal organization, or an old one with a new grudge against the AG?"

"I'd have to check, but I have to stress, it'll be for your eyes only. Your clearance is still valid, but nobody else in your unit has that privilege."

"I get it, and that's where the big ask comes in."

"This should be good," Bull said with heavy sarcasm. "Hit me."

"How fast can you have the team spun up and ready to deploy when we figure out what this is all leading to?" Cross still wasn't sure what the mission would be, but he was becoming more convinced by the day that this wouldn't be solved at the conventional level.

"A few hours, maybe less, depending on the nature of the mission. Are you thinking of making a comeback tour?"

"The thought had crossed my mind. I'm worried 'Big Coast Guard' will screw this up. It would be better if we took it on. Once we figure it out, there's less risk of blowing it on logistics or bad information."

"You're telling me I get to hunt down some real bad guys?" Bull's exuberance at the prospect of taking out this threat himself was why Cross knew he'd called the right guy.

"Unless I'm way off, it sure looks that way."

"Your instincts were always better than most. Let me start digging, and I'll let you know what I find."

"Signal only, zero risk, don't want to blow it this close."

"Copy that. I'll reach out when I have something."

Cross took a moment to catalog what he knew. There was a lot to sift through. So much violence. So much death. So many people Cross knew and cared about were pulled into the ever-expanding threat. Now the attorney general? This was all adding up to something big, dangerous, and still unknown. He had to continue working on the problem if he wanted to find the answers.

UNITED STATES COAST GUARD STATION
GLOUCESTER, MASSACHUSETTS JULY 2022

THE PIPE for him to the OIC's office was expected, Cross told himself after he heard it. CGIS hadn't given Grayson the answer he wanted. In line with Chief Drazen's warning, the old man still had a bone to pick. Chief Halverson confirmed the OIC was still griping about it earlier in the morning. Cross had a feeling he knew what was coming.

He walked into the building, expecting to have a confrontation with Grayson. He took a few calming box breaths to lower his heart rate, as he would for a controlled rifle shot. He needed to be peaceful about this, knowing it wouldn't go well. He couldn't allow himself to get emotional, to lose his composure, or to show a weakness to this man, who was, without a doubt, targeting him. He knocked on the door a moment later and was called in by a growling, "Enter!"

As he squared his corner, Grayson said, "Close that damn door."

Cross closed the door and stood in front of the OIC's desk. He didn't offer Cross a seat and stayed standing himself. Though he knew what was coming, Cross didn't expect the brutal onslaught of Grayson's venomous words.

"We both know CGIS *fucked* this up," Grayson started. "And

were it not for your reckless behavior, Petty Officer Sutter would still be working today."

"Sir, CGIS did their—" Cross started.

"The *fuck* they did!" Grayson quickly countered. "They went soft on you. Sutter's wounding is entirely because of you, your cavalier attitude, and your cowboy approach to carefully crafted operations. *You* are the reason your crew nearly got killed. They should have locked you up!"

Cross felt the rage and remorse boiling up and took a breath. "Sir, there was nothing—"

"Nothing you could have done differently?" Grayson wouldn't let him get a word in. He had hit Cross like a rogue wave, giving him no chance to recover.

"How about positioning so you could see both occupants, keeping your head up and on the boarding? You're supposed to be experienced with this, *Mister Tactical Law Enforcement!* You couldn't protect your crew, and one is in a hospital bed because of you, because of *your* failure!"

Cross took another breath. These were not the words of a concerned leader trying to ensure the best for his crew. Grayson was outright attacking him. The contempt in the words 'tactical law enforcement' was meant to rattle him. Grayson was trying to make him break. Make him lose control.

"Aye-aye, *sir,*" Cross said with some contempt bleeding through and leveled an icy glare at Grayson that made the old man visibly shudder.

"And you put your pregnant wife at risk," Grayson continued, despite feeling like Cross was staring a hole through his head. "What kind of fucking horrible husband would do that? You don't deserve your rank, your position, or your letter. But since I can't do any of that, expect paperwork by the end of today for putting your crew at needless risk!"

Cross felt his rage briefly consuming him at the mention of

Melanie and their unborn child by this piece of shit. He took a quiet breath and suppressed the feeling before he leaped across the table and snapped Grayson's neck. He replied coldly, "Aye-aye, *sir.*"

Finally, Grayson seemed to realize there was nowhere he could go. Cross was not going to react. He stated bluntly, "Get the *fuck* out of my office!"

Cross about-faced and walked out, slamming the door behind him so hard it almost came off the hinges. It was the only outward sign of his rage that he would show in this confrontation.

●●●●●

After walking into such a devastating ambush, Cross could only think of one thing to do. He walked right into Chief Drazen's office and closed the door to a confused look from the XPO. He sat down to detail the whole event.

"I heard the old man yelling from all the way down here. What the hell was that all about?"

"Remember how you said he still had it out for me? That was putting it mildly. He tried to burn me to the ground on the boarding. He told me CGIS are a bunch of hacks, and I should be in prison right now. He said I was lucky he didn't pull my quals, rank, all of it."

"He wouldn't have the grounds to do it, especially if CGIS detailed why they cleared you. Sector, district, they wouldn't back him up on that."

"I think he knew that. That's why he's writing paperwork for putting the crew at risk. He even tried to say I put Melanie and our unborn child at risk by being a cowboy. I damn near jumped across the desk at him on that one."

"I think he wanted you to lose it. That's not good. He's trying to bury you under administrative charges. Why?"

"I think we're sniffing too close to something he doesn't want us to find out. Whoever he's working with must not take kindly to failure."

"Fuck! They must be some seriously dangerous people."

"I'm starting to think that, which is why I've got someone on the dark side looking into who they might be. We need to figure out the who and the why, and preferably the what, damn quickly."

"Definitely," Drazen said with a look of concern and a hand to his chin. "Keep digging but watch your six."

"You too, Chief." Cross swiftly walked out to resume his duty period after clearing his head with some brief combative practice in the gym.

21

BEVERLY, MASSACHUSETTS, JULY 2022

CROSS ARRIVED home after a roller coaster of a duty period. His face was sunken, robbed of its usual energy. This was eating him alive. Melanie immediately took charge and kissed him.

He felt the tension slowly ease.

She guided his hands straight to the curves of her butt, which he willingly grabbed. His love and attraction for Melanie rapidly replaced the stress of the present circumstances. They moved to the bedroom as the cats watched them with curiosity. In minutes, their moans of pleasure echoed through the house as they melted together.

●●●●●

As Melanie rested her head on Cross's shoulder, she twirled a lock of her brown hair in her fingers and asked, "So, what happened exactly?"

"Grayson lit me up and told me Nate's wounds were entirely my fault. He claimed CGIS fucked up and took it easy on me. He said I put you and our unborn child at risk."

"Good God," Melanie said as she put a hand to his cheek.

"That couldn't be farther from the truth. You put yourself in harm's way to protect us."

She put her hand on her belly to include the new life growing in her womb. Cross touched her hand with affection, and they locked eyes briefly. Cross felt exactly what Melanie was trying to convey from the warmth in her eyes and felt compelled to acknowledge it.

"Thank you. It means the world that you have such trust in me. You and our child are and will be my grounding force. You're both the reason I'll always come back, no matter what happens."

Melanie had a few tears in her eyes. "I know you will."

They embraced in silence for a few moments, and then Melanie asked, "Do you know what's coming yet? I mean, something must be, right? This wasn't random."

"And I don't believe in coincidence. But no, not yet... not exactly. All I know is it has something to do with the attorney general and his yacht in Salem Harbor."

"Why him, and why his boat? What does he have to do with all this death?"

"Not a fucking clue, but I have a few folks trying to find that out."

His phone rang. The caller ID displayed "CGIS Rick," and Cross held it up for Melanie to see as he said, "Speak of the devil."

Cross answered, "Special Agent Lozaro, what can I do for you?"

"Logan, this is big. The ID you gave me? I passed it to HSI through my agency contacts, and they damn near blew a gasket."

"What do you mean? Why were they so excited?"

"Because this name was populated against a list of folks who are connected to a criminal syndicate, no one seems to know much about it. They've been waiting for one of these chuckle-heads to pop his head up. They're anxious to play whack-a-mobster."

Cross had to chuckle at the visual of the old arcade game brought to life in a law enforcement context. "Whack-a-mobster... nice. Okay. That is big. Next steps?"

"They're routing it to ATF and FBI. Maybe they can roll him and his buddy and make them flip for immunity, get some information about the syndicate."

"Holy shit! That's exactly what we need."

"I know, that was a good pull. I wish we could thank Petty Officer Sutter for holding onto the ID."

"Me too. I think he'd be happy we were pursuing this with such ferocity."

"Anyway, I'll let you know what happens. It might be very soon if the address isn't a fake. Sounds like they're confident in a good result. Nothing new on Grayson yet, but I should have more soon."

"Thanks, Rick, and good luck."

He hung up a moment later and looked at Melanie. "Road trip?" She smiled brightly and stepped into the bathroom to get ready.

Boston Medical Center, Boston, Massachusetts

Cross and Melanie entered the room. Lindsay was in her usual chair by his side and stood to greet them, looking a little less forlorn this time around. "Hey, Logan. Hey Melanie, how are you?"

"We're all right," Melanie said. "How are you? Are you hanging in there?"

"Yes," Lindsay said. "But it's been rough."

"Have the docs given you any updates?" Cross asked. "Any idea what to expect?"

"Not exactly. They've replaced the blood he lost, but they're waiting to make sure there are no other problems."

Cross took a deep breath and considered his next words. "Have they made it sound like he'll recover?"

"You know," Lindsay said. "While they haven't been very direct, they've been sounding more optimistic by the day. I'm feeling that energy. I get the impression he'll be okay, once they pull him out of the coma and his body recovers."

"That sounds really positive, Lindsay," Cross said. He was still stuck in the feeling that he was the reason Nate was in a coma. "I'm really happy to hear it."

"Listen," Lindsay said. "I can tell this is still weighing on you. So, tell me something good. Maybe it can take the pressure off all of us."

Melanie glanced at her husband with a soft smile.

Cross took a deep breath. "Well, Lindsay, we're pregnant."

"No way! Congratulations! Honestly, I can tell. You've both got a glow. If Nate were with us now, he'd ask if the kid was going to come out holding a karambit."

Cross shook his head. "Nate was always giving me so much flak. Still, he's probably not wrong."

Lindsay immediately moved to Melanie and gave her a gigantic hug, and then she moved to Cross for the same.

After they broke the hug, Lindsay's face became serious once more.

"Logan, I have to ask. Have you figured out anything new?"

Cross knew he couldn't leave Lindsay completely in the dark, but he hesitated to go too far. He wasn't going to put anyone else in harm's way.

"Lindsay, I can't tell you much," he started. "What I can say is that the piece of the puzzle Nate supplied has already done some significant good. I've got other agency partners trying to nail the guys who attacked us. That's all I can say, I hope you understand."

"Of course I understand, Logan," Lindsay said with a solemn nod. "Operational security. Nate always said that loose lips sink ships. You don't have to say more. I know you're doing what needs to be done to find answers and justice for Nate."

"Everything in my power," Cross said firmly. "I can't rest until this threat is behind us all."

"How dangerous is all of this?"

Cross felt his violent alter-ego nudging him from the dark corners of his conscience. His next words came from the most savage corner of his conscious thoughts. "Lindsay, that doesn't matter. They've never come across anyone like me... not in their wildest dreams."

●●●●●

On the way home from Boston, Cross was lost in thought.

After some time, Melanie asked, "Hey, honey, what's going on? You've been quiet and distant since we left."

Cross took a breath to clear his head and avoid coming across sounding completely insane. "You're right, I have been. Speaking with Lindsay puts things in perspective. Well, talking with Bull, then Lindsay."

"What do you mean? How so?"

"I'm starting to think...," Cross carefully chose his words as he felt his chest tightening. "Whatever this all is, no matter how dangerous, it might be on me to end it."

"You mean in uncovering the bigger threat?"

"Not just that," Cross said as he touched a hand to her thigh. "But eliminating the threat entirely."

"I thought you were done with all that. I thought we decided you wouldn't go back?"

"I thought we had, but this fight chose me, chose us... and it's not going to stop. The only way I can protect you and our family, our future, is to find that part of me that's still lurking under the surface and bring him back to finish this fight the right way."

"Logan," Melanie said with a cautious look at her husband. "This is too dangerous. You can't take them on yourself."

"I'm not going to be alone. I'm making sure of that. Did I ever tell you about my nickname on the team?"

"'Iron Cross', I know, but—"

"I told you how I got it, right?"

"No, but I think you'll need to fill me in for my own peace of mind."

Cross proceeded through the story of the tanker takedown, beginning to end, leaving no detail untold. At the end, Melanie stared at her husband in disbelief and then said, "It sounds like they've met their match."

Cross glanced at Melanie from behind the wheel with a look of fierce resolve, and then stated bluntly, "They're going to find out the hard way."

22

CROSS SPENT a couple of good days enjoying time with Melanie, realizing that those moments together would come to an end for a while after they became parents. Selfishly, he wanted as much time with Melanie as he could get, enjoying her calming presence, the warmth of her affection, her smile, and her incredible body. He watched as it filled out to raise their child in her womb. She would always be beautiful to him, and he would make sure she felt it, knew it, even when he was gone.

The next duty period arrived; Cross put on his prepared uniform and all his gear in the 4Runner and went to the station on Wednesday morning, ready to do his job and lead his crew. They still needed him sharp and ready, despite everything he was already shouldering, and he wasn't going to let them down a second time.

When he sat on the briefing, he realized he hadn't seen Lauren. He asked Cody about her.

Cody informed Cross that Lauren had a medical appointment and would be in shortly. Cody looked like he was hiding something, but Cross couldn't figure out what it could be.

Finally, Lauren returned after 0900, and Cross saw her car

pull up and stop. He went out to meet her in the parking lot. "What's going on? Everything all right?"

"Yes and no. Can we talk privately?"

Cross had an instant flashback to his first unit and felt his jaw clench and his blood boil. He took a calming breath, reliving the pain he felt that day, the anger at not being able to help a shipmate when she needed it most. Cross hoped more than anything that he was wrong, and that whatever this was didn't mirror the past, which still haunted him. They walked to the deck office, the nearest private location, and Cross opened the door, waving Lauren in.

Once inside, Cross asked hesitantly, "Did someone—"

"No," she interrupted with an abrupt shake of the head. "Thankfully, no. But while you were off, Mr. Grayson called me into his office."

"Why would he do that?" Cross already knew the answer as he breathed a sigh of relief that he hadn't helped create another Emma all over again.

"He had some harsh words about what would happen to my career if I followed your example. He cautioned me against learning from you, even encouraged me to move to the other section."

"Interesting, and what did you say to him?"

"Nothing really, I wasn't sure I should. It's like he thinks I can't make my own decisions."

"I'm sorry to hear that. That's not a good feeling, not to be trusted."

"What's the alternative, though?" Lauren asked with resignation in her tone. "Do I fight the OIC? I'm a non-rate; he won't listen to me."

"I have a different idea, if you're open to it."

"I suppose," Lauren said dubiously. "It's not like I have much of a choice."

●●●●●

Thirty minutes later, the 29183 was underway outside Gloucester, Cross at the sticks, when he brought the throttles down. He knew one of the best ways for him to balance the rage he was feeling toward Grayson and whatever he was involved in was to jump back into training others. With Lauren seemingly undecided again about staying in, he wanted to try to boost her confidence, making her feel like she had a bright future, which of course she already did.

"Okay, Lauren," Cross said as he unclipped the kill switch lanyard. "Come on up, clip in, take the sticks. The boat is yours. I'm going to stand back and coach you through how to drive this machine."

"Seriously? You want me driving?"

Cody looked at Cross for a moment, and then back at Lauren with a grin and said, "Does he look like he's joking? Time to make you a boat driver!"

Lauren clipped in, adjusted the seat in the RBS, and adjusted the helm angle so she could steer effortlessly. Finally, Cross stood to the side and said, "Grayson thinks your future is in jeopardy; we're going to prove him wrong. Clutch ahead, then push those levers as far forward as they'll go." The RBS took off a moment later, and Lauren steered toward the sea buoy.

The instruction continued into the morning, with Lauren becoming increasingly confident. "Okay, see how when you bled off your speed on approach, the wind started grabbing the back end of the boat, and you went for a ride? If you push the boat where you want it, then chop speed at the last second, the wind doesn't have much chance to take over. Again." Lauren backed down smoothly, trying another approach to the sea buoy, acting like it was another boat.

Her driving continued to improve until the new engineer,

MK3 Alcott, spoke up. "You guys usually skip lunch, or was that for my benefit?"

There were embarrassing glances around the boat crew from one to another, realizing they had been so in the zone. They were so invested in Lauren's skill-building that they had completely lost track of time. It occurred to Cross that he needed these quiet moments of training, improving the lives of those around him, more than he realized. He would keep training Lauren, hopefully convincing her how good an operator she already was in his eyes.

● ● ● ● ●

The next day, Cross set Lauren up with another driving opportunity. Grayson seemed particularly cold and distant, and Chief Drazen had passed down the order from Grayson to conduct extra boardings around Rockport, almost the farthest point from Salem. He quietly called Cross in, trying to get his thoughts on the situation.

"He's trying to distract us," Cross said when he closed the door. "It's a shell game. Has to be."

"Any new indications of what the real threat is?"

"No," Cross said, a neutral expression on his face. "That's what makes me nervous. I might hear back from Special Agent Lozaro soon, but until then, we're stuck."

Cross felt his phone buzz.

> Lozaro: Rolled up operator and the shooter, they lived together. Working them shortly.

Cross turned his screen quietly to face Drazen so he could see the same update.

Drazen nodded soberly.

Cross: Nice work, let me know when there's
any progress.

"That might get their attention," Drazen said with a grim look on his face. "This might accelerate their plans."

"Good point. I think we need eyes on the objective."

"Meaning what exactly?"

Cross had been training for this most of his life in one way or another. Cross pulled up his phone and punched in a number. It only rang once and was picked up. "Hey, Bull, yeah, need part of that favor. How soon can you have ISR assets over Pickering Wharf here in Salem? End of day? Perfect, and how long can they remain detached from command without questions? That's a long time, but that sounds like some outstanding bullshit. I'm sure they'll buy it. Thanks for the help, Bull. We'll be in touch."

Drazen looked at Cross inquisitively, then asked, "Are you going to tell me what that was all about?"

"Sorry, Chief," Cross said with a shake of his head. "That was a buddy attached to MSRT. He's going to send a guy with a drone to monitor Pickering Wharf. They'll be detached for up to a month if we need them. He's going to tell command down there that it was a last-minute request from MSST Boston. They will hold some electronic threat detection training with Boston SWAT. He's going to call a few contacts to make it sound legit. We'll have eyes shortly on anything that moves on Pickering Wharf, anywhere near that yacht."

"Jesus! Nicely done. I'm inclined to ask, though. Are you thinking about kicking in a door yourself if something goes down?"

Cross saw no point in lying to his chief. 'Iron Cross' was starting a return to the fray, no matter how much Cross had tried to stay out of the fight. Doing the right thing simply meant getting hands-on when it was needed. "Yes, Chief. I don't think I'm going to have a choice. They made this personal. I should be the one to end it."

"No way of talking you out of it?"

"Melanie already tried, Chief," Cross said with a chuckle. "Good luck."

"I've got nothing on her, so we need a way to detach you from this command temporarily that the old man will buy into. I'll think of something."

Cross was stunned by the instant backing and couldn't think of much to say. "Thank you, Chief." He walked out to the pier and his waiting mission, teaching Lauren about how to approach law enforcement boardings as a coxswain.

●●●●●

Lauren picked up the boat-driving quickly, as Cross thought she would. It helped him as much to mentor someone instead of thinking about his old life that kept calling him from the dark edges of his soul. He knew the fight was coming, and he knew he would need to put himself and others at great risk to some unknown end, at a time yet to be determined. For now, he needed to focus on something to subdue his rage about the fight he was in.

He was knocked away from his thoughts as they contacted their first recreational boat, and Lauren backed off the throttles to let the crew handle lines. She didn't say much to them. "Nice approach, Lauren, but next time, more communication. It comes with time and practice, but the more you're saying what's in your head and what you want those guys to do, the better they'll do it. Eventually, they'll be ready to do it long before you give a command. It'll be like breathing. You'll say it, and it'll already be done."

"Roger that, BM1," Lauren said, smiling at how much confidence she seemed to be acquiring in two short days. "Thank you for the feedback. I'm glad you're letting me do this. It's fun! Difficult, of course, but a worthy challenge."

"You're damn good at it," Cross confirmed with a rare smile for the current stress load he was under. "Keep it up, we'll make a coffee-guzzling boatswain's mate of you yet."

Lauren chuckled and said, "Sounds like a good life. Sign me up!"

They completed eight boardings before the end of the day, breaking at the Rockport pier for lunch halfway through. Lauren continued to improve her driving skills. Cross felt for his part like he was, at least for the moment, making a difference where it mattered. He would try to stay under the radar as a seasoned boat driver, training and mentoring his crew until the time was right for greater action on the developing threat.

23

BEVERLY, MASSACHUSETTS, JULY 22, 2022

CROSS'S RETURN home was met with a hug and kiss from Melanie, and a request to go to the range. After all their amazing conversations while shooting lately, Cross readily agreed. Subconsciously, he recognized that weapons practice was going to make all the difference in the coming fight. These weren't random thugs with guns. The organization would likely send some very serious people to achieve their mission. He would need to be ahead of that curve, because being behind or right at the edge could mean death for himself or someone else. He had to come home for Melanie and their unborn child.

They arrived at the range and checked in, went to their assigned lanes, and unlocked their weapons. Burned gunpowder hung in the air like a cloud; the constant pop of rounds being fired at paper targets formed their soundtrack. As Melanie was setting her Sig on the bench, she turned toward Cross and said, "So, I want you to know, I did some thinking while you were on duty."

"Oh," Cross asked with a hand on her shoulder. "About what?"

"Your place in whatever's coming and finishing it."

Cross was nervous that he had started driving a wedge

between himself and his wife, until she finished her thoughts. "I know you're not like others. You excel at everything you do, and being on the team was natural for you. You always came home, despite the odds, and now I understand why. Your dark side is the cold, calculating, operational expert, the one who can win any fight. The one that doesn't think about the odds, only coming out on top, winning the fight, and coming home. I know now I'm your reason for always coming home, and that needs to remain the case. Whatever happens, whatever you need to do to make this right, I have your back. Just come home as you always do."

"Yes, ma'am," Cross joked with a smile. "I promise, I'll always come back to you."

"Good," Melanie said, with a grin of her own. "Now let's see if I can give you a run for your money."

•••••

After a couple of hundred rounds fired, Cross and Melanie returned home to clean weapons and have lunch. As they stripped their weapons down, Cross asked Melanie, "How are you feeling? I feel like I haven't really had any time to ask."

"Things have been chaotic. I get it. Feeling a little better after the incident here. I still wake up reliving it, but it's not as traumatizing as it was. It'll fade in time."

"That's really good to hear, and the pregnancy?"

"Honestly, I feel great! I thought I'd be feeling some morning sickness, but it's been nonexistent. It's still hard to believe I'm pregnant; it doesn't seem real yet, but I figure when my jeans don't button, it will be."

Cross laughed as he cleaned the grit out of the frame and moving parts, then said, "Yeah, I mean, I'm sure it'll seem real before then, but it'll feel very real at that point for both of us.

Have you thought about how you want to give birth, or is it something you'll figure out as it gets closer?"

"I thought about that years ago, and I'd prefer it to be a natural and traditional birth. Lots of moms seem to want a water birth, C-section, or something. I want it straightforward."

"I guess that makes sense. You're not a complicated person at all."

"Wait," Melanie joked. "Are you calling me a simpleton?"

"That's not..." Cross stuttered. "That's not what I—"

"I'm kidding, sweetie," Melanie giggled. "I know you didn't mean anything. I was trying to mess with you."

"Thank God. You had me worried for a second."

Melanie leaned in for a kiss, then said, "I love making you squirm a little. Apparently, I've still got it!"

"Yes," Cross said with a smirk. "I'll be sure to remember that when you start snoring and waking up five times every night to pee."

Melanie giggled with an adorable smile on her face. "It's cute that you think it'll only be five times every night."

They sat down to lunch after the cleaning, and Cross's phone immediately buzzed. He pulled it out expectantly and saw a Signal message from Lozaro.

> Lozaro: Broke them. Call me ASAP.

Cross stepped into the garage a moment later and then called Lozaro through Signal. He answered in two rings.

"Logan, you're not going to believe this."

"Hit me," Cross said, his pulse suddenly racing, the anticipation building like a burning dynamite fuse. "What do you have?"

"It happened quickly; I didn't expect that. Apparently,

loyalty isn't a top-shelf commodity in an organization that kills anyone who falls astray of the path."

"You don't say," Cross said, the statement dripping with sarcasm. "So bottom line, what did they give the interrogators?"

"They were hired to attack your crew by the syndicate, who allegedly received the order through someone in uniform."

"Fuck!" Cross said in disbelief as he felt his fists tightening. "But they didn't say who?"

"They didn't know who. They knew it was a well-placed individual with some relative anonymity. We can't figure out who the hell that is, and it won't pay to find out. It doesn't get us any closer to finding out what else they're planning."

"We know Grayson is involved; the list of payments, the suspicious absences, the deaths of three known traffickers in an area this normal, then the attack on me and my wife, and the shooting. He was paid for everything."

"You saw notes of the payments?" Lozaro hadn't heard about that.

"Yes," Cross admitted. He still felt guilty lashing out at Chief Drazen in the OIC's office. "I was keeping that quiet until we figure out the real threat, because three dead pushers isn't the endgame. We act now, and we'll spook them. We need them to keep thinking they're winning."

"I wholeheartedly agree. Can you send me any pictures of the payoff notes?"

"Absolutely, but I think we need to ensure we don't handle Grayson until we know what he's into. He's dangerous, but he's a piece of the puzzle. If we bag him now, the game is up."

"I get it, but what I don't understand is why the dead pushers."

Cross had a sudden vision of Jake Harper, buried in a coffee mug and a notepad. "I'll ask someone else I trust. I'm thinking they can shed light on that."

"You do that and let me know what comes of it. In the meantime, we need to figure out what they're planning. They only said it has to do with a high-level government official."

"Attorney General Scott," Cross said, catching Lozaro completely off guard. "Our home invaders keyed us into that."

The insight caught Lozaro completely off guard, and he nearly choked on his next words. "Okay, that's bigger than I thought. Logan, we need to let Scott know what's happening."

"No. Rick, we can't say anything yet. All we're doing is creating a spin, crying wolf."

"Logan, that's a very dangerous move! Playing it that close? What if we wait too long, and Attorney General Scott takes a bullet to the head?"

"Rick, that's the problem. What's happening? We don't have enough information for even a rudimentary target package. We don't know what they're planning, when, or how."

Lozaro calmed down upon hearing the assessment. "Okay. You're not wrong. So, if we're not telling Scott yet, what's the play?"

Cross paused a moment. "We need to think like we're targeting him ourselves. We need to think like pirates. I'll dig in and see if we can tie up any loose ends here."

"Okay, we're in agreement. Keep me updated if anything else knocks free, and I'll do the same."

"Thanks, Rick. We'll talk soon."

Cross hung up and then tried to focus hard on the information he had so far. There was a small piece still missing.

UNITED STATES COAST GUARD STATION GLOUCESTER, MASSACHUSETTS, JULY 25, 2022

CROSS AND MELANIE enjoyed a great weekend together. They made love, relaxed, and watched some of their favorite movies. They even went on a short-distance day hike. They visited Nate once more, and the prognosis was significantly improved from the last visit. Lindsay had heard directly from one doctor that Nate would most likely be just fine. Cross was still plagued by the thought that he had caused harm to his crew by getting them involved in such a dangerous situation. As he returned to duty, Cross made a vow to keep quietly chasing down the loose threads of this looming danger. He refused to back down from doing what was right, no matter the cost. The threat needed to be stopped, and no one was better equipped to handle it. He would not let this threat harm anyone else if he still drew breath.

Lauren caught up to Cross as he was unloading the 4Runner and asked if she could drive the RBS again. She was energized, and it was obvious to Cross that he was helping her find her purpose. It was one more piece of good news to him amid so much trouble and pain. "Yes, Lauren, you can absolutely drive. Every time that boat moves, you're at the sticks unless I need to demonstrate something."

"Thank you, BM1!" She ran off into the main building without a further word.

Cross finished unloading his gear, walked into the station, and changed into uniform. He paused with the karambit, making a couple of quick practice attacks, remembering his training under Pak Hendra all those years ago. How he had pushed for growth, for the karambit to be an extension of one's body. The tiger stripe karambit he had been gifted from the old master had been secretly hidden in a gear case and was currently residing in his house, on a ready access display mount on his bedroom wall. The Fox folder had been a necessary shift, as carrying a fixed blade karambit in uniform was simply not an option. In mid-thought, Cross had a more disturbing thought slip into his mind.

Cross worried he was subconsciously preparing to kill. This was a threat unlike any he had faced before, and he promised Melanie he would return to her. The disturbing nature of the thought pulled his attention from the world around him, almost like a weight attached to his foot in the combat pool at Camp Lejeune.

After a few moments of collecting his thoughts, Cross headed to the morning brief. The other duty section had done a ton to catch up on station and boat maintenance. Cross felt compelled to give them early liberty and subsequently a little extra time with their families. He also felt compelled to share that Nate was still in his coma, but the doctors were more optimistic by the day that he would recover fully. The new information seemed to make a lot of people happy, despite the unfortunate circumstances that landed him in a hospital bed in the first place.

Cross left the brief, did his quick double-check of station cleanliness, and then walked into Chief Drazen's office to ask for early release for the starboard duty section. The chief immediately called the watchstander to have them announce early liberty, and the pipe over the station announcing system started a moment later, "Now, liberty, liberty, liberty. Liberty is hereby granted for the starboard duty section to expire no later than—"

Chief Drazen motioned to Cross to close the door and asked with the noise of the announcement covering him, "Anything new?"

"The boat crew broke and confirmed they were hired by a syndicate to keep us off their tail. They were put on by someone in uniform, but they didn't know who."

"More than the person we know? Someone above him?"

"That's how it sounds," Cross confirmed as the announcement ended, and they quieted their voices. "Special Agent Lozaro agrees we would only spook them by taking down Grayson or hunting for his contact now. Our best chance seems to be letting it play out, hoping for a capture-kill option to present itself and start uncovering the syndicate from within."

"This is not good, needing to let it play out, but I trust your instincts. The only part I can't figure out is why those three traffickers. What's the significance of killing them?"

"I—" Cross started when his phone buzzed. It was a Signal text from Harper.

> Harper: HSI conferred with FBI, they think those first three were a message, 'Stay out of our way.' All from different organizations on their watch lists, known names that have been elusive so far, and someone kills them first? It's not a coincidence. They were telling other organizations to back off and using the Coast Guard to facilitate the message. They probably wanted the investigations buried so no one started digging further. Everyone would take a win. You kicked the hornet's nest; hope you're ready for what comes next. Still can't figure out what their endgame is or when, though. Stay safe.

Cross felt a look of concern pull on his face.

Chief Drazen asked. "What is it?"

Cross silently turned his phone toward Drazen and said nothing as his chief read the text. His response was exactly what Cross thought it would be.

"Holy shit! Taking out their competition? These are some seriously dangerous people."

"I know," Cross said as he put his finger to his chin in contemplation. "I'm starting to think their endgame will be dramatic. I need to make another call to Bull."

●●●●●

"Talk to me," Bull answered with his usual enthusiasm. "What do you have, brother?"

"The FBI and HSI think the three murders were a message to other organizations to back off. They're taking out the competition while covertly burying the investigations so no one could dig further."

"Christ! We heard some rumblings, but these guys are way more ruthless than even we thought."

"They are, and it may come down to us to stop them. Any word on how the attorney general is involved or what they want with him?"

"We've been kicking that around the shop, and the prevailing narrative seems to be that he's likely their target, though we don't know exactly why. If they're trying to take him out, we don't know when. There's been no movement in Salem since we put the ISR team in. No one was watching, and no one was coming or going other than an occasional security round from a handful of rent-a-cops. No idea who they would send to do it."

"Okay," Cross said. The weight of the unknowns felt like it caused his chest to constrict. "Intel isn't saying anything that might confirm your narrative?"

"Not exactly. There's nothing much out there identifying anything this group has a hand in. They're darker than dark. Practically invisible. No name or any identifiers. I've honestly seen nothing like it."

"Doesn't leave us much of anywhere. I guess we keep an eye open and ear to the ground and wait for them to make some mistakes?"

"Like the trackers of old," Bull said with a slight air of confidence and a chuckle despite the tension in the situation. "Don't you worry, brother. We'll come up with something. In the meantime, I've got a trailered boat that is packed with goodies, including a set of gear for you off your old 538. You know, just in case you decide you want to step down out of that palace you call a station to kick in the door with the rest of us knuckle-draggers."

"Thanks, Bull. I really appreciate the support. I can't do it alone, and there aren't many people I trust right now."

"Least we can do," Bull said, chuckling. "You saved our asses a few times over. Everyone here owes you one... or three."

"Hey, I was doing my job. The same way anyone else would."

"Always so humble, except you weren't just anyone, Iron Cross, were you?"

"Fine," Cross said. The vivid memory returned once more of the brutal end to a hijacker who may have... should have... killed him. "You win this one. Let's keep digging. I know there's a piece missing here."

"Agreed, we'll find it, stay safe."

"Thanks, Bull. You too." Cross hung up then, thinking over the information. There was a reason the attorney general was a target. There had to be.

● ● ● ● ●

Cross needed some perspective on the issue and knew the best way to get there. He woke up early Thursday morning, put in his earbuds to some classic rock, and started a punishing workout. Lauren managed to walk in just as he was about to start, and she joined him. Pushups, pull-ups, kettlebell swings, squats, lunges, and multiple Krav sequences followed. Two hearts raced, sweat soaked their shirts, stung their eyes, but neither backed off even an ounce. As they finished, the only thoughts in Cross's consciousness were Melanie, the new life growing inside her, and Lauren's training.

As they stretched, Lauren asked, "BM1, what's been happening with Grayson?"

"What do you mean?"

"Well, since the attack on our crew it seems like things have been very quiet. Have you figured out what's really going on?"

"In part," Cross said. "It's a little complicated. I think there's something at play bigger than some dead traffickers. I just don't know what."

"Whoa, that's pretty heavy," Lauren said as she took a sip of water. "Anything we can do?"

"At the moment," Cross said. "No, not really. I need to wait for some further answers from others. Until then, we're dead in the water."

"I understand, BM1. Just let us know if we can dig in. We can all see how heavily this is weighing on you. There isn't a single person here who hasn't said something about it. Don't feel like you're alone. You'd look out for us the same way if we were in your shoes."

"Thanks, Lauren. I appreciate the support." They parted ways as Cross continued thinking about the conversation.

He showered and got into his uniform. As he was putting on his GoRuck boots, he realized part of what he was missing. He might be able to dig into Attorney General Scott and see if there was any connection to why he might be targeted. What would make him an object of a criminal syndicate's wrath, other than the obvious? He wouldn't be able to do it until he got back home. He resolved to put it out of his mind for now, focus on the immediate, and started planning what kind of drills he would run for Lauren to boost her confidence at the sticks.

BEVERLY, MASSACHUSETTS JULY 27, 2022

CROSS ARRIVED HOME ON WEDNESDAY, plagued with questions whose answers were eluding him, as well as apparently anyone else who had any piece of this puzzle. It could be said that any United States attorney general would always have a target on his or her back with all the organized crime in the country, but this felt more directed, and no one could seem to figure out why.

As Cross grabbed his backpack and closed the door of the 4Runner, it occurred to him that if no one could figure out the answers to these last little pieces of the puzzle, the syndicate could easily succeed. All the death, the pain, brought into his life and the lives of those he loved would be for nothing. What was missing? The last pieces kept eating at the edge of his conscious thoughts, taunting him like an elusive target hidden behind the haze of a smoke grenade. The veiled information was maddening to a man so used to being fully in tune with his surroundings.

He expected Melanie would be waiting with her usual affection, but when Cross walked in, she was at her computer, seemingly deep in thought. She was, in fact, so deep into what she was doing that she didn't notice him walk in and jumped a little. A squeal escaped her as she turned to him and yelled, "Don't scare a pregnant lady like that. We pee easily!"

Cross laughed so hard he almost fell over and dropped his backpack. After he caught his breath, he said, "Sorry, I didn't mean to scare you. I didn't realize you were researching the meaning of life over there!"

"Not the meaning of life," Melanie said with a grin that belied the importance of what she was into. "But something that might help."

"Sweetie, what do you mean? Helping what?"

"The thing that I already know is distracting you, eating you alive... the fight that chose us."

Cross looked at Melanie with a smile, realizing she had found her peace with what he had to do. She was ready to help fix it herself. It simultaneously made him love her even more and broke his heart that she had been sucked into this evil for simply being married to him.

Cross pushed the ugly thoughts aside and asked, "So, what are you looking at exactly?"

"Well," Melanie said, looking like she was still lost in thought. "I got to thinking about the why of all this. Everyone's trying to figure out the endgame, but what if this is strictly personal?"

Cross suddenly knew exactly where she was coming from and realized she was on to something. "Keep going."

"This feels personal, and no one can figure out why. So, I started digging into the person at the center of it all. Good place to start, right?"

Cross was blown away. He always knew Melanie was exceptionally smart, as evidenced by her degree in forensic psychology, but now he was about ready to defer to her completely. She was onto something that veteran operatives, investigative agents, and cops had so far missed, including himself.

"Okay," Cross said with a hand on her shoulder. "So what have you found?"

"Not much, but it still might help. Attorney General Griffin Scott was a California attorney turned senator and was plucked for AG a few years ago. Most of the stuff I found says he's got a spotless record, one of the strongest picks for AG we've had in a long time. He has a military record in the Marines to back up his career as a litigator and politician."

"Okay," Cross said as he folded his arms over his chest. His mind sorted through the details like it was on autopilot. "So, loved by us, hated by criminals. That's nothing new."

Melanie gestured with her hands like she was stacking cups side by side on her desk as she continued explaining. "That *alone* isn't, but here's where it gets interesting. Years ago, he bought this mega yacht with his extra pocket change. None of it made sense until a reporter picked up on the name, *Second Chance*, which he claimed was for his son. His son Matthew has been dead for years. Cause of death? Organized crime violence, wrong time, wrong place."

"Holy shit!" The enormity of the situation suddenly hit Cross with the force of a Nor'easter. "He boosted his career off the death of his son. He's hunting these guys down using the law, making a run at revenge for his personal loss."

Melanie's face turned serious once more. "It certainly sounds that way. It's no wonder he's a target of their wrath. He's got the gloves off, hunting them down with reckless abandon."

"Christ! I guess that—" As if the universe had spontaneously grabbed Cross's brain and shaken it, he stopped mid-sentence, his eyes wide, his heart racing, realizing exactly what the missing piece was, the one nobody had figured out to this point.

"Logan, what is it? What are you thinking?"

"Honey," Cross said, his voice concise, measured, confident.

"I think you cracked this one wide open for us. You're a genius! You've got a career in investigations if you want it."

"Wait, what?" Melanie asked, hands behind her head, confused slightly but smiling at the sudden compliment. "What did I figure out?"

"Let me drive. I'll show you."

Melanie slid her chair aside as Cross worked his way to the mouse and keyboard, quickly scrolling and clicking other links in the Google search results.

Melanie watched carefully and asked, "What are you looking for exactly?"

"We agree he's a target," Cross said, his eyes locked on the screen like he could stare a hole through it. "And his whole career..." He paused as he read, then exited another page. "His whole career has been a calculated rise fueled by the tragic death of his son. That's significant to him. The son is the key."

Melanie was seeing a side of her husband she had never witnessed. He was zeroed in on this like she had never seen from him before, and she suddenly realized what he was looking for.

"There, stop, look," Melanie said abruptly. "His son was born in February, nowhere close to summer."

Cross scrolled further down, and he felt his breath catch in his lungs, his throat tightened, and the alarm bell screamed in his head. "He died August 5, 2012. This is the tenth anniversary of his son's death. Jesus! They're looking to make a symbolic statement with their plan for him. They're going to take his yacht and assassinate him on a date critical to his career and personal life, send a message that it doesn't matter how much motivation you have; they'll still win."

"Good God." Melanie gripped Cross's arm tight enough to whiten the flesh. "You need to let someone in on this. They need to keep him from getting on that boat!"

"Actually," Cross said with a dark grin. "I have a better idea."

●●●●●

For the first time since June, Cross felt like his head was clear about everything happening.

The only way to stop this was through a careful game of chess, like he was playing against Grayson. The syndicate had to think they were still winning; they had to believe they had a chance.

As Cross snuggled with Melanie in their bed, he said, "I hope you know I'm going to come back from this. I know the dangers, but I can handle it. We can handle it. And I've got the team on standby to help me end it."

"I know you will," Melanie said, rubbing her belly as she looked in Cross's eyes. "I'm worried about what comes after."

"After?" Cross couldn't mask his confusion.

"You'll need to confront Grayson. Are you sure he's not going to try to kill you himself?"

Cross let out a deep sigh. Grayson couldn't be avoided. "He might, but it'll end badly for him."

"That's what I'm afraid of. I'm afraid that you'll go a step too far after all the pain he's caused you. You won't be able to come back from that."

"I know. I'll have to channel my inner Zen master with him, but he's not exactly a real threat. I don't expect much fight from him."

"Still, be careful. I don't want our children to grow up seeing you as nothing but a killer."

"They won't," Cross said as he put his hand to her belly, imagining the tiny life growing inside. "I promise."

●●●●●

The next day, after sitting on the new development overnight to make sure he wasn't jumping the gun on an emotional reaction, Cross made several calls.

Bull, as always, praised Cross's ability to read through the fog and see the big picture, and said he and the boys were itching for a good fight against a serious threat. Things were too quiet in Chesapeake, training for fights that weren't happening. They needed a real mission, and they were going to get one. Bull agreed to get the team ready to deploy to Boston, claiming to their command that the MSST wanted to play around for a couple of weeks to enhance their readiness stance in the area. They were more than happy to get the team out of the shop. That the team had quietly filled an 1149 form to transfer a case of MK18 Mod 0 rifles, over 500 rounds of 5.56x45mm ammunition, a couple of Barrett M107 sniper rifles and .50-caliber ammunition, a case full of Sig 229DAK handguns with over 200 rounds of .40 S&W ammunition, flashbang grenades, smoke grenades, and enough tactical gear to invade a small country would fly under the radar until the next monthly inventory. By that point, they would have saved a senior government official from certain death. They would be ready for a fight, and they would win at all costs.

The next call was to Commander Matthews. "Potshot, ready for a real mix-it-up?"

"Always. When and where?"

Cross filled her in on the details. She was blown away by the complexity of the syndicate's plans, but this was a fight she wouldn't back down from. After Cross saved her life on that go-fast op last year, she was anxious to return the favor. She promised air coverage, no matter who she had to duct tape and throw in a gear locker. That part made Cross smile, as Matthews was always such a straight shooter, never one to mince words. Her wounding last year hadn't slowed her down at all.

Lozaro was the next call, as he would need to be up to speed on all the details Cross and Melanie had pieced together. Also, as a rule, it was better to inform a trusted ally that you were about to venture way off the reservation to save a high-level government official. Lozaro agreed tentatively that the bigger Coast Guard would screw this up, force the syndicate to go to ground, disappear, and come back twice as strong. The best shot, at the risk of career suicide for everyone involved, was a covert operation to stop the threat to Attorney General Scott, and a follow-up arrest of Grayson, whose interrogation Lozaro would personally oversee. Lozaro wished Cross good luck and happy hunting, having served in law enforcement for many years before joining CGIS. He knew the odds the team would be up against, but he told Cross he couldn't think of anyone more suited to the challenge.

The final call was to Mendez, as she would need to be in the loop to arrest anyone captured alive in the yacht takedown. She would also need to be available for the inevitable arrest of Chief Warrant Officer Bill Grayson when Cross confronted him after the failure of his organization's assassination attempt on the attorney general. All the Ts would need to be crossed, all the Is dotted if this were to find its way to a courtroom to bring the syndicate down. Cross was not going to leave any stone unturned.

Finally, Cross texted Harper with all the details, how they had come to their conclusions, and Harper jokingly responded.

> Harper: Well, Melanie was always the smarter of you two.

He reminded Cross to be careful and to stay true to himself. It was not a mission of vengeance, but a true mission of justice, doing the right thing because it was the right thing.

Cross jokingly said he'd go Zen master on Grayson.

> Harper: Remember... two graves.

UNITED STATES COAST
GUARD STATION GLOUCESTER,
MASSACHUSETTS, JULY 29, 2022

CROSS JOINED the brief that Friday morning, feeling confident in what was coming, although the trick was now pretending like he was going through the motions like normal. Serving, training, mentoring, cleaning, running SAR and LE operations as a boatswain's mate of his rank and knowledge with not an ounce of his plan flagging visually for anyone to see—least of all the traitor, Grayson. Cross needed the OIC to think he was untouchable, that his subordinates were in line, and that no one was on him. He needed to think the syndicate was going to succeed in its mission against the attorney general, and that it was because he was still in charge of Station Gloucester.

During the brief, everything almost seemed normal, despite the veil of evil hanging over the place. The rest of the crew, including Chief Drazen, had almost no idea what was about to take place in their own backyard. Given the necessity for secrecy, none of them would likely find out about it until after the fact.

After the brief, cleanup, and liberty for the starboard duty section, Cross walked into Chief Drazen's office and quietly pointed to the deck office. He held up one hand with all fingers extended. Then he walked out without a word.

A few minutes later, Chief Drazen walked in, trying not to

appear like he was about to have a covert discussion with Cross about the looming threat. He looked at Cross, seated on the small couch along the back wall, and asked, "What's with the sneaking around?"

"Because Melanie and I figured it out. If we give away even a hint that we're on to them, it's game over, and we lose our shot."

"Wait! Figured what out?"

"All of it," Cross said with a grin. "The whole thing."

"Fuck! Tell me—quickest version."

"Attorney General Scott is absolutely the target. Here's how we know. He came up through the California law scene after some time in the Marine Corps, became a senator, then made a run at AG. About ten years ago, he lost his son to an organized crime hit. His son was in the wrong place at the wrong time. The AG buys a boat, *Second Chance*, paying homage to the son, Matthew. He commemorates the anniversary of his death every year. His rise to power is a revenge-fueled hunt to disrupt organized crime to the maximum extent the law permits. He's made enemies in abundance."

"Okay," Drazen said as he held up a hand. "You mentioned the anniversary of the son's death, Matthew, was it? When was that?"

"Yes, Chief. That's right. He was killed on August 5, 2012."

"Holy hell! The tenth anniversary of Matthew's death is a week away!"

"I know, Chief, and you can thank Melanie for tying that thread together next time you see her."

"Damn! I owe her dinner for this one, and maybe a medal from the Oval Office."

"I told her she could easily get a job at CGIS. I'm not sure she bought it."

"No shit, she's smart. You've done well. So, what's next?"

"What's next?" Cross asked, his brow furrowing, eyes

narrowing. "I'm set up to end this, but I can't do it attached to this unit."

"Wait, are you saying you've got resources already lined up to save the attorney general?"

"And arrest any live subjects on the yacht... and Grayson when I come back for him after the yacht killing fails. He'll be in a corner with nowhere to run."

"Christ, Logan, you've been busy."

"I'm not going to let my crew or family be targeted again; this ends for good." There was a fire in Cross's voice that Drazen recognized immediately. He was going back to his MSRT roots, becoming a cold, calculating tactician and warrior.

"I get the impression a bunch of people are going to be doing some mildly illegal shit in the coming days, am I wrong?"

"Maybe not illegal, simply not routed through the proper channels. Rick Lozaro knows it all, in case we fail. That way, you have plausible deniability. You've been sticking your neck out for me too much already."

"And I'll continue doing it if I can, because I trust you. You're not going off-reservation for fun. You're doing it because it's the only right play. When the time comes, you've got my support. I'll knock down the commandant's door myself, if I have to, for you and anyone helping you to end this. I don't care what it takes. You guys will not pay the price for anything. The Coast Guard failed to flag this; you're doing the job they should have done a long time ago."

"Thank you, Chief, for everything. Now we've got to figure out how to detach me from this command long enough to go take down a yacht."

"Any ideas, or are you going to walk away and hope he doesn't notice?"

"I've got one idea," Cross said with a devilish smirk. "But you're not going to like it."

●●●●●

It was a training day, and Cross needed the outlet—the distraction. He knew this might be his last opportunity before committing career suicide on an unsanctioned operation. He wanted to go out on a high note. The wind was kicking up Saturday morning, driving choppy seas off Cape Ann, which were creating havoc for Lauren behind the sticks. The spray from the wave tops obscured the view through the windshield. The other RBS was out, and the crews took turns practicing towing approaches to each other, taking advantage of a windy and choppy day to dramatically improve their skills. Maintaining a good position relative to the other boat was extremely difficult.

Cross saw Lauren struggle to hold a good line; the RBS fell out of position each time she tried to approach the other boat. She was serious but smiling. Still, Cross saw no need to keep beating her up for no good reason. "Demo time. Back into good water and unclip, then we'll switch spots while you watch me."

"Copy, Boats," Lauren said, then communicated to her crew. "Backing down!"

The crew acknowledged the call and repeated it. Then Lauren placed the throttles in stern propulsion and backed down deliberately, getting in a safe position before unclipping and handing the kill switch lanyard to Cross.

"Nice comms and movement. Well done. Now, I'm going to demo the approach once to show you how I handle weather like this, and hopefully it helps you put some things together."

Cross clipped in, settled into the seat, and took a quick look around at his surroundings. When he knew the wind direction off the chop pattern, he observed the other boat as he explained to Lauren that looking at the other boat could do as much to guide your approach as reading the water. Maneuvering alongside another boat was more artistry than science, but sometimes science became your only option. "If I cross the T, put us down-wind and cross their bow, they're going to drift into us hard and fast, and I won't have a good way out. Let me show you that quickly, then we'll do it another way."

Lauren nodded as Cross yelled to the crew, "Coming around to approach!" He pinned the throttles to ahead propulsion, favoring his port engine with a little extra power, turned around in a tight arc, and lined himself up with the wind on his star-board. The other boat drifted bow-first from right to left a hundred yards ahead.

Cross turned the wheel slightly counterclockwise to adjust his end position to port, then yelled, "Coming up, starboard approach!" The crew immediately repeated the command, and Cross clicked the throttles into forward gear, then jammed them ahead to get a boost out of them. "Speed is life," Cross said to Lauren with a grin. "You lose that in any wind or current, Mother Nature takes you for a ride."

He gained a good position in front of the other boat in a matter of seconds and stopped himself with the other RBS closing distance rapidly. Cross looked at Lauren. "See? Bad spot. Always leave yourself an exit strategy. Backing!" He swiftly kicked the boat into stern propulsion while giving it a slight turn to starboard to keep his bow away from the rapidly closing second boat. He boosted the throttles hard for a moment before easing off and letting the other boat cruise right by where their own boat had been seconds earlier.

"That would have been hard contact if I had stayed there, and that breaks boats. Let's look at this from another angle."

Cross repositioned himself parallel to the other boat and then yelled, "Making my approach!"

"Making your approach, aye-aye!" The crew responded with practiced speed.

Cross pinned the throttles once more and boosted himself

forward to position along the other boat's port side. He stopped his way, using the strong and steady wind to hold himself about twenty yards off the side of the other RBS.

Cross took his hands completely off the controls and said confidently to Lauren, "I can sit here all day." Then he asked the crew, "Do you have a shot?"

The reply was instant, "Got a shot!"

Cross yelled back, "Send it!" A large orange ball attached to seventy feet of bright yellow polypropylene line went hurdling through the air. It slammed into the windshield of the other RBS with an echoing thud before the other crew grabbed the line.

Cross then demonstrated an opening maneuver to gain distance, and then a closing to shorten the distance to the other boat. "Read the environment," Cross said to Lauren as he was breaking contact with the other boat and slowly motoring to safe water under the hum of the twin Honda engines. "Read your contact, then use the prevailing force to make your approach as smooth for your crew and as uncomplicated for you as possible."

Lauren replied, "Thank you, Boats. That was something else. Can I try again?"

Cross smiled at her determination and replied with a grin, "I was wondering if you were ever going to tell me to move my ass! Yes, get in here, do it again. Both approaches."

"Aye-aye, Boats," Lauren said confidently, then yelled to her crew. "Coming around for approach. Let me know when you're ready on deck!"

UNITED STATES COAST GUARD STATION GLOUCESTER, MASSACHUSETTS, AUGUST 1, 2022

AS THE DUTY period came to an end, Cross felt good about where things stood. He heavily trained Lauren, putting her on a track to be an even better boat driver than himself. Things were lined up to take down the real threat, but he needed to be free to act. That part would come next. He hoped it would work and not blow up in his face like a poorly fused breaching charge.

Cross packed his gear into the 4Runner uncharacteristically early after a brutal workout to keep his head in the game. As the morning brief started, he was nervous but ready.

Cross spoke about the maintenance and training opportunities they had utilized, the couple of cases they handled, and then the engineering department did their pass-down of expected big-ticket maintenance items coming up. Finally, the command pass-down started, and Chief Drazen detailed all-hands requirements, folks needing medical, other metrics updated, and big events coming up.

When Drazen discussed medical metrics, he mentioned Nate, who was still absent. "Looks like Petty Officer Sutter is due for dental. Would help if he wasn't laid up in a coma, but I guess we lost *that* opportunity when someone walked him into an ambush." He glanced at Cross. There was a sudden palpable tension in the air that turned the room into an instant icebox.

Cross looked straight at the chief with cold condemnation in his eyes as he said, out of turn, "And what the fuck is that supposed to mean?"

"Try putting 'Chief' at the end of that statement, you insubordinate piece of shit." Drazen was in attack mode, shutting Cross down in front of the stunned and bewildered crew.

"Fine," Cross said, the rage building in his voice by the second. "What the fuck is that supposed to mean, *Chief?*" Cross spat out the last word with venomous contempt.

Chief Halverson spoke up. "Hey fellas, maybe we could lower it down a—"

"I mean," Chief Drazen said as he attempted to burn a hole in Cross's head with his fiery eyes. "You fucked things up for everyone by getting him shot."

Chief Warrant Officer Grayson tried to get a word in, but it was like he wasn't even there. His words went unnoticed.

"The *fuck* I did, you read the CGIS report. It was unprovoked."

"Maybe you're too reckless," Chief Drazen continued, lowering his voice, appearing somehow more threatening. "Maybe you had it coming."

In the blink of an eye, Cross launched himself across the table like an Olympic hurdler. He let loose with a series of punches straight at Chief Drazen's chest and face, the hits landing with practiced precision and force as Drazen attempted in vain to block. He tried to return with a couple of punches of his own, but Cross blocked easily. It was evident to everyone watching that their chief was outmatched. Cross was more savage and aggressive.

The shock of the moment prevented an immediate response,

but after several exchanges of hits, Chief Halverson and a couple of the biggest guys at the station jumped to the aid of Chief Drazen, pulling Cross off him. Cross, for his part, was largely silent, breathing heavily. The hatred in his eyes was directed squarely at Drazen, whose lower lip and nose each had small glistening rivulets of blood trickling out of them.

The room fell silent for a moment; no one was quite sure what to do or say. Then Chief Warrant Officer Grayson snapped out of his own shock and spoke again as the senior man in the room. "Cross, get the fuck out of my station! You're on administrative leave until we can figure out what the hell to do with you."

"But, sir, I—" Cross started to say, but he was cut off.

"Not another word. Get the fuck out of my station before I have you arrested!"

Cross spoke with rage and contempt as he responded only with, "Aye-aye, *sir.*"

•••••

Cross got in the 4Runner, looking around him at this station that had become his new home. Despite everything that was happening, he still loved being here. It was a beautiful area, a busy enough unit to be fun and challenging, and he had been able to teach and mentor others. He couldn't ask for more. He knew he had put it at risk, but it had to be done. As he was lost in thought before leaving the station grounds, Lauren suddenly appeared at the driver's side window. Cross lowered the window, not wanting to leave her confused.

"What was that?" Lauren shook her head in disbelief. "Why was that necessary?"

Cross held his tongue for a moment, thinking about how he wanted to respond. In the end, he simply responded, "What's right is right, regardless of the personal sacrifice." It wouldn't become clear to her until a week later, but she somehow knew there was a reason behind it all.

●●●●●

Beverly, Massachusetts, August 1, 2022

Cross arrived home shortly after the incident, grabbed his gear from the 4Runner and walked in. He realized he would need to tell Melanie the entire truth. It was risky no matter how he played this, but down to the very fiber of his being, he believed he had made the only right play. It wouldn't work any other way. If his career was now at risk, he would find a way to work through that. He had the support he needed from Chief Drazen. He told himself he needed to trust his allies in Chief Drazen, Special Agent Lozaro, and State Trooper Mendez to prevent his career from being thrown out the window. They knew his character; they all knew there was no other way.

Melanie gave him a warm hug and asked, "What's wrong?"

Cross hesitated for a moment, trying to pick his words, and then said, "I made a judgment call, and I hope it's the right one. I strongly believe it is, largely because it was the only way."

"This doesn't sound good," Melanie said, a look of concern on her face. "What did you do?"

"Actually, we, Chief Drazen and I. We agreed the only way for Grayson not to immediately become suspicious of my sudden absence was if he had to do it himself."

"Oh shit! You guys are going to get yourselves dishonorably discharged, aren't you?"

"I think we played it perfectly, but the next few days will tell the tale."

Melanie's face was etched with deep concern. "Care to elaborate?"

"Pretty simple, really. We staged a fight. Chief accused me of being reckless with Nate, and it led to bloodshed. Grayson had no choice but to put me on administrative leave. Now I'm free to act, prevent the threat on the AG, and stop Grayson."

"Jesus, that's a huge risk! What if Grayson figures it out early? What if you and the team fail? We can't afford to have you in prison for a mutiny with our first child coming!"

"I know," Cross said, the concern on his own face evident. "I'm scared shitless that this won't work, and I'm trying my hardest to think only about how to beat Grayson and the syndicate for good. I know I need to come back to you. I promised I would, and I will. It's a risky move, and I fully understand that. The only hope I have now is to be one step ahead of Grayson and his backers, because they've been a step ahead of all of us from the moment this started."

Melanie paused with her hand on her belly and one on the back of her neck. "This turns the tables. He's not counting on you throwing yourself on your sword, and he thinks it's going to help him with you out of the picture."

Cross smiled as Melanie caught up to the gamble. "He set up his own downfall just by being greedy for a win."

"It's a chess game, and you just put him in check. He doesn't realize it. You know, I don't like it, but I think it was the right play. We all better hope it works."

"That's my only focus now," Cross said, with an affectionate smile and a hand to her belly. "Other than coming back to my stunning wife and unborn child one more time."

•••••

On a last-minute whim, Cross and Melanie made the decision to go backpacking. It was a retreat from the stress they were feeling and that which was coming. It was one last opportunity to connect before things really went off course. They spent the morning packing, then started the drive shortly after lunch.

They followed their usual patterns, finding a campsite a few miles in, secluded enough that no one would accidentally stumble on them. Cross built a fire pit while Melanie set up the tent, and they sat down together at the fire to talk after it was all done.

"I'm nervous about all this," Melanie confided in her husband. "There are so many moving pieces."

"I am, too, if it makes you feel better. You're not alone."

"It does. I worry this is too much for even you to handle."

Cross thought about that for a moment before answering. "Is there some way I can make you feel less nervous about it?"

"I don't know. Maybe reassure me that the team has your back, and that you'll win and come back to me no matter what."

"I've never been more driven to succeed in my entire life, and these assholes simply will not win. They haven't come across someone like me, and they'll regret it."

"It helps to know how committed you are. Logan, I—I want to make sure you're with me when our child is born."

Cross wrapped his fingers with hers, looking her straight in the eyes as he said, "I will be, no matter who I have to take out to get there."

Melanie smiled, then asked, "Have you thought about what you want to do when this is all over?"

"I need a vacation, that's first."

Melanie giggled at the bluntness of Cross's statement, then said, "Wait, you're telling me you're not a robot? You don't eat, sleep, and breathe work?"

"Not exactly, and these have been a crazy couple of months."

"Tell me about it," Melanie said. "It's been wild."

"Honestly, I'm trying to survive one day at a time."

"Well," Melanie said with a seductive grin. "I happen to know a way to take your mind off all that."

Cross smiled and kissed Melanie as she stood up, motioning with a single finger for him to join her.

28

BEVERLY, MASSACHUSETTS, AUGUST 3, 2022

ONE DAY PASSED without any word from Bull, and Cross worried that their information and conclusions may have been off. There was no movement at the yacht, or Bull would have notified him immediately.

The details from the informants had been clear, though. This had everything to do with Attorney General Scott and his yacht. With the dots that he and Melanie connected, it was obvious enough.

Finally, later that morning, Cross got a Signal text.

> Bull: ISR showing movement on the yacht, maybe underway soon, will advise.

Cross had to clarify something, so he sent a text back to Bull.

> Cross: Any signs the boat is being watched?

> Bull: Only two guys we've seen multiple times, must be marina staff.

> Cross: Can you send me a couple of clips of each from the overhead feed?

Bull: Standby.

Cross waited for what felt like an eternity, then a few short videos came through, one after another. He scanned one, nothing catching his eye, and then another. Still nothing. Then he watched the third one. Second guy, but he didn't appear to be doing a safety round; he was on a small pocket monocular, looking... where? His focus was on the attorney general's boat. It occurred to Cross that he might be looking at an advance scout element. Then Cross watched the next video of the same guy. He looked more normal now, but as he walked past the *Second Chance*, he looked inside for what seemed like a very long time for an innocuous safety round. He was casing the interior layout. He was getting a picture of where everything was located.

Cross: Double-check those last two. Scouting party, he's casing it. Keep an eye out for him as they get underway and afterward.

Bull: Copy, marking him for further viewing. Good eye!

Cross: Team and boat ready?

Bull: Combat parked at Sector Boston, ready to roll on a moment's notice.

Cross: Copy, let me know if you see additional movement.

Bull: Will do, be ready to meet us in Salem if we see anything close to a boarding party.

It was a waiting game now. Once the team noticed a boarding party, they would sweep the marina and make their move.

● ● ● ● ●

Cross tried hard not to overthink the plan. He was confident he had accounted for everything. He still had a natural inclination to this kind of work, and his highly trained brain tracked every little detail now. Iron Cross had a firm grasp on the wheel. He simply had to wait for the right moment to take decisive action. As he always did at the MSRT, Cross's next moves revolved around a well-known key phrase: speed, surprise, and violence of action. He was as ready as he would ever be for this fight.

Cross was deep in thought, sitting on the couch, when Melanie sat down next to him, grabbed his hand and leaned into him in a way that nearly made him forget what he was thinking about. It always amazed Cross how deeply Melanie affected him. "Thank you. I'm so lost in this thing. I'm not here for you at all, and I'm sorry."

"I know you will be once it's over," Melanie said with a soft and beautiful smile on her face that broke Cross's toughness down instantly. "There's too much to process all at once, and you need to be focused on the fight ahead if you're going to win."

"You're right. I need to stop this for good. You don't deserve to be trapped in this danger. You're the only reason I function every day. If not for you, there wouldn't be anything left in this life for me. Thank you."

"I'm glad I can be your anchor, your reason for living. I want all of you back when this is over."

"That's the plan," Cross said with a grin. "As long as I have any say in the matter."

● ● ● ● ●

Beverly, Massachusetts, August 4, 2022

The next morning, Cross was up before Melanie, hitting the gym to clear his head. He got a Signal text from Chief Drazen.

> Drazen: Still no clue, you're in the clear. Well done, and happy hunting!

> Cross: Thank you, I hope I didn't bang you up too badly?

> Drazen: Remind me never to get on your bad side!

Cross tried hard to focus on a punishing workout while he attempted to stay present in the moment. He recalled his workout the morning after the first murder scene. He was unfocused then, drawn between past and present. He was off rhythm, off-balance, out of sync. Now, he knew what he had to do.

He pushed his earbuds in and started his workout playlist. The first song on the shuffle was "Sad But True" by Metallica. He started with a short run to warm up. He felt his body synchronize with the fast pace he was holding.

He truly felt the lyrics speak about betrayal as he started his run. Grayson had betrayed everything the uniform stood for. The words assaulted his senses as he realized that Iron Cross had to lead this final mission.

His feet pounded the treadmill belt. His lungs pumped vital oxygen into his legs. He was centered and focused. Still, his mind drifted to the past. He pictured all three dead traffickers: Rivetti, Valero, Lombardi. He could see their images from their dossiers, and their dead bodies from pictures after each of their murders. None of it had been an accident, he knew that now.

His mind cast those images aside like smoke through an open window. He suddenly had a vision of his first major training operation years ago at the Port of Norfolk. Crouched in the delivery boat, eye to his optic, as he watched the suspicious activity they were tasked to stop. He thought back to how finely tuned his senses were then, how ready he was to deal death and destruction and serve a higher calling for his nation.

He moved to weights. He tore through rounds of bench press, overhead press, pushups and lunges. His drive was as strong as a battering ram. His focus could have cut stone.

The lyrics continued to echo in his ears like the sound of thunder. Pain when he couldn't feel, and dreams turned real.

His mind replayed the home invasion, the fight with Apollo and Ox. He pictured every gruesome injury he gave the two intruders, every jarring impact to his body as he fought them off. Then he pictured Melanie behind him as she shot Apollo in the shoulder. He pictured her when she broke down afterward, emotionally and psychologically compromised. Then his mind cast out the image like a casing ejected from his handgun.

His mind moved backward to his karambit training under Pak Hendra. All the times he was beaten and slammed to the mat. The bruises all led him to a greater mastery of the weapon. By the end, he was formidable, though he still had more to learn. He had started becoming Iron Cross, the darkest, most violent part of himself.

The lyrics continued to burn in his ears about reasoned alibis. He focused harder as he moved to the heavy bag, and fired off round after round of palm strikes, punches, elbows, knees, and kicks. He hit the bag harder than he ever had, each strike vibrating the vinyl like a jackhammer, followed by continuous rounds of strikes with the karambit. It was then that his past came fully into focus. He continued to slash the air with the curved blade and had a sudden vivid image of the night he acquired the moniker 'Iron Cross.' He pictured the EMP detonation, his instantaneous kills of the first three hijackers, and the rattle of his rifle as he ended three hostile lives. The final fight with the eighth hidden hijacker flickered to life in his subconscious. He felt his pulse race as he remembered the feel of his karambit slowing against flesh when he sliced the man's throat open, ending his life instantly.

The final lyrics vibrated in his skull with astonishing clarity: "I'm you."

Cross slowed his attacks and paused. He inhaled heavily, hands on his hips. The images of his past, both near and far, were meant to tell him something. He quickly recognized it was a message to channel 'Iron Cross' once again. In order to save his family and his team, there was no longer a decision to make. As he was finishing his stretch, his phone buzzed again.

> Bull: Lots of movement this morning, TOI getting underway likely within the hour. Our guy has been cycling in and out of the area since yesterday, changing outfits to throw us off, but it's still him.

> Cross: Copy, pass any updates soonest, I'll be ready to meet you there. Advise staging the boat locally but covertly if possible. Boston traffic could delay us too long.

> Bull: Copy, passing the word now. We'll have it ready and waiting.

Cross left the garage then and walked in to find Melanie, who was sipping a glass of juice and fixing breakfast. He wrapped his arms around her and then touched her breasts and belly.

She moaned then said, "Good morning to you, too!"

Cross caressed Melanie for a few minutes longer, and then they sat down to breakfast together. Cross gave Melanie as much affection as he could that day, knowing she wasn't handling this one well. It didn't surprise him. Things were different. He was taking on a significantly more dangerous adversary than he ever had. He was doing it with only part of a team cobbled together through phone calls on not enough information. It wasn't the cleanest mission he'd ever run, and there was a high margin of error. The stakes were high, and the result of failure could be death for him, his team, and the attorney general. It could be jail time even if they succeeded. He hoped he had lined up enough support and evidence in the right places to prevent that for himself and everyone else. The thing that weighed on him, and clearly on Melanie, was the pregnancy. She wanted him around, needed him around to start their family, and there was a chance this mission would cost them all of that. No amount of reassurance would quell that fear. He had to go out there, channel his inner warrior, let 'Iron Cross' take over, and make it back to Melanie and their unborn child no matter what price he had to pay.

●●●●●

It was sometime after lunch when Cross got the texts that made his breath catch in his lungs.

> Bull: TOI was underway a little while ago. There's an increase in foot traffic around an open console we haven't seen before, identity and motives unclear but it looks like our guy has linked up with them. Might be our crew and boat. Loaded some unmarked Pelican cases on the boat under the seats. One guess what those are.

Cross: We'll link up tomorrow unless they move out sooner, keep eyes on.

29

BEVERLY, MASSACHUSETTS, AUGUST 5, 2022

CROSS AND MELANIE woke up around the same time on Friday morning. Neither was able to sleep all that well. Both had their nerves about what was coming, and there was only so much they could do to mitigate those fears. Cross would succeed or fail, and there were consequences for each. Cross did some extensive stretching that morning, loosening up to prepare for what he knew would be the toughest mission of his whole career.

They sat down to breakfast together, letting the silence radiate between them as they said quiet prayers that everything would go the way it needed to. Cross hoped this wasn't a suicide mission. Then again, if the mission went well, there was still a looming confrontation between Cross and Grayson. Cross had said he wasn't worried about Grayson. He could tell Melanie wasn't entirely convinced.

As they were finishing breakfast, Cross got another Signal text from Bull.

> Bull: Traffic coming and going from the unknown boat. Looks like they're close to getting underway. Might need you down here quickly if they start loading.

> Cross: Copy. Heading out shortly.

Then Cross thought of something else he could do inside the bounds of his resources. He pulled up Lauren's info on Signal and texted her.

> Cross: Before you leave, can you pull up AIS on the 183 and see if you can find a boat named Second Chance? Send me all the pertinent position info.

> Lauren: Sure, I suppose, give me a couple of minutes.

A few minutes later, she passed the information off the Automated Identification System, and Cross thanked her. Based on his knowledge of the area, and the AIS not giving an exact position, the *Second Chance* was in open water well south of Baker's Island, probably holding position for the memorial that night if his guess was right.

There was no sense delaying any further. It was time to get to business.

He looked at Melanie, who had a knowing look on her face as he finished the text with Lauren. It was time. They stood and embraced, the moment seeming to last forever as tears welled in Melanie's soft brown eyes, soaking her cheeks. She let go, and Cross gave her a long kiss. He put on his blue concealment jacket, a ball cap, and sunglasses. He grabbed his Eberlestock bag organized with all his gear for the mission ahead.

"I love you," he said, trying to maintain his composure despite his racing heart and shortness of breath. "See you on the other side of this thing."

"I love you," Melanie replied, her composure barely intact with tears still streaming down her face. "Be safe and come back to us." She touched her belly once more to emphasize the point, and Cross looked like he'd been punched in the gut.

Inwardly, he felt 'Iron Cross' nudge what little remained of his inner family man into the back seat as his fists clenched with focused fury. Capture-kill, but only if they allowed it. Otherwise, he'd send every one of these assholes to the afterlife with a smile on his face. The real "capture" target was sitting in an air-conditioned office on 17 Harbor Loop in downtown Gloucester, and he'd deal with that scum-sucking traitor next. He smiled at Melanie as he turned and walked to the 4Runner, feeling confident in his chances of success. Though he thought he had left the high-stakes operator's life behind, he would do it one last time to protect his family and save a life. Then, he would end the violence for good.

●●●●●

Salem, Massachusetts, August 5, 2022

Bull waited at the appropriate spot, casually sitting on a bench a block away from Pickering Wharf. He observed the comings and goings of people, but mostly anyone around the monitored open console. Cross almost missed him at first. One thing about Bull was that while he was a tough operator who could take down any opponent, he could still blend in anywhere. He was a big guy, which should have made that hard, but he had a knack for looking like any local gym rat anywhere. The local meathead who would attract attention from literally no one. There was always one more meathead, and Bull could be anyone and no one all at the same time. Cross was slightly envious of his ability to hide in plain sight as he nearly walked right past his teammate.

"Where are you going, brother?" Cross turned to see a casual smile on Bull's face, partially obscured by a ballcap. Once again, he was all but invisible to the crowd.

"Damn, you're good at hiding," Cross said with a chuckle. "You missed your calling with the CIA."

"So, I can have my martini shaken, not stirred, and miss out on the mission of a lifetime? No thanks. They can do spook shit— we can go kick in a door."

"Fair point. Any changes?"

"Plenty of traffic to that boat, but no indication they're getting underway yet. What're you thinking?"

"Night op. It's what I would do. Element of surprise, fewer eyes on what they're going to do to Scott and his wife if we aren't there."

"See, that's why you're paid the big bucks, and that's why we *will* be there."

"Damn straight," Cross said as the two bumped fists together. "Here's to doing something stupid and dangerous for the history books."

"Think they'll teach this at West Point, or maybe Quantico for those FBI pukes?"

"Never know. Stranger things have happened."

As Cross and Bull finished their conversation, Cross's phone rang. Bull stepped away as he answered the call. "This is Cross."

"It's Rick. That favor you asked about after the shooting. I finally got somewhere with it."

Cross listened intently. "Rick, tell me something interesting about Grayson."

"Okay, Logan. This is a doozy. You might want to be sitting for this one."

"Just tell me, Rick. What's his deal?"

"Plain and simple, his career was headed down the drain years ago. Divorced, reviews not all that good, he didn't have much left in the tank. Then, a few years back, his career suddenly picks up steam again."

"Any indication why?" Cross was confused and hoped Lozaro had more than just some vague career trajectory information.

"Well, it seems like he must have had a mentor of some kind. There were sudden increases in his review scores, and he tested for chief, then warrant. Then he lands in Gloucester."

"And no clue who this mysterious mentor is?"

"Unfortunately, no."

Cross thought hard for a moment, trying to connect dots that never should have connected. "Rick, hold on a second. Bear with me. Grayson met with a lieutenant after the first death. We never identified him. Cody overheard Grayson getting his ass chewed after the third. Grayson disappeared a bunch throughout those couple of months. Could he have been visiting someone at Sector Boston? Maybe a lieutenant?"

"Hell, I suppose so. But without a name... what's the connection?"

"I don't know, but I think it's worth looking into once this is all over. I'm starting to wonder if this is just the start of something far more deadly. I don't believe in coincidence."

"I don't either. This needs a fresh look. For now, good luck with the attorney general, and I'll be ready to handle Grayson's interrogation when I get the green light. Stay safe."

The rest of the morning and afternoon, Cross checked in with the rest of the team. The snipers were conspicuously missing, but Cross knew that was part of the plan. The assault team was in a coffee shop down the street, at a corner table, acting like they were having a reunion of SWAT cops or something equally unremarkable. Cross sat down with them, reviewed current intelligence on the op, and the position of the *Second Chance* he received from Lauren. He passed the same information to

Commander Matthews for her awareness, and would inform her of their underway time, their time to contact, and the execution timeframe. Hopefully, things would line up the right way. After his brief, Taters and Hooker gave each other a look, and Hooker turned back to Cross and said, "Nice to have you back, Iron Cross. Let's go ruin their night, huh?"

Cross looked Hooker in the eyes and said with a sour look, "I'm not back; this is a one-off."

As Cross stood to leave, Taters said, "Yeah, boss. Sure, it is. No such thing as a normal life for guys like us."

Maybe not, but Cross was sure as hell going to try.

●●●●●

Sunset gave way to civil then nautical twilight. Bull got a text from the drone operator saying that the small boat was loading up, and there were between ten and twelve men he could see joining the crew. That was a large number of men. Bull relayed the information to Cross, who had walked off to get an hour of sleep in the back of one of the team vans. He responded within a minute, "Standby to bring the boat up. We'll gear up at the marina office."

Bull continued to watch from his perch, counting the men as they continued to load the boat with more gear and finally got in. Twelve men, a dozen hostile targets. They would have a serious gunfight on their hands if these guys were all on the yacht. Tight confines, lots of targets, at night, but they'd done worse before. Bull texted the final count to Cross, who ordered him to stand by to move until the small boat had left the pier and was at least at the channel buoys.

●●●●●

Ten minutes later, the small boat pushed off the pier and motored away from Salem. Bull informed Cross when he saw their lights pass into the buoy line. "Rally at the marina office," Cross said. "Gear up and be ready to move."

The entire team converged at the marina office moments later to the stunned look of the marina attendant at the sudden appearance of a bunch of deadly-looking guys holding giant bags of gear, asking to use his office. He willingly complied, too confused to offer any resistance.

A few minutes later, the team slowly emerged, one by one, dressed in their dark blue assault uniforms with matching dark blue covered ballistic helmets with attached NODs topping them like ominous-looking hood ornaments. Within moments, Bull had pulled several large Pelican cases from the boat, unlatching them to reveal enough weapons to equip a small army. Each man loaded full magazines into pouches, flashbangs went to hip holsters, Sig P229s to drop-leg holsters, and there was the sudden rattling symphony of four handguns and four rifles all simultaneously going 'condition one' and loading live rounds in chambers to prepare for a major gunfight. Safeties were engaged, gear checks started cycling around the team, and they suddenly heard the attendant say in a stiff Boston accent, "Looks like you boys have a wicked interesting night ahead of ya."

"That depends," Cross said dryly as he shot an ominous look at the attendant. "On whether they're stupid enough to shoot back."

The boat drivers detached from MSRT tactical delivery jumped in behind the team. Lighting off the three 300-horsepower outboards, everyone shared looks with each other. Nox Noctis est Nostri... it was time to own the night once more.

30

SALEM, MASSACHUSETTS, AUGUST
5, 2022, 1800 HOURS LOCAL

THE THIRTY-SIX-FOOT SPC-BTD, special purpose craft –
boarding team delivery, slated for replacement early next year,
was serving its intended purpose better than ever. Its three 300-
horsepower Mercury outboards screamed, propelling it at close to
its maximum speed. The hostile boat and team had a bit of a lead
on them, but that lead would easily be cut down by the SPC-
BTD and the highly-capable drivers of MSRT-East. They had no
intention of being late on target and letting their critical mission
fail. Their only concern was a storm brewing off Cape Cod. The
distant flashes of lightning flickered threateningly in the dark,
distant sky. It wasn't a deterrent, but something to look out for.

As they sped from Salem Harbor, Cross got on the encrypted
communications channel and keyed into his portable radio.
"Reaper, Reaper Actual. Radio check."

"Reaper One, Lima Charlie."

"Reaper Two, Lima Charlie."

"Reaper Three, Lima Charlie."

The team had clear comms. Cross keyed again for the boat
team, "Neptune, Reaper Actual. Radio check."

"Neptune, Lima Charlie."

"Talon," Cross said last to Matthews. "Reaper Actual. Radio check."

"Reaper Actual," Matthews replied over the radio. "Talon is loud and clear, standing by in orbit."

Cross took a deep breath, centered himself, and keyed his radio once more. "All teams, thank you for being here. You're a credit to the uniform, and no matter what happens, I'm proud to have you all with me. We all know the stakes if we fail, and even if we succeed, we're all likely getting masted. Worst case, see you in the afterlife, best case, see you at the green tablecloth."

There were hearty laughs around the boat, then Matthews spoke up. "We're on the righteous path here. That will play well in the investigation. Don't forget why we're here. I feel the medal write-up starting already. Stay sharp; let's finish this."

Cross laughed to himself and then keyed up again. "You heard the lady. Kick in some teeth." There was more laughter, and then things turned serious as the yacht became visible on the eastern horizon.

"Talon," Cross said. "Reaper Actual, making our approach. Five mikes ETA, standby for cover action."

"Reaper Actual, Talon," Matthews said. "Standing by."

As they approached the yacht, the delivery team called a small boat off the starboard beam, about two hundred yards beyond it. Everyone confirmed the sighting, and Cross smiled at what was about to happen. *Nox Noctis est Nostri, the night is ours.* He reported the contact to Matthews over team comms, telling her to proceed as briefed. She radioed back that she copied.

The SPC-BTD stealthily approached the still-moving yacht on the port side to avoid the small boat on the starboard. As the delivery team approached the yacht, their lights were off to prevent detection. They quietly reported a sentry on the top deck of the yacht, which Cross and the team saw at the same time.

Cross needed to preserve the element of surprise. "Reaper, Reaper Actual, check fire." The repeat was instant and sharp from the team, despite every one of them wanting to smoke the sentry immediately. They would engage only if the sentry spotted them prior to boarding. They silently stepped onto the lower swim platform of the *Second Chance* with MK18s up and ready to engage any additional roving sentries, but none were evident in their approach.

"Reaper, Reaper Actual. Stay low. Stack on rear and port doors to main salon. Prepare for flash entry."

"Copy, stacking for flash entry," came the crisp read back. The team slipped like blue-suited ninjas to their doors, preparing flash grenades to blind the hostiles to secure the salon.

Small flashes lit up the night sky around them, letting them know they were about to be in a storm.

From inside they heard the leader say, "If you don't denounce your targeting of our organization, we will be slowly removing pieces of you until there's nothing left, but not before you watch as we rape your wife and strangle her."

The brutal inhumanity was torture for the team to hear and watch. They knew they had to stop what came next. The unspoken truth was that these bad actors would need to die. There would be no room for a capture on this mission. This had instantly turned to a kill mission. No remorse. No hesitation. No chance for Attorney General Scott and his wife to die, only a rapid trip to the afterlife for some gun-wielding dirtbags.

The calls came back seconds later from the team. "Stacked and ready for entry. Seeing five targets in the room," Bull called. "Four innocent, flex-cuffed, center of the room." Cross did the mental math on that call.

Five in the room, one on top, six unaccounted for. It was time to prioritize and execute. The math would work itself out.

"Copy," Cross said. "Standby to go loud. Talon, you're up. Reaper, standby to flash and clear on Talon's fire."

"Reaper copies," came across the radios a second later. "Standing by to go loud."

"Talon copies," Matthews replied. "Inbound on my run, ETA sixty seconds. Rifles are counting three in the boat."

The team stood ready at their doors, with Cross and Hooker at the back and Bull and Taters on the port. Cross silently held the count until about ten seconds, when he announced, "Ten seconds, standby to execute."

Under ten seconds later, there were three booming cracks as the team snipers led by Donkey took three.50-caliber precision shots at the hostiles in the small boat, instantly turning three chest cavities into mostly liquid as their lifeless bodies slumped to the deck. Then there was an even louder explosion as Donkey put one more.50-caliber round through the sentry, and his head exploded like a watermelon at a county fair. "Four down," came the call from Donkey a moment later. He followed up with, "Assault team, you're up."

The team saw the men in the salon turn their heads with the sudden and abrasive noise, but before they could figure out what it was, Cross said over the team radio, "Execute, execute, execute!"

On the second repeat, two flashbang grenades were already twisting through the conditioned space toward the hostiles, exploding within milliseconds of each other.

WHOOSH-WHOOSH

Both doors silently opened simultaneously as the four heavily armed team members executed a pre-planned entry into the salon.

Cross button-hooked right; Hooker made a cross-entry to the left, as their optics eclipsed the first two targets. There was a violent clatter of more than five 5.56x45mm rounds into each of the first two hostage-takers as they dropped in bloody heaps on the deck. A second rattle of rounds exploded into the second pair of hostage-takers lined up by Bull and Taters fractions of a second later. Cross shifted fire instantly and acquired the fifth and final target in the room, unloading a controlled burst into his stunned face at less than ten yards before he fell backward onto the carpet.

By Cross's quick count, there were nine hostiles down. Where were the rest?

Cross commanded, "Clear compartments, three tangoes still unaccounted for!"

Bull moved forward with Cross to his right, when a shot rang out from above them, and suddenly Hooker unleashed a controlled burst at an unseen attacker who moments later fell lifeless down the stairs from above.

Cross and Bull both turned briefly to see it, and when they came back around, they found themselves suddenly staring down the barrels of a pair of pistols.

●●●●●

Bull took the first round to the plate carrier and stumbled backward. Cross thought his friend was dead. His rage filled his heart and lungs. It was unbridled and reckless. He shoulder-charged the attacker in front of him, taking a grazing shot to his left arm in the process. The man stumbled and fell, the two of them rolling in a single mass across the floor for a moment until Cross got his bearings and swept his legs under him in a powerful scissor kick, knocking the man to his feet as he was trying to get the upper hand. Cross jumped on top of him, surprising his opponent. The man tried to throw some wild punches, but Cross outmatched him, grabbing and breaking one arm at the elbow. He then pinned the other arm as he reached for his karambit. The deadly curved blade clicked open and locked as he drove it through the man's neck.

As the blood poured from the open wound, Cross leaped to his feet again, just in time to see the second man pointing his handgun at his chest. With fractions of a second to respond, Cross lunged at the man, closing the distance offline of his target to spoil any shot he might get off.

With practice and precision born in the crucible of constant, relentless training, Cross grabbed the handgun slide and barrel. He whipped it outward from his opponent's body, breaking fingers with a sickening crunch and disarming him. The man howled in pain and then tried to tackle Cross, but he grabbed the man's shoulder, throwing two knees into his core with enough force to wind him. He followed that with a downward elbow to the back of the head, making his opponent stumble backward. Balance lost, the enraged man staggered toward Cross.

Cross prepared to send a front snap kick into the man's chest; his opponent shadowed the coming charge, and a blur crossed into his vision from left to right. His brain barely registered the most Bull move ever. Despite being shot in the chest, Bull rose like the mythical phoenix from the ashes, charging at the last man and picking him up off the ground by his belt and arm. Using the man's head as a battering ram, Bull slammed him through the nearest exterior door.

"Fuck *you!*" Bull spat in anger at the unconscious and bloodied man on the deck. He slowly, painfully staggered back in. In response to the shocked Cross, Bull said sarcastically, "*Yes,* I got shot in the chest. *No,* I'm not dead. Slowed against a magazine and dispersed on the vest. Still hurts like a motherfucker though. I'm sure it broke something."

Cross closed the gap and wrapped his arms around Bull in a tight hug, thankful for small miracles. "I'm glad you're okay, Bull. I thought he had you for sure."

"Ah, fuck! Watch the ribs! Nah, think about it, brother. If I died out here, my wife would bring me back to life long enough to kill me herself for being such a selfish prick. I wasn't about to let *that* happen!"

"Fair point," Cross said, then turned and yelled. "Clear!"

Heads turned to assess the room and surroundings, then immediate clear calls came back from the team moments later. After Bull repeated the call, Cross finally yelled, "All clear!"

Quickly snapping back into mission mode, he got on team comms. "Neptune, Talon, Reaper Actual, objective secure. I say again, objective secure. Eleven EKIA, one for detention. Moving to secure Eagle and Osprey."

Bull moved to flex-cuff the unconscious man.

Cross then stepped across the deck and used his karambit with its now clean blade to slice the flex-cuffs from the wrists of both Attorney General Griffin Scott and his wife, Madeleine, as the team freed the yacht crew. Kneeling, he asked, "Mr. Attorney General, Mrs. Scott, are you two all right?"

"Jesus," the attorney general said. "Against all odds, it appears so. And who the hell are you guys?"

Cross held out a gloved hand, and as they shook, he said, "Logan Cross, United States Coast Guard, nice to meet you, sir." Then on the team's comms, Cross radioed, "Talon, Neptune, Reaper Actual, Eagle, and Osprey secure. Say again, Eagle and Osprey secure, all objectives secure. Mission complete."

"Neptune copies, standing by to extract."

"Talon copies, RTB, scuttling enemy vessel."

● ● ● ● ●

It was done. Well, part of it. As Cross looked around at the devastation they had brought down on this hostile force, he turned to his right, and Attorney General Scott touched Cross on the left arm and said, "Son, you're bleeding." Taters heard it a few feet away and was ready with his IFAK personal aid kit and treating the wound seconds later.

Cross calmly said to Scott, "It's okay, I'll survive."

"How the hell did you know we were out here anyway?" Suddenly, there were a few booms that made everyone jump as the snipers punched holes in the enemy's small boat.

"Well, we got wind of a plot when some traffickers started winding up dead near Gloucester, and the fallout painted a very grim picture."

"But how did you know what they were planning, and how did you know they'd be out here?"

"There was more than enough suspicion to take them at the pier, but we needed to let them think they still had a chance of success."

"Wait," Scott said, somewhat incredulously. "Are you saying you used us as bait?"

"I know it sounds like that, sir, but let me explain. There are at least two traitors in the Coast Guard, covering the syndicate that took your boat. One of them is my next target. To keep him in the dark, I had to make it look like their plan would succeed, maintain surprise, and finish it outside the chain of command. Everyone you see around you, including the folks in that Jayhawk, and on our boat outside, risked their lives and a potential court-martial, going off-reservation to save you and your wife because it was the right thing to do. If we had done it by the book, the syndicate would go to ground and then pop back up six months from now with a plot we won't see coming and can't stop. This way, we have a way in."

"Thank you for clarifying. Don't worry about that court-martial part. I'll cover all of you on that. You did save my ass, after all."

"Thank you, sir," Cross said with a chuckle. "Much appreciated. Now, if your crew is up to it, I recommend they bring it back to Pickering, moor it up, and we'll have medics and state police meet you at the pier for statements, medical attention, and to secure the scene. Sound acceptable to you?"

"Yes," Scott said with a firm nod. "I'll brief the crew now. My wife and I will steer clear of all the dead bodies. Thank you again, Mr. Cross. We would have all been dead without you and your team."

Cross didn't correct him, the wise-ass response of working for a living slipping quietly from his thoughts.

Finally, Scott asked, "Now, what are you going to do?"

Cross's face suddenly betrayed his inner rage at his next move, as he said coldly, "I'm going to go confront a traitor to everything this uniform stands for. This ends tonight."

UNITED STATES COAST GUARD STATION
GLOUCESTER, MASSACHUSETTS,
AUGUST 5, 2022, 2000 HOURS LOCAL

BILL GRAYSON HAD every reason to believe the plan would succeed. He was working with a ruthless organization that didn't tolerate failure, and this assassination would send a message loud and clear to those trying to hunt them down, "Back off, or else." He was pushed to power with their influence, and this would give them reason to continue to trust him in the long run.

He expected to hear through internal Coast Guard networks of something happening off the coast of Cape Ann, even if no one quite knew what it was. When the notification didn't happen promptly, he reached out to the lieutenant. There was no answer. Grayson would wait it out and call back a little while later if he hadn't heard back. It wasn't like the lieutenant leaving him hanging; they had long been allies if not friends.

Half an hour passed before Grayson wondered if something was wrong and called the lieutenant again. His call went straight to voicemail. Why was the lieutenant unreachable? He'd try again in a few minutes.

●●●●●

Cross's drive back to Gloucester was consumed with thoughts of those who had been dragged into this terror with him. Melanie, pregnant with their first child, had nearly been killed by home invaders. Nate took two bullets on a boarding that meant to hurt his crew. Bull, Hooker, Taters, Commander Matthews, Donkey, Mendez, Lozaro, Drazen, Cody, and Lauren. The list seemed to get longer the more he thought about it. All the death, the destruction, the upheaval of lives now centered around one man: Chief Warrant Officer Bill Grayson.

The lightning flashes illuminated the night sky, more brightly than ever, fueling the fire in Cross's soul. He couldn't help but feel like he had no choice but to end Grayson once and for all. He could call it self-defense if Grayson attacked him, but Cross felt like he would be justified in killing the man. But he wasn't a killer. He did it only because he had to as part of his job. It didn't define his nature. The psychological seesaw effect was torturous.

He wasn't sure how this would go, but he knew he had to end it. Grayson was the last real piece of the puzzle. The lieutenant and the syndicate were likely untouchable, and more likely someone else's problem now. As he pulled into the station, rain pelted the roof of the 4Runner, and lightning flashed every few seconds. Cross told himself that Grayson needed to live to stand trial and, in turn, give up his sponsors.

●●●●●

Grayson tried the lieutenant once more. The call went to voicemail once again. Something about this didn't sit right. He sat at his desk a moment longer, thinking through the possibilities, options, and next moves. He finally realized his only option was to escape. He would sort out the details after figuring out why he couldn't reach the lieutenant.

Grayson grabbed his coat and quickly walked to the door,

stepping around the frame and entering the darkened hallway. He was about to reach back to turn off the light when something caught his eye. He saw the faint outline of a figure cloaked in shadow. The unknown figure wore a ball cap, jacket, jeans, and then a flash of lightning briefly illuminated the hallway. Grayson recognized the figure of Logan Cross staring at him, cold, unflinching, soaked with the rain that had started falling in sheets outside the station.

"Grayson," Cross bellowed down the passageway, sounding like a demon of vengeance. "Don't you fucking move."

Grayson stood his ground, staring down his subordinate as he walked down the passageway, closing the distance until they were mere feet from each other. Grayson slowly backed into his office, like he was a trapped animal.

"It's over, you traitorous *fuck,*" Cross barked. "Your plan against the attorney general failed. We killed every one of the assholes you sent except for one. They'll make him squeal. It's only a matter of time."

"I was wondering why you suddenly attacked Chief Drazen," Grayson spoke calmly as he backed toward his desk. "I thought you had saved me a major headache, but I guess I had that wrong."

Grayson seemed unusually calm, and Cross couldn't figure out why.

"You're coming with me," Cross said coldly. His shoulders rose a touch with the confidence of a man who was about to close out a threat for good. "No one else gets put in the line of fire for a piece of shit like you."

Cross approached Grayson, who acted like he was going to comply. Maybe he was only trying to act tough? As Cross went around the large hardwood desk and put a hand to Grayson's left shoulder to sweep the arms for cuffing, the man's right hand twisted, shoulder flagging for a millisecond as his right fist came up to Cross's face so quickly, he didn't have time to dodge or block. The hit landed on his left temple with such speed and force, Cross saw stars and stumbled across the office into the bookshelf.

Grayson took the momentary hesitation in his opponent to square off against him, a boxing guard stance replacing the relaxed demeanor he held moments ago.

Cross rapidly reassessed the man, suddenly realizing he was up against someone who was not ready to give up.

Cross shook his head to clear the ringing in his ears, then locked onto Grayson with a look of resolve on his face. His body slipped into his fighting stance as he slowly maneuvered toward the office door to give himself an exit strategy.

Grayson followed, his guard tight and his body radiating the amateur boxing career he held before he entered the Coast Guard. Cross picked up the trained fighter in the man's stance; his body positioning, his eyes. Cross knew Grayson was in a dangerous position, like a caged animal. He might have nothing to lose, especially if he knew what had just transpired on the yacht.

As the fight moved to the darkened hallway, Grayson lunged for Cross, a powerful straight punch from an extended right arm missing Cross's face by inches as he skillfully deflected and fired a right palm strike straight to Grayson's right temple. The force that would normally have dazed another opponent caused nothing more than a frustrated grunt from Grayson. A mild shake of the head gave way to a jab and an immediate cross. Cross blocked both with extended forearms, elbows locking at ninety degrees to absorb the crushing impact. Grayson lunged again, a tight uppercut that Cross dodged backward against, followed immediately by another jab and cross. The jab was blocked, but the next punch caught Cross in the sternum, briefly knocking the wind out of him as he stumbled over one of the folding tables. He crashed to the ground with it. He recovered quickly, sweeping his legs back under him and standing to catch his breath in time to catch a jab to the right side of his jaw that knocked him backward into the wall hard enough to dent the wood paneling.

Cross propelled himself from the wall in a shoulder-charge, catching Grayson in mid-cross and sending him off-balance into a table on the other side of the room. He grunted, stood tall, shook his head, and locked eyes with Cross. "You can't win, son. I'm going to bury you."

Grayson closed the distance once more. Cross looked for the telltales preceding his punches. He wasn't using his legs other than to move, like a boxer. He wouldn't be prepared for a lower-body counterattack. As predicted, Grayson threw punches. Strong, precise, but still predictable. After a couple jab-cross combinations and an uppercut that Cross deflected, he felt like he had a pattern established on the old boxer. Grayson's jab was solid, but his shoulder dipped slightly a fraction of a second before. His cross was damn near perfection, with no flagging at all. During the uppercut, his body sank to the side of the arm used for the strike, and while it provided ample power, it was easy to counter.

Cross countered Grayson with hardly any of his renewed attacks landing. Cross could feel the energy bleeding out of his opponent. Grayson was experienced and strong, but not invincible, and no match for Cross's combat training.

The battle entered the Can-Do Café. Cross kept looking for an opportunity to use Grayson's speed and ferocity against him. Grayson was losing his edge but was still dangerous.

Grayson twisted for a jab. As the jab landed and his cross started, a glint caught Cross's eye. His senses registered brass knuckles. Cross brought up his left forearm in time to block the deadly concussive weapon. Cross's right arm flew forward in a blur, landing a strong punch to Grayson's sternum, winding him.

Grayson returned the favor with one of his own as he swung the brass knuckles low into an uppercut. Cross blocked low and shoved Grayson's arm away.

Cross attempted to interrupt Grayson's next jab, deflecting and counterattacking with an elbow to the head, but was met with a cross to his temple. The brass knuckles had the intended effect. He stumbled, seeing stars, back to the wall as he twisted. By the time he brought his hands back up, another cross landed on his cheekbone. Cross heard and felt the crack and returned fire with a snap kick to Grayson's groin. As he bent forward, Cross saw his opportunity and capitalized on it. He sprang upward on his left leg, grabbing Grayson's shoulder and pulling his face into his quickly rising right knee, shattering Grayson's nose on his kneecap. Grayson stumbled backward, the brass knuckles slipping from his fingers, as blood poured from his face. He released a guttural groan. In the momentary gap in his opponent's onslaught, Cross lunged forward off his left leg, landing a straight kick directly in the center of Grayson's knee, shattering the knee and bending the leg back at an unnatural angle as the old man collapsed in a piercing howl of agony.

Cross's rage took over, and he jumped into top mount, unleashing palm strikes at a blistering speed. Causing more damage with each strike, the blood covered Grayson's face. Grayson frantically moved his right hand to his waistline. A folding knife locked open with a click as Grayson used his last remaining energy to aim the knife into Cross's ribs. Cross saw the move in slow motion and swiftly blocked, slamming the arm across his leg with brutal force, snapping Grayson's arm in half. He screamed. Cross instinctively brought his karambit to Grayson's throat.

It was at that moment that Cross caught movement in the doorway and glanced up. Melanie was there with a look of shock and terror on her face. Mendez put an arm across Melanie's chest to keep her from rushing to her husband and getting caught in the fight.

"Do it, you fucking coward," Grayson screamed, the pain bleeding through his voice. Blood spat onto Cross's face. Grayson's broken and mangled limbs dangled beside him. "Kill me! You know you want to!"

Cross stared at his tormentor for a moment that seemed to stretch into eternity. The man deserved to die.

"Don't listen to him!" The words came through in a fog and then became clearer as Cross brought the surrounding environment into focus. The blood pumped in his ears but slowed to a mild thumping, and he heard Melanie's voice cut through his rage. "Logan, think about me. Think about our child. Please, don't do it!"

He raised his knife. Cross fought to see through the rage in his eyes. His jaw clenched. Then, as suddenly as it came on, his rage dissipated, and Cross lowered his karambit. He unlocked and folded the blade closed. Cross looked Grayson in the eyes and spat contempt. "Death is the easy way out. You can burn, motherfucker." He motioned for Mendez and stepped off Grayson as she flipped him, swiftly cuffed him, and read him his Miranda rights.

Cross moved to Melanie, his thoughts racing, but his heart rate slowly returning to normal. He embraced her in a tight hug.

She spoke in a whisper. "I knew you'd need me, so I had Stephanie come over with me. I somehow knew he'd try to corrupt you."

"I'm still here," Cross reassured her. "I'm not going anywhere."

THE CONFERENCE ROOM was as spartan as Cross had come to expect of the Coast Guard. He was called there by a captain after the events of the last couple of months were unveiled by Chief Drazen. Melanie was at his side, as was Chief Drazen. Also present were the members of his team that night: Bull, Hooker, Taters, the snipers, the delivery team, Commander Matthews, and CGIS Special Agent Rick Lozaro. A pair of salty-looking master chiefs sat in the back of the room.

After a brief time, the captain entered the room, and Commander Matthews called, "Attention on deck!" All uniformed members stood crisply at attention.

The captain said, "Please, folks, take your seats."

Everyone sat down again, and the captain looked around the room. "This is quite the group of rebels. You all know you acted without any authorization, right?" There was silence. No one was going to admit fault or guilt for doing the right thing.

"Okay," the captain said with a shake of his head and a raised hand. "Let me back up. You all helped save Attorney General Scott, and that can't be ignored. He wanted me to thank each one of you personally, for him and his wife. What also can't be ignored is that you all acted outside the bounds of the law, Coast Guard regulation, as if you were vigilantes."

"Captain," Chief Drazen offered. "If I can—"

"No, Chief," the captain said sternly, cutting him off. "I'm not finished. That was completely reckless and in no way consistent with the core values. What did you all think would happen if you sent proper notifications?"

Cross spoke out of turn. "Captain, it would have taken too long to act, and Attorney General Scott and his wife would be fish food." There was some light chuckling around the room.

"You still acted outside authority," the captain barked, "Now we have to figure out what to do with all of you! In my estimation, you should all be court-martialed!"

"But Captain—" Commander Matthews started.

"But nothing, Commander," the captain bellowed. "You all should have known better! Expect your careers to all be over after this stunt!"

The door suddenly slammed open with so much force it almost came off the hinges. The former Marine lieutenant turned Attorney General Griffin Scott stood in the doorway and barked at the captain, "Like hell they will!"

The looks of shock around the room could have been cast in marble. Scott took the moment of stunned confusion to clear the air. "Here's what is really going to happen, Captain. These folks acted with the highest honor and integrity. Their careers should be honored as much as the sacrifices they made. So, Captain, no more political bullshit. I want advancements and promotions for every man and woman here. Can you handle that, or do I need to find someone who can?"

"Sir, I...." the captain stammered. "I don't know that I can—"

"Then leave the fucking room. Go find me someone with a spine."

"Okay, it's difficult, not impossible. It's a big lift."

"You call me," Scott said with an abrupt finger pointed at the captain's chest. "If you get any legal pushback or hit any roadblocks. I'll blast a clear path for you, whatever you need."

"Thank you, sir. I'll get started right away."

The master chiefs made the rounds, asking for statements from all involved. Scott approached Cross and Drazen. "Nice to see you again under better circumstances Mr. Cross."

They shook hands and Cross briefly corrected, "Actually, sir, I'm only a boatswain's mate first class."

"Goddamn boatswain's mates. All the same, with all the 'I work for a living stuff.' To be honest, I think you look more like a chief boatswain's mate. And Chief Drazen? You look more like a senior chief. I understand Station Gloucester needs a new commanding officer." Scott grinned, lightening the mood.

"Yes, sir," Drazen said. "That's correct."

"Then I'll pull strings and put you in charge of Station Gloucester with Chief Cross as your second-in-command. Any objections?"

"No, sir," Drazen responded. "Thank you, sir."

Scott turned to Melanie and said, "I'm sorry, I've been remiss, ma'am. I'm Griffin Scott. You must be our new chief's better half!"

"Yes, I am," Melanie said, blushing at the unexpected compliment. "Melanie."

They shook hands, and Scott leaned in and said, "A couple of questions for you, if you don't mind."

"Please, sir," Melanie said. "Go ahead."

"I understand from Chief Drazen that you were the one to piece together what they were planning. Is that true?"

"Well, Logan was a big help, but I had a hand in it. Yes."

"I may be able to get you a civilian award for your actions. Presidential Seal, the works. How's that sound?"

"Sounds like more than I deserve."

"You don't stop a threat like that and casually walk away. You earned it. I'm told you're expecting your first child?"

"Yes, we found out the day they tried to kill us at home."

"Jesus! Hell of a day to find out. I know your husband is probably too humble to ask, and so are you, it would seem, but if you need anything, please call me anytime, day or night. You've got a permanent ally in me." He handed her his card, and they shook hands.

●●●●●

Stephanie Mendez coordinated the state police response to the yacht takedown, sending troopers to Pickering to conduct statements on the four survivors. They took custody of the lone survivor of the team's precision takedown. Though Mendez hadn't expected much, the solo hijacker did unveil some extra details about the criminal syndicate behind everything, including the name, Blackwake. It was a starting place, and all organized crime takedowns started with something small.

When Cross stepped away from Bill Grayson at Station Gloucester, she said nothing to him. She proceeded professionally with the arrest of Bill Grayson. She called immediate medical support to attend to his graphic wounds. He was transported to Boston Medical Center shortly thereafter for surgery on his mangled leg and arm and remained under armed guard until he was recovered enough to move to the United States Disciplinary Barracks in Leavenworth, Kansas to await trial for his part in the plot to assassinate Attorney General Scott and his wife, and the trail of bodies and lives ruined on the way to that objective. He would pay a high price for his actions because he was alive to answer for his crimes.

●●●●●

"The anchor is emblematic of a chief. It is stability and security..."

The moment felt surreal. It had barely been a month since the events on the yacht and then the showdown at the station. Cross stood next to Melanie as she and Senior Chief Drazen pinned anchors to his dress shirt. The crew watched with pride as their former port section leader took the executive petty officer position at the station. Chief Drazen advanced to senior chief a few minutes earlier and was put in charge of the unit. Part of Cross felt like he didn't deserve his promotion. He didn't want it. He felt he wasn't fit to lead the crew after what happened to his family, to Nate, and to his boat crew in the preceding months. The presiding captain made it very clear. If not for his actions and those of his crew, a senior US Government official and his wife would have been murdered. It was only fitting to advance Cross to a position of leadership and influence hearts and minds in blue uniforms.

As the ceremony ended, Cross approached Drazen. The job was done; the universe was right, at least for the moment. "Thank you, Senior Chief," Cross said. "For everything. I couldn't have done it without you."

"Hell, Chief, I hardly did a thing. You took a bullet for the attorney general and his wife. Enjoy your success, celebrate it, and spend time with Melanie. Hopefully, you feel the little kicks in her belly soon."

Cross realized then he had a promise to keep, and asked with a grin, "Right, Senior Chief, about that time to enjoy..."

AIRSTA – Air Station
AIS – Automated Identification System
ATF – Bureau of Alcohol, Tobacco and Firearms
CGIS – Coast Guard Investigative Service
CO – Commanding Officer
EKIA – Enemy Killed in Action
ETA – Estimated Time of Arrival
FBI – Federal Bureau of Investigation
GSW – Gunshot Wound
HSI – Homeland Security Investigations
HVI – High-Value Individual
IFAK – Individual First Aid Kit
ISR – Intelligence, Surveillance, Reconnaissance
LEPO – Law Enforcement Petty Officer
MSRT – Maritime Security Response Team
MSST – Maritime Safety and Security Team
NOD – Night Optic Device
OIC – Officer-in-Charge
OOD – Officer-of-the-Day
OTH – Over-the-Horizon Cutter Boat
RBS – 29-foot Response Boat Small

RTB – Returning to Base
SAR – Search and Rescue
SPC-BTD – 36-foot Special Purpose Craft – Boarding Team Delivery
SSE – Sensitive Site Exploitation
SWAT – Special Weapons and Tactics
TACLET – Tactical Law Enforcement Team
TOC – Tactical Operations Center
TOI – Target of Interest
VHF – Very High Frequency
WEPO – Weapons Petty Officer
XPO – Executive Petty Officer

ACKNOWLEDGMENTS

I would like to acknowledge the following for their contributions in creating this work:

Jocelyn, Ben, and Bonnie — for your unwavering support through every stage of this novel. I know how deep I dove into this project at times, and I wouldn't be here without each of you.

Stacey Smekofske, my exceptional editor — thank you for treating me like the next great thriller author, long before I ever felt like one.

J.K. Wolfe — for the countless conversations, shared struggles, and mutual encouragement as we wrote our first novels side by side. Logan Cross and Jake Harper are one hell of a combo; here's to seeing how far we can take them.

My parents — for believing in what I was capable of and supporting me every step of the way, even when the details didn't always make sense.

The United States Coast Guard and the Department of Homeland Security — for invaluable research assistance and support throughout this process. A special thanks to **MSRT** and **CGIS** for their direct input in helping me keep this debut as authentic and balanced as possible.

ABOUT THE AUTHOR

For almost twenty years, D.M. Webber has served in the United States Coast Guard, standing duty in Search-and-Rescue, Maritime Law Enforcement, and Afloat Operations. His time across both Active Duty and Reserve service has shown him the hardships, the sacrifices, and the remarkable courage found in every corner of the fleet. He continues that service today.

His fiction is shaped by those lived moments—the midnight radio calls, the chaotic seas, the underway meals grabbed between evolutions, and the missions where blood, sweat, and silence told the story better than words ever could.

Because behind every uniform is a human being who chooses service over self, again and again. These novels are a tribute to them—their bravery, their sacrifice, and their stories that deserve to be told.

Follow D.M. Webber and Logan Cross at
DMWebberBooks.com

You can also find Logan Cross in the Detective Harper Series by JK Wolfe.

ENTER THE DETECTIVE
JAKE HARPER SERIES

To read more about Logan Cross's ally from the Coast Guard and the man who still carries a badge stateside...

Detective Jake Harper isn't just chasing killers; he's carrying the weight of every case that cuts too close to the bone. A former Coast Guardsman turned Oregon detective, Harper is relentless, scarred, and unwilling to look away when justice is on the line. A decorated officer with a reputation for seeing what others miss, Harper is a husband, a father, and a man still reckoning with the cost of doing the job the right way.

Shadows of the Badge introduces Harper at a crossroads. A brutal murder tied to institutional betrayal forces him to confront his own mistakes—and the line between loyalty and justice. As the case deepens, Harper learns that the truth doesn't always bring relief...sometimes it only sharpens the blade.

In *Shepherd's Wake*, a missing Coast Guard officer and his pregnant wife pull Harper back into federal waters when a pristine yacht is found abandoned in Puget Sound. What begins as a missing persons case spirals into something darker: entangling cult manipulation, financial crimes, and predators hiding behind faith. With his own family growing, Harper is forced to stare down the kind of evil that doesn't raise its voice—only tightens its grip.

Hostile Intent pushes Harper into the heart of a multi-murder conspiracy where revenge masquerades as justice. As bodies surface and the truth fractures across jurisdictions, Harper must navigate a case built on grief, custody battles, and hired violence —while the past he's fought to bury threatens to resurface.

Justice doesn't come clean in Harper's world.

It bleeds.

It costs.

And walking away is never an option.

Because for Jake Harper, the badge isn't just a job.

It's a promise.

Follow at www.jkwolfebooks.com

The Storm Front Literary Universe, in chronological order:

Cold Front – D.M. Webber

Storm Warning – D.M. Webber

Shadows of the Badge – J.K. Wolfe

Nor'easter's Wake – D.M. Webber

Shepherd's Wake – J.K. Wolfe

Hostile Intent – J.K. Wolfe